*Praise for Susan Conant's
Dog Lover's Mysteries*

THE BARKER STREET REGULARS

"Sherlockians especially will enjoy Conant's latest dog mystery featuring journalist Holly Winter in her most intricate case yet." —*Publishers Weekly*

"Dog lore and Sherlockiana will keep Conant's audience interested. . . . Recommended." —*Deadly Pleasures*

STUD RITES

"An intimate knowledge of Alaskan malamutes isn't necessary to appreciate Susan Conant's *Stud Rites*. . . . Conant's characterizations are dead-on and her descriptions of doggy kitsch—most notably a malamute-shaped lamp trimmed with a dead champion's fur—are hilarious."
—*Los Angeles Times*

"Conant's doggy tales . . . are head and shoulders above many of the other series in which various domestic pets aid or abet in the solving of crimes. . . . Should appeal to everyone who is on the right end of a leash."
—*The Purloined Letter*

BLACK RIBBON

"A fascinating murder mystery and a very, very funny book . . . written with a fairness that even Dorothy Sayers or Agatha Christie would admire." —*Mobile Register*

RUFFLY SPEAKING

"Conant's dog lover's series, starring Cambridge freelance dog-magazine reporter Holly Winter and her two malamutes, Rowdy and Kimi, is a real tail-wagger."

—*The Washington Post*

BLOODLINES

"Highly recommended for lovers of dogs, people, and all-around good storytelling." —*Mystery News*

"Lively, funny, and absolutely premium, Conant's readers—with ears up and alert eyes—eagerly await her next." —*Kirkus Reviews*

GONE TO THE DOGS

"Conant infuses her writing with a healthy dose of humor about Holly's fido-loving friends and other Cambridge clichés. The target of her considerable wit clearly emerges as human nature." —*Publishers Weekly*

ANIMAL APPETITE

"Swift and engrossing." —*Publishers Weekly*

"Invigorating . . . Conant gives us a cool, merry, and informative look at academic Cambridge." —*Kirkus Reviews*

EVIL BREEDING

A Dog Lover's Mystery

Susan Conant

BANTAM BOOKS

New York Toronto London Sydney Auckland

This edition contains the complete text
of the original hardcover edition.
NOT ONE WORD HAS BEEN OMITTED.

EVIL BREEDING
A Bantam Book

PUBLISHING HISTORY

Doubleday hardcover edition published April 1999
Bantam paperback edition / February 2000

ISBN 0-553-58052-3

Published simultaneously in the United States and Canada

Bantam Books are published by Bantam Books, a division of Random House,
Inc. Its trademark, consisting of the words "Bantam Books" and the
portrayal of a rooster, is Registered in U.S. Patent and Trademark Office and
in other countries. Marca Registrada. Bantam Books, 1540 Broadway, New
York, New York 10036.

PRINTED IN THE UNITED STATES OF AMERICA

OPM 10 9 8 7 6 5 4 3 2 1

To my handsome, prancing boy, Frostfield Firestar's Kobuk, CGC, whose radiant optimism now brightens even the valley of the shadow of death. Take careful note of the route, my sweet dog. One day, you will light the way for me.

Acknowledgments

The Alaskan malamute called Tazs, mentioned in this book, is Ch. Foxfire's Szatahni Tosah, WWPD, WTD, WPD, WLD, WWPDX, CGC. Tazs is owned and adored by Delores Lieske. Thank you, Delores, for letting me borrow this miraculous combination of sweetness, strength, beauty, and charm. I am once again grateful to Chris and Eileen Gabriel for graciously letting me name a fictional cat after their legendary Alaskan malamute, the late Tracker, Ch. Kaila's Paw Print. For help with the background of this book, I want to thank Janice Ritter and her highly accomplished and sweet-tempered German shepherd dogs, especially SG-Jagger vom Mack-Zwinger, SchH1, AD, CGC.

Many thanks also to Jean Berman, Dorothy Donohue, Alice Gerhart, Roseann Mandell, Emma Parsons, Phyllis Stein, Geoff Stern, Margherita Walker, and Anya Wittenborg. I am blessed with the perfect agent, Deborah Schneider, and the perfect editor, Kate Miciak. Huzzah!

EVIL BREEDING

Chapter One

F. SCOTT FITZGERALD was right. The very rich really are different from you and me. They can afford more dogs. Geraldine R. Dodge, for example, had opulent kennel space for a hundred and fifty. Ten or twelve dogs always lived in the house with her. The house had thirty-five rooms.

Geraldine R. The *R* was for *Rockefeller*. She was me with money.

Or that's how I'd always thought of her. From her birth in 1882 until her death in 1973, she broke record after record for looniness on the subject of dogs, dogs, and more dogs, exceeding even the most maniacal excesses of yours truly, because she could afford to indulge this joyful madness, and I can't. Speaking of dogs, as Mrs. Dodge, I am sure, habitually did from woofy sunrise until late into the drooly, furry night, I was raised with, and to a large extent by, golden retrievers. I eventually emerged from a belated psychosocial identity crisis with an independent sense of self, by which I mean that I got a new dog of a new breed. He was and most vibrantly remains a male Alaskan malamute named Rowdy. He, together with my malamute bitch, Kimi, is overwhelmingly who I am. Should you lack fluency in the dialect of purebred dogdom, let me point out that in calling my lovely Kimi a bitch, I am not talking dirty about her. I myself, I might add, am a female dog person and a bitch only when the situation warrants it.

The daughter of William Rockefeller, John D.'s brother, Ethel Geraldine Rockefeller didn't exactly start out poor. In 1907, when she married Marcellus Hartley Dodge, the Remington Arms heir, the two were heralded as the richest couple in America. The groom, at the age of twenty-six, was worth about sixty million dollars. His fortune was rumored to be smaller than his bride's. Miss Rockefeller had no need to marry for money. Love? Or was it perhaps animal magnetism that drew her to a man with a name—M. Hartley Dodge—composed of letters that could be rearranged to spell *Tamely herd dog* as well as *They dream gold?*

Geraldine R. Dodge: *Indeed, larger dog.*

Anagrams aside, Mr. and Mrs. M. Hartley Dodge are still semifamous not only for enjoying stupendous wealth but, weirdly enough, for sleeping apart. Wouldn't you think all that money could have bought privacy? But as I'll explain, the arrangement would have been difficult to keep secret, and in fact, it's public knowledge. I found it on the World Wide Web in an article about the health benefits of sleeping alone. Mr. and Mrs. M. Hartley Dodge were cited as an example, perhaps because they carried the practice to an extreme: They inhabited separate manor houses on adjacent properties in Madison, New Jersey. She lived at Giralda Farms, he at Hartley Farms. The marriage lasted until the death of M. Hartley Dodge at the age of eighty-two. He died on Christmas Day, 1963. His widow outlived him by almost ten years. She died on August 13, 1973. M. Hartley Dodge bequeathed most of his money to charities, including his alma mater, Columbia University, and to various cousins. His widow got personal effects, family portraits, assorted jewelry, an unspecified number of automobiles, and a house and some of his property in Madison, plus small change: a paltry hundred thousand dollars in cash. When she died, her estate was valued at eighty-five million dollars. I know these details, you see, I made it my business to research them.

My actual business, to which I have already alluded, is the unprofitable enterprise of writing for what my editor at *Dog's*

Life magazine facetiously refers to as "money." Maybe you've seen my column? Holly Winter? The photo on the masthead is better of Rowdy and Kimi than it is of me. When knowledgeable readers write to me, they often remark on the dogs' beautiful heads. No one ever mentions *my* head. My kind of reader is too busy studying the fine points of my dogs to give me more than a glance that swiftly passes once it's clear that I am human. If you meet the dogs and me, you'll see that the photo hasn't set you up for the kind of rude surprise I had recently when I went to a book signing in Harvard Square and discovered that the author didn't look like a movie star at all. What I'd mistaken for the woman's literary cultivation of a stylishly evocative out-of-date hairdo turned out to have another and simpler explanation: The photo had obviously been taken fifty years ago. I wouldn't want to let my readers in for that kind of horrid shock. As shown in *Dog's Life*, I'm in my mid-thirties and perfectly ordinary-looking. Rowdy and Kimi really are gorgeous.

Once I started working on the book about the Morris and Essex dog shows, however, I became so overidentified with Mrs. Dodge that I longed to replace the accurate photo with a new one that would make me look rich or, failing that, one that showed me wearing a hat. This topic is not the non sequitur it may seem. Mrs. M. Hartley Dodge was the president of the Morris and Essex Kennel Club, and the benefactor of the famous Morris and Essex dog shows, which, except for a hiatus during World War II, took place each May from 1927 through 1957 on the polo fields of Giralda. Polo: She raised horses, too. Also, pheasants.

My coauthor, Elizabeth Kublansky, who, I might as well emphasize right now, is a photographer, not a writer, was restoring and arranging photographs for a book about the Morris and Essex shows. The project was Elizabeth's idea. She invited me in on it when she discovered that to get a publisher for the book, she'd need to submit a proposal. In writing, of all things. Worse, the book itself would need words, sentences, maybe entire paragraphs. Horrors! Elizabeth wanted to *do* the book; she just didn't want to *write* it. I did, and not only because I was already slightly obsessed with Geraldine R. Dodge. I saw the book as a belated opportunity to fit in with my fellow residents here in Cambridge, Massachusetts, where I had previously distinguished myself by being the only postpubescent person who neither was writing a book nor had already written one. I'd have been less embarrassed if my breasts had never developed and my periods hadn't started yet.

So I wrote the proposal, and Elizabeth got us a contract with a publishing house that specializes in lavishly illustrated and wildly expensive books about dogs, horses, and gardening, earthy subjects all, but groomed, trained, curried, weeded, or mulched, as the topic dictates, for coffee-table ostentation. Elizabeth and I were thrilled. We shot e-mail congratulations and self-congratulations back and forth—she lives in Seattle—and we posted our news on Dogwriters-L, the e-mail list of our profession, and I posted an announcement on Malamute-L and wandered around public places in Cambridge and dog shows all over New England creating occasions to refer to "my book." We were worse than new parents. I hadn't made myself so obnoxious since Rowdy finished his championship, but I didn't have e-mail then, so there were limits to the number of people I could inflict myself on. Now I took advantage of boundless possibilities.

Elizabeth and I decided to concentrate on the shows of the late thirties. After the war, the shows were limited to a comparatively small number of breeds. Before the war, they were all-breed shows that grew more lavish each year. The first show, in 1927, drew about 600 entries. By 1934, there were 2,827 dogs "benched," as it's said, meaning present and on exhibition. Since some competed in more than one class, the total entry was 3,590. In 1939, there were 4,456 dogs on the benches, with a total entry of 5,002 from forty states and Canada. The show drew people, too, of course, and in great numbers. On Saturday, May 27, 1939, a crowd of more than 50,000 watched the judging in sixty rings. All in a single day! And a beautiful day it was. The night before, rain threatened, and McClure Halley, who managed the show for Mrs. Dodge, had to scurry around getting the rings set up under the grooming tents. But in the morning, the sun rose on tents and pennants in the Morris and Essex colors, purple and orange, and on the huge orange beach umbrellas Mrs. Dodge thoughtfully provided to offer shade to stewards and judges. Or was the color not orange after all, but gold? Maybe even *real* gold? The trophies, in any case, contributed by Mrs. Dodge, of course, were sterling silver. And the cash prizes! More than $20,000 in all. These days, you're lucky to get a ribbon and a piece of silver plate. Mrs. Dodge herself always presented the Best in Show trophy. In 1939, it went to a black cocker spaniel, Ch. My Own Brucie. A picture in the *New York Times* showed Mrs. Dodge as she handed it to the famous cocker's owner-handler, Herman E. Mellenthin.

She wore a hat. I wanted a hat and smiled her gracious smile. Mrs. Dodge met Rin Tin Tin. She bred 150 AKC champions. With a coauthor, she wrote two books, one on the English cocker, one on the German shepherd dog. She used her four-story mansion at 800 Fifth Avenue mainly as a convenient place to stay with her dogs when she showed at Westminster. By the 1950s, the mansion had fallen into such a state of neglect that the neighbors complained. If one of Mrs. Dodge's dogs bit an employee, it wasn't the dog she fired. Most of the world saw her as eccentric. I had always thought she was wonderful.

Chapter Two

O N AUGUST 29, 1930, Marcellus Hartley Dodge, Jr., was killed instantly when his car hit a tree just outside the tiny French village of Magescq, on the road between Bordeaux and Bayonne. His skull was fractured. The carotid artery was severed. His companion and college classmate, Ralph Applegate, was lucky to get off with a broken leg and severe bruises. If it hadn't been for two French motorists who came on the scene and dragged the young men from the car, Applegate would have been burned alive. It was Mrs. Dodge who had sent her son on this and other automobile tours of Europe. Young Hartley Dodge had what the *New York Times* called a "predilection for aviation." His mother hoped to divert him from the hazards of flying. He had graduated from Princeton in June.

B. Robert Motherway was reputed to have known M. Hartley Dodge, Jr., as well as Mrs. Dodge. Motherway had shown at Morris and Essex in the thirties. He was my source of a firsthand account of the grand show in its heyday, my living link to Geraldine R. Dodge and her very own dog shows. What's more, he lived about a half hour's drive from my house. If he hadn't been nearby, I'd have had to settle for a skimpy phone interview. Our publisher had been tightfisted about funding research for the book. I, at least, consider a budget of nothing to be rather ungenerous.

Mr. Motherway had to be a thousand years old, or so I'd assumed when I'd called to request an interview. Young Hartley Dodge had, after all, died in 1930, and Mrs. Dodge's gigantic and fabulous shows had taken place before World War II. Mr. Motherway's voice surprised me. There was nothing frail about it. And after I made my request, it was clear that he wasn't too old to want his name in a book. The names of his dogs, too. Their photographs. His own photograph. To say that he agreed to the interview is a bit of an understatement. I let him set the date and time. He picked the next day at ten A.M. The conversation left me with a glorious sense of authorial power that lasted until the next morning when I tried to set out for Mr. Motherway's and my old Bronco refused to start, and without one of its usual excuses, either: subzero temperature, rain. This was a dry, sunny morning in early May. If the Bronco had been a dog, I'd have known how to rev it up. Cars, however, fail to respond to even the most enticing motivational approaches; neither dried liver nor rare roast beef does a thing for them. The man from Triple A recharged the battery. He suggested getting a new one. He mumbled something about wires and alternators. I knew his diagnosis was wrong. The engine simply had to be clogged with dog hair. When something breaks around here, that's always why.

I called Mr. Motherway to explain that an important editorial conference required me to postpone our appointment. Would tomorrow morning be convenient? It would. It was foolish of me to lie. When I drove up, he wouldn't exactly mistake my battered four-by-four for a chauffeured Rolls. And I wasn't going to park the Bronco down the road from his house and pretend to have walked from Cambridge. Besides, there's nothing shameful about having your car refuse to start. It happens to rich people, too, especially rich people with big, hairy dogs. Mrs. Dodge's limousines were probably as unreliable as my old Bronco. What made me fib was Mr. Motherway's address. He lived in what always emerged in Boston newspaper and magazine surveys as not only the wealthiest but the most prestigious and altogether splendiferous community in the Commonwealth. It had more millionaires, more green space, better schools, and less pollution than anywhere else in Massachusetts. Higher taxes. No lottery ticket sales at all. If you lived there, you already had so much money that you didn't throw it away trying to win more. Not that absolutely every person there was loaded.

Oh, but *he* was. I knew it even before I got to his house. Well, I didn't exactly *know* it. But I can take a hint. Hints there were: the acres of pasture surrounded by neat white fences, the stables, the horses, and the colonial houses that, gee whiz, actually dated to the days of the Colonies. B. Robert Motherway's was a white saltbox screened from the narrow road by a row of lilacs. More lilacs bloomed on either side of the front door. Beds of perennials took the place of foundation shrubs. Lupine and columbine were in bloom. The beds were weeded, but not too perfectly weeded, and certainly not mulched with wood chips or fir bark. There wasn't a rhododendron in sight. The horticultural testimony was irrefutable: This wasn't just ordinary money I was dealing with; it was serious Old Money. The newly moneyed in the Boston suburbs buy what are cruelly called "tract mansions": four-story, twenty-room mock palaces pitifully set on quarter-acre lots. Mr. Motherway's house didn't have a tract mansion jammed next to it. It had woods on one side and, on the other, a vast stretch of roughly mown acreage that looked like a lawn from a distance, but was, up close, a field. Attached to the house by a substantial extension was an immense white barn with kennel runs along the side. From the closest run, a shepherd ordered me to go home. I should perhaps add that by "shepherd" I do not mean a biblical fellow with a flock and crook. In my world, as in Mrs. Dodge's, a "shepherd" is a German shepherd dog. In writing, the breed is often the "GSD." "Alsatian," the British *nom de guerre* after both world wars, never really caught on in the United States and has almost vanished. What no one who's anyone in dogs ever calls a shepherd is a "police dog." Dahlings, it's simply not done.

The front steps of Mr. Motherway's house consisted of massive slabs of granite. Before I had a chance to ring the bell, fierce woofing from the opposite side of the door loudly announced my arrival. I rang the bell anyway. The door opened to what looked like a museum of Early American decorative arts and furnishings. Without saying a word, a tall woman in her early fifties with broad, stooped shoulders and pale skin ushered me inside. She was not dressed in colonial attire. Furthermore, to my relief, she did not wear a black dress with a frilly white apron. Maids in mufti are less intimidating, I think, than maids in uniform. In any case, this woman's appearance and manner were so unthreatening that even if she'd been in full regalia, with a frilly white cap on her head, she wouldn't have scared me at all. As it was, she wore a plain white blouse, a blue denim skirt, clean white running shoes, and a pair of yellow rubber gloves. She should have been five foot ten or maybe even six feet tall, but her head dropped forward, and she had what in dogs, maybe in people, too, is called a "roach back." In dogs, however, the problem does not stem from the postural efforts of tall teenage females to shrink themselves to the median height of their peers. Her odd shape could have resulted from untreated scoliosis or possibly osteoporosis, I suppose, but the cowed expression on her face suggested a sincere desire to squeeze herself into less space than nature had intended. Her pale blue eyes blinked rapidly, and she kept her rather full lips puckered, as if she were trying to suck them inside her mouth. Her long, straight brown hair was shot with gray. It parted itself down the middle, and was unflatteringly secured at the nape of her neck by a wide elastic band.

The dog who'd been barking now lay silently but vigilantly just inside the door on what I thought must be his rug. I had the impression that in dropping to this down-stay, he had obeyed no one but himself. He was a large black shepherd. To my eye, he looked oversized, but I am no expert on the breed. The shepherd I know best, India, belongs to my vet and my lover, Steve Delaney. India has her UD—Utility Dog obedience title—and is working on her UDX. The X stands for *excellent,* which is what India already is in all possible respects. She defines her work as taking care of Steve by doing whatever he wants. India is beautiful, intelligent, obedient, well trained, protective of Steve, friendly to almost everyone else, and good with other dogs. Also, as does not go without saying in her breed, she is blessedly free of congenital joint disease. India is such a paragon that she'd be almost intolerable if it weren't for her infectious interest in everything. If she could speak English, her characteristic utterance would be a buoyant, ''I wonder what *this* is? And *this!* Oh, and what's *that* over *there?*'' Like India, this big black male monitored his surroundings. India's eyes and ears, however, are alert with curiosity. This fellow had a guarded, wary expression. He didn't growl. His hackles weren't up. Still, I reminded myself to do everything he expected and nothing he didn't. My pockets were, as usual, full of dog treats. I didn't offer him one.

''I'm Holly Winter,'' I told the woman. ''I have an appointment with Mr. Motherway.''

She still said nothing, but nodded pleasantly before picking up a plastic bucket and a spray bottle of all-purpose cleaner and heading up the staircase that rose opposite the door. In her absence, the black dog continued to observe me. Normally, if you were to set me in the middle of the Louvre and turn loose some scruffy, mangy little street dog, I'd be on my hands and knees making friends with the fascinating creature, and I'd be subsequently unable to remember a single art object in that particular gallery or maybe in the entire museum, because the living work would have stolen my rapt attention.

Now, reluctant to make eye contact with the black shepherd, I studied the hallway and admired the living room, visible through a doorway to my left. The house had the low ceilings and uneven floors of its era. The walls of the long, wide hallway, which stretched to the rear of the house, were covered with what looked like the original flower-patterned paper, miraculously preserved. The paper simply had to be a reproduction of an authentic pattern, didn't it? Except to install electricity and radiators, no one had done any visible updating since about 1800. All the woodwork, including the banister, doors, door frames, baseboards, and window trim, must have been stripped to the raw wood and freshly painted in these bright and unusual shades of blue, green, yellow, and a soft, rich red. The furnishings were American antiques. On the walls were American primitive paintings, including the kinds of oil portraits done by traveling artists who turned up at the doors of prosperous colonists with painted canvases missing only the particular faces of the family members to be immortalized. Displayed on tables and in cabinets were not the rustic, rusty kitchen implements it's become fashionable to collect, but pieces of silver and pewter that had certainly been valuable in their own time. On the sparkling floors lay the kinds of Oriental carpets imported for wealthy colonists who wanted their establishments in the New World to look as much as possible like gentlemen's residences in England. Everything looked scrubbed, dusted, vacuumed, shaken out, ironed, or polished, as needed. I don't share the popular objection to a house that looks like a museum; the absence of a VCR and a mess of old newspapers in the living room didn't bother me at all. I was wowed. By comparison with Mrs. Dodge's Giralda Farms, I reminded myself, this place was practically a hovel. I was still wowed. And if the black male shepherd didn't ooze charm, he at least refrained from oozing bodily fluids and leaving chew marks on his master's showplace.

Footsteps sounded overhead. The feet and long legs of a man began to descend the stairs. Mr. Motherway was tall, lean, and fiercely upright. He had a bullet-shaped head and thick white hair cropped almost to his scalp. His eyes were a deep, bright cobalt blue. His unobtrusively well-tailored gray wool suit struck me as the perfect attire for an American Kennel Club judge on an important assignment. Reaching the bottom of the stairs, he stepped forward, extended his hand, and said, "Miss Winter, a pleasure. Jocelyn should have asked you to take a seat. You shouldn't have been left standing here."

As we shook hands, the dog rose and went to Mr. Motherway's left side. Even in his master's presence, this was not an ears-up, eyes-bright animal. The shepherd held his head low and moved as if completing a boring but necessary mission.

I said that I'd been enjoying myself admiring his house. I'd always liked American primitive paintings, I added. I liked the sweetness and the naïveté. What I actually liked, although I didn't say so to Mr. Motherway, was the depiction of dogs in American primitives. I loved the ones that showed a child or a group of children cuddling a stiff-looking, formal lapdog. Mr. Motherway didn't have any of those, at least that I'd seen. I settled for saying that he had a wonderful collection.

"Family legacy," he replied modestly as he led me into the living room. "My stepfather collected in a small way. He introduced me to dogs, too. He had shepherds. He was the one who first took me to dogs." The reference to his stepfather caught me off guard. Barbara Altman, the fellow dog writer who'd put me on to Mr. Motherway, had warned me that he'd had a sister who died in Germany in the thirties. He never discussed her; the topic was off limits. I'd somehow assumed that the taboo extended beyond the sister to the rest of Motherway's family—obviously, I'd been wrong.

Mr. Motherway motioned me to a love seat that faced the immense fireplace. He took a wooden chair by the hearth. The dog lowered himself to rest at Mr. Motherway's feet.

"Do you remember what year that was?" I asked.

"Well, it must have been 1928. I know it wasn't the first year. Compared to what Mrs. Dodge did later, it was small. But even back then, it was an exhibitor's show. She always went out of her way to make everything convenient. The trains that brought in the dogs had special baggage cars, and she arranged to have the dogs and the exhibitors transported from the trains. The estate, Giralda, was . . . Well, I wasn't much more than a boy, and to me it looked like a castle out of a fairy tale. In later years, it got . . . Well, the word is *spectacular*. She kept enlarging the polo fields to make room for more rings and more tents, and the lawn would stretch as far as you could see. And there'd be trees all around, dogwoods blooming. It was extraordinary. Everything was tented. There was a luncheon tent. If you showed, Mrs. Dodge provided lunch for you. Don't see much of that these days, do you?"

On cue, I laughed. "These days, you're lucky to be able to park in walking distance of the rings."

Mr. Motherway smiled. He had good teeth, obviously his own. "One year, can't remember just when, she had a special area reserved for toys." Toy breeds, I should perhaps add. Little dogs. "Special parking area," he continued, "right by a big tent reserved for toys, so no one had to lug anything. And the whole area was at the edge of the field, in the shade, as I recall. The show was always in May, late May, and it can get good and hot and humid in New Jersey in May, so she had tents everywhere and these orange beach umbrellas. There was a tower for the photographers to go up to get panoramas of the whole scene. I talked my way up that tower one time, and it was a sight to see: the trees, the acres of lawn, thousands of cars, fifty or sixty rings, dozens of tents, umbrellas, dogs, exhibitors, gawkers. Even from the ground, it was a remarkable site, like a giant carnival."

"I'd give anything to have been there," I said truthfully. "What did she give the exhibitors for lunch?"

Mr. Motherway looked taken aback. "Well, don't know that I recall. Chicken, I suppose. It must have been chicken."

I'd always been curious about those lunches. These days, the club sponsoring a dog show provides a good lunch for the judges and either the same lunch or a less lavish one for the stewards, the volunteers who help the judges. Exhibitors pack their own picnics, or eat at cafeterias or concession stands. I couldn't get over the idea that Mrs. Dodge had served a civilized lunch, presumably a delicious one, to *everyone* who entered her show. Before I could press Mr. Motherway for details about the menus, a loud, horrible scream rang through the house. If the black dog hadn't still been motionless at Mr. Motherway's feet, I'd have assumed, I hate to admit, that he'd dug his teeth into someone, probably the maid, Jocelyn. There was something elusively female about the scream.

Mr. Motherway rose from his chair by the fireplace. "My wife," he explained. "Christina is dying at home," he added with dignity. "Everything possible is done for her here. If you'll excuse me, I'll see that Jocelyn is with her. Jocelyn has orders to stay within close hearing distance of Christina, but she does not always follow orders.'' Glued to Mr. Motherway's left side, the shepherd followed him from the room. The dog hadn't shown any reaction to the startling cry. He must have been used to it. To some extent, I was, too. My Rowdy is a certified therapy dog. We visit a nursing home. A few of the very old and ailing people there cried out now and then in a way that had initially alarmed me; I thought I was hearing shrieks of pain. Some may have been. Others were not. One day I took Rowdy to the bedside of an ancient, frail woman named Betty whose mind wandered. On some days, she loved to see Rowdy. I'd guide her thin hand through the safety bars that surrounded her bed, and she'd rest her palm on top of his big head and finger his soft ears. Occasionally he'd gently lick her fingers in what I took to be a canine effort to heal a wound. One day when Betty's mind was somewhere else, I tried to rouse her by following our usual routine. I guided her hand to Rowdy, who must have sensed that she was failing and decided to help. The second his damp tongue touched her skin, she broke into wails of terror. Someone should never have done something; she screamed. Never on earth! Never on earth! She cried out to God to save her. Hauling Rowdy with me, I ran for a nurse. What Betty suffered now was an attack of ancient psychic pain revived by her illness and dementia. I felt terrible about having unintentionally aroused some mental monster.

Having apparently restored his dying wife to comfort, Mr. Motherway returned. Over coffee supplied by the still-silent Jocelyn, we had a long talk about Morris and Essex. Mr. Motherway had actually been there in 1935 when Johnny Aarflot, the famous Norwegian breeder, judged Norwegian elkhounds. In 1935, Mrs. Dodge brought from England Mrs. Cecil Barber, who judged Scottish terriers, and Mme Jeanne Harper Trois-Fontaines, who judged Great Pyrenees. In 1937, Forstmeister Marquandt, president of the Dachshunde Club of Germany, drew a big entry: nearly three hundred dogs.

Mr. Motherway also wandered into tales of his youth. In the thirties, he'd led student tours of Europe. He'd been teaching art history at the prep school from which he was now retired, and in the summers he and a band of students would wander in France, Italy, Spain, and Germany. It was hard to connect the freewheeling character he'd evidently been with the staid, upright gentleman I saw now. In the summer after his sophomore year in college, he informed me, he'd gone to Montana with a party of friends. "On a dare," he confided, "I entered a rodeo. Had no idea what I was doing. I ended up on a wild steer, and darned if I didn't ride it to the finish!"

"That's amazing," I said.

"Won my spurs in range fashion! Foolhardy. I was lucky to get off without breaking my neck."

"But you're glad now you did it?"

He beamed. "Shall we meet again? Somewhere, I've got a few pictures from the old days that might interest you. I'll dig them up."

"That would be great." I also had some questions I hadn't been able to fit into my allotted time. "How would next Friday be? At ten or so?"

"Ten," he said firmly. I should have realized that he wasn't an or-so type.

Before I left, he offered me a tour of his kennels. I accepted. I expected him to show me around himself, but he departed in search of someone called Peter, to whom he was evidently delegating the task. This time, the black shepherd stayed by the hearth when his master left. I hadn't seen Mr. Motherway give any signal to the dog. He certainly hadn't issued a spoken command. The dog apparently did what he felt like doing, and since he mostly just put himself on long down-stays, there was no reason for anyone to object.

Jocelyn appeared carrying an empty tray that she rested on a side table. I picked up my cup and saucer and started toward the tray, but she rapidly took the china from me. Mr. Motherway's cup and saucer lay on what I think is called a piecrust table, a small side table with the top fluted around the edge. The black shepherd was still on his voluntary down by Mr. Motherway's chair and directly in front of the table. When Jocelyn leaned over him to get the cup and saucer, he stirred, eyed her, and growled. The cup and saucer rattled in her trembling hand.

I couldn't keep my mouth shut. "He shouldn't be allowed to get away with that," I told her.

"It's not my dog," Jocelyn said meekly.

"So what? No one should have to tolerate being growled at."

"If I stay away from his places, he doesn't do it. It was my fault. I put my foot too close to——"

"You are a person. If you need him to move, he should move, and he shouldn't growl at you. There's no excuse for that kind of obnoxious behavior."

Before I could ask Jocelyn whether she had ever discussed this situation with her employer, he reappeared with a sullen-looking man at his side. "Peter will do the honors," Mr. Motherway said pleasantly. Before excusing himself to sit with his wife, he said how happy he was to have the opportunity to reminisce about the grand old shows and how glad he was that we'd be meeting again.

Peter glared at Mr. Motherway's retreating form. He might as well have said outright that he resented being stuck with me. He was a wiry man in his fifties, I guessed, shorter than either Mr. Motherway or Jocelyn, with sun-reddened skin, blue eyes, and blond-gray, scraggly hair that fell to his shoulders. He wore work boots, dark-green work pants, and a matching work shirt too hot for the spring day. His expression suggested that since he had yet to meet a human being he liked, I shouldn't waste any effort in trying to make myself the first. I trailed after Peter as he stomped by the row of sixteen or eighteen spacious, sturdy chain-link kennel runs attached to the freshly painted barn. The shepherds, being shepherds, ran to the ends of their runs to bark at me. Peter made no effort to silence them. Rather, he ignored them as diligently as he ignored me. The dogs made so much noise that even if I'd wanted to ask a question or make a comment, I wouldn't have been able to make myself heard. The kennels had concrete floors and were as clean as any I'd ever seen. The dogs looked healthy and were as clean as their living quarters. In the distance, I noticed two more outbuildings, also with kennel runs attached, but Peter didn't offer me a tour of those, and I didn't ask.

When I'd driven up, the doors to the big barn had been shut. I'd parked my car on the gravel by the side of the house. Now the barn doors stood open to reveal not only the interiors of the dog runs and a collection of farm and kennel equipment, but an old black Ford pickup, some sort of unpretentious little foreign car, a luxurious black sedan that stopped maybe a few inches and a few thousand dollars short of being a limo, and exactly the kind of shiny new van that would let the dogs and me travel to shows in safety, comfort, and style.

I thanked Peter, who was already too far away to hear me, climbed into my old Bronco, and hoped it would start. It did. On the way home, I kept seeing glimpses of my battered car, my modest house, and, indeed, myself through the unflattering eyes of the rich. Whenever I signaled a turn, the car's wipers swept across the windshield. The upholstery had triangular rips on both front seats. The tape player would work for weeks and then unpredictably destroy a cassette that I couldn't afford to replace. When I opened the windows, dog hair flew out, but the dog smell stayed. Pulling into my own driveway again, I wished that I had a garage and that I occupied all three floors of my house instead of just one. Brushing undercoat off my denim skirt, I wished I'd had something better to wear to Mr. Motherway's than an outfit almost identical to his maid's. The back stairs to my house needed painting. I'd have to do the job myself. As I put the key in the lock, I realized that I had the hands of what I often was: a manual laborer. And I wished for something I'd ordinarily have laughed at: a professional manicure.

But when I opened the door to my kitchen, Rowdy and Kimi came bounding toward me. Their lovely ears were flattened against their heads, their dark eyes smiled, their wolf-gray coats gleamed, their beautiful plumy white tails wagged across their powerful backs, and they sang in unison the universal malamute song of joy: *Woo-woo! Woo-woo-woo!*

"I am richer with you," I solemnly told the dogs, "than I would be with other people's money. I wouldn't trade with anyone."

If I'd been Geraldine R. Dodge, I wouldn't have had to trade. I could have had my perfect dogs. And money, too.

Chapter Three

LIKE GERALDINE R. and Marcellus Hartley Dodge, Steve Delaney and I maintain separate residences. The Dodges had adjoining estates. Hers covered about two thousand acres. His? I don't know. Those were just their country homes. They also shared a Fifth Avenue town house. *Shared* is probably the wrong word. Mrs. Dodge always had ten or twelve dogs with her. Consequently, I suspect that occupancy of the Dodge town house was more a matter of taking turns than of actual sharing. A dozen dogs wouldn't drive Steve away. There are often more than that at his clinic, and his own dogs, India, the shepherd, and Lady, the pointer, live with him above the clinic, which is in Cambridge and, come to think of it, probably closer to my place than Mr. Dodge's house was to Mrs. Dodge's. Our Cambridge estates, alas, cover less than a quarter acre each and do not abut. Because the noise from Steve's patients and boarders disturbs my sleep, he often stays with me. Rowdy and Kimi howl at sirens once in a while, but are otherwise remarkably quiet. My cat, Tracker, sleeps on the mouse pad by the computer in my study, so even if she purrs loudly, no one but the PC hears her, and so far it hasn't complained.

Alaskan malamutes being the pack-oriented creatures that they are, Rowdy and Kimi like to sleep in the bedroom. Rowdy's favorite spot is under the air conditioner, which he regards as a totemic object to be worshiped year round because even when its motor is turned off, it still leaks cold air. Both dogs are supposedly allowed on the bed only by invitation, but Kimi gets away with assuming that the invitation is open, and I don't object because she is an excellent bed dog, meaning that she cuddles without shoving you onto the floor. When Steve is there, we banish the dogs; caring nothing about privacy themselves, they fail to respect other people's. Enough said.

Anyway, the siren-induced howling of the exiled dogs was how Steve and I ended up at the Isabella Stewart Gardner Museum. The whole episode was the fault of the latest craze in canine education, a technique called "clicker training." A clicker is a little plastic device with a metal strip that emits a sharp click when pressed. The first step in clicker training is to pair the *click* with food: *Click,* treat, *click,* treat, *click,* treat, and presto! The sound comes to mean that food is on its way; it rapidly becomes a secondary positive reinforcer. Since malamutes are totally obsessed with food and go utterly bonkers at dinnertime, I speeded up the initial phase of clicker training by clicking just before the dogs' dinner bowls hit the floor. The next step was to pick a behavior to reinforce with clicks and treats. What I chose was howling. I selected this target for the excellent reason that when it came to Northernbreed vocalizations, Rowdy had always distinguished himself as a Pavarotti among malamutes, a canine Caruso, if you will, and while Kimi was more given to what malamute people call "talking" than to actual singing, she was perfectly capable of joining Rowdy in gloriously melodious evocations of the Land of the Midnight Sun. The only problem was that the dogs seldom showed off this prodigious talent. Also, they wouldn't sing on command. Suppose you're the young Glenn Gould's mother, okay? Except that he hardly ever sits at the piano, and when your friends drop by, he won't so much as rattle off a little tune, never mind launch into a Goldberg Variation. Such was my frustrating position until along came clicker training. The only impediment was that since the dogs hardly ever howled, they gave me blessed few opportunities to reinforce the target behavior with clicks and treats.

So at two o'clock in the morning on a Saturday in May a few days after my first visit to Mr. Motherway, as Steve and I lay asleep in my bed, a terrible fire or possibly a major false alarm—I never found out which—sent what must have been dozens of fire trucks, cruisers, and emergency medical vehicles speeding down Concord Avenue past my house with their sirens wailing and blaring so loudly and insistently that Rowdy and Kimi felt compelled to answer back. Their chorus was utterly beautiful: eerie, chilling, and heartwarming, all at the same time. Dedicated dog trainer that I am, I leaped out of bed, grabbed a clicker and dog treats from the pockets of my jeans, which lay on the floor by the bed, and dashed naked into the kitchen to reinforce like mad now that I finally had the opportunity. And let me tell you, clicker training really works. You know those dolphins at Sea World? That's how they're trained, not with clickers and dog treats, of course, but with whistles and fish. Still, the method is the same. And the results are just as spectacular as those I was getting right in my own kitchen at two o'clock in the morning—*Ah-wooooooooo! Ah-wooooooooo!* Click! Treat!—until Steve staggered in and, after a few efforts drowned out by the dogs, managed to convey his displeasure at having been awakened.

I was surprised. "You can always sleep through anything," I reminded him. Steve never looks better than when he's just reaching consciousness. His brown hair was curling all over his head. His eyes were especially green, probably, it occurred to me, with envy. After all, my brilliant dogs were learning a trick that his dogs hadn't mastered. He was unselfconsciously naked. My desire to clicker-train the dogs subsided, replaced by a new and more compelling longing.

The green in his eyes was apparently not caused by envy after all. "You have neighbors," he said sternly. His tone silenced the dogs, who eyed him with puzzled disappointment.

"Rita takes out her hearing aids before she goes to bed," I replied. "Otherwise, she gets ear infections." Rita is my second-floor tenant. She is also a close friend. She is young to wear hearing aids, and she uses those tiny ones that don't show, so people tend to forget that she has a hearing loss.

"Holly, for Christ's sake! Helen Keller couldn't have slept through that racket."

"Steve, the sirens were not *my* fault. *I* didn't call the fire department. And *I* didn't tell the dogs to start howling. All that would've happened anyway, even if I'd stayed in bed."

Steve had wandered to the refrigerator and was swigging directly out of a milk bottle. "In this situation," he said slowly and patiently, "a normal human being tells her dogs to shut up. She does not jump out of bed in the middle of the night to pretend she's Karen Pryor and that her dogs are porpoises." Karen Pryor is one of the principal proponents of clicker training. She was a founder of Sea Life Park and Oceanic Institute in Hawaii.

"I was *not* pretending I was Karen Pryor," I said huffily.

"But you were pretending that the dogs were porpoises."

"Dolphins," I admitted.

"In the morning," said Steve, returning the germy milk bottle to the refrigerator, "you owe this entire neighborhood an apology."

As it turned out, the sirens had awakened all my neighbors anyway, and everyone, with one exception, was wonderfully understanding and, in a few cases, complimentary about the dogs' howling. The exception was Rita. She was also the one person to whom I admitted that I'd inconsiderately prolonged the howling by seizing an unparalleled opportunity to apply a new and fashionable method of dog training.

This was over a late breakfast. To buy forgiveness, I'd arisen early and driven all the way to Brookline for Kupel's bagels with cream cheese and nova lox. When I returned, Steve refused the bagels and fried himself two eggs. Then he left for his clinic. After that, I apologized to my third-floor tenants and to the people in the nearby houses, including Kevin Dennehy and his mother. Kevin is a Cambridge cop. He really can sleep through anything. He swore he had. Mrs. Dennehy said that the dogs had put her in mind of the voice of the turtle—she's very religious—and that she had gone right back to sleep. Rita said that I did indeed owe her an apology, but that in place of groveling she would accept Kupel's bagels, provided that I had bought cream cheese and lox as well. Once Rita settled herself in my kitchen, however, she fell victim to one of the many occupational hazards of being a psychotherapist—that's what she is—by trying to persuade me to examine the meaning of what I'd done.

She spread a thin layer of cream cheese on what she refers to as a *goyische* bagel: plain, and especially not garlic or onion. Rita is a New Yorker. She gets her medium-length brown hair lightly streaked with blond and has the kind of expensive cut that would cause the average Cambridge woman to wrap her head in a scarf until her hair grew out. To hang around with my dogs and me on a Sunday morning, she wore a navy wool pullover she'd bought in Scotland, dry-cleaned jeans with sharp creases down the legs, and a pair of ankle-length Joan and David boots sturdy enough to withstand a one-block hike on Fifth Avenue. As I understand it, her concern with superficialities is a necessary counterbalance to her personal and professional preoccupation with such heavy psychological matters as life, death, and what to do with the time in between if it isn't automatically filled by dogs, dogs, and more dogs. Rita has only one, a Scottie named Willie. Still, if she didn't give a damn about things like having her eyebrows waxed, the weight of her concern about love, fear, depression, and madness would throw her completely off balance, and she'd topple over like an old-fashioned scale with nothing on one end and a ten-ton bar of lead on the other, not that she views her clients' problems or anyone else's as leaden, in the sense of dull or worthless. On the contrary, human suffering and conflict are Rita's pleasure as well as her business, but only because she is always certain she can help.

"The principal victim of this lunacy," Rita now declared, "was Steve. He was asleep only a few yards away. And you chose to act as if the noise wouldn't disturb him, or as if he wouldn't care if it did. Or"—here Rita paused to place a slice of nova on her bagel—"as if by comparison with your dogs and with your desire to train your dogs, Steve's needs did not count one whit with you.''

Noise! I ask you! The music of the spheres. I said nothing.

"And when I say *noise*,'' Rita continued, ''I mean noise. I know that to your ears, when the dogs howl, it's the music of the—''

"Spheres,'' I finished. ''As the hymn says: 'All nature rings.' ''

"Do you want my professional opinion on this matter?'' Rita demanded.

With what her clients pay, I'd have been a fool to say no. She told me to think of the most romantic place in Greater Boston. What sprang to mind was the Bayside Expo Center during the Bay Colony Cluster dog shows. Unfortunately, the Bay Colony Cluster takes place in December, this was May, and a May-to-December romance was not at issue. Steve and I are about the same age. Besides, according to Rita, if I didn't make Steve feel loved, important, and central to my life within the next few hours, there wouldn't be any romance left.

Even if you rule out the Bayside Expo Center during the Bay Colony Cluster shows, Boston is rich in romantic places. The North End, Boston's Little Italy, with its winding, narrow streets and pastry shops, is ideal for romantic wandering, but the sky had darkened and rain was predicted, so it seemed like a poor choice, as did the Public Garden, not that riding in a swan boat in the rain was outright unromantic, but it felt childish to visit the setting of *Make Way for Ducklings*. Also, Steve, being a vet, might take a more anatomical than romantic view of the boats and realize that we were nestled in the swan's liver or in a section of its large intestine.

So that's how Steve and I happened to spend the afternoon at the Isabella Stewart Gardner Museum, Fenway Court, which is so outrageously romantic that the Boston papers are always reminding us that Mrs. Gardner did not, in fact, import and reassemble an Italian palace stone by stone. As myths do, this one contains a truth that overrides reality: Fenway Court feels exactly as if its pink marble had been imported stone by stone from Italy, especially if, as in my case, you've never actually been to Italy. The building is four stories high and constructed around a big central courtyard with a mosaic floor and, high above it, a gigantic skylight. The upper floors have galleries that let you peer down into the courtyard, and especially on a rainy day, the filtered light that pours through the immense glass roof feels and tastes like some tangible form of grace given by one of the ancient gods depicted in the museum's statues and paintings. All year round, the courtyard displays plants and flowers, including what must be the longest and most luxuriant nasturtium vines in the world. Isabella Stewart Gardner built the house between 1899 and 1901 to display her art collection. She always intended it as a museum. But she didn't just turn it over to the public. She lived on the top floor. You can see why.

Mindful of Rita's advice, I stood next to Steve just outside the courtyard and said, "There! Doesn't this make you feel special?"

Because of the soft light, we looked special. In some parts of Fenway Court, the light was better for looking at live people than for examining the works of art, many of which were hidden in dark corners. According to art experts, that's where some belong. Some pieces in the eclectic collection are considered to be, ahem, not in the best taste, which is more or less what Brahmin Boston thought about Isabella Stewart Gardner, too. Anyway, the central courtyard was a big hit with Steve, especially when he discovered a promising-looking café a few steps from it on the ground floor. But I persuaded him that having come to the Gardner, we were obliged to do more than ooh and ah at the courtyard, eat, and go home. Didn't he want to see the scenes of the famous robbery? He did. In fact, it crossed my mind that Steve's idea of the perfect museum would be one from which all the art objects had been filched and nothing remained but the coffee shop. I more or less dragged him up one flight to the Dutch Room, which I remembered from childhood visits with my mother.

As everyone in Boston knows, on the night of March 18,

1990, two robbers dressed as Boston police officers convinced the museum's two guards to do exactly what they had been ordered never, ever to do: open the door. The guards promptly found themselves bound, gagged, and handcuffed. The robbers got away with art worth between two and three hundred million dollars. The most valuable piece was taken from the Dutch Room: Vermeer's *The Concert*, one of only thirty-two Vermeers in the world. The Dutch Room also lost two Rembrandt oil paintings, *A Lady and Gentleman in Black* and *The Storm on the Sea of Galilee*, as well as a Rembrandt etching, a bronze beaker, and a painting by someone named Flinck once attributed to Rembrandt. Six additional works of lesser value were stolen from the second floor. One was the finial from a Napoleonic flag. The robbers also took a Manet painting that was in a room right by the entrance. The total was thirteen objects. All were uninsured. A one-million-dollar reward was offered for the safe return of the stolen art. By now, the reward had been increased to five million. Not a single piece had been recovered.

Steve was gazing at the frame that had held Rembrandt's lady and gentleman. "Is this your idea of an upbeat afternoon?" he asked.

"Romantic," I corrected. "Not necessarily upbeat."

"Can we eat now?"

In spite of the Sunday-afternoon crowd, we lucked into a small table by the window. The view was of a section of the garden thick with ivy that sprawled over the ground and climbed heavily up the trees. It was raining hard now, so the trees and plants were dripping, and we were warm, dry, and hungry. The menu was a little too ladies'-lunch for Steve's taste, heavy on light quiche, but he ordered homemade soup and spicy cold linguine and didn't complain. And he wasn't the only man there. In fact, there were a lot of other couples. At a table close to ours, a man sat alone. We decided that he had to be an art student. The Gardner is right near the Museum of Fine Arts and the Boston Museum School, so the area is full of art students. This one had thick, dark, curly hair. On his left forearm was a tattoo embellished with such elaborate curlicues that I couldn't tell what it was supposed to represent.

"*He's* eating quiche," I said quietly to Steve.

"Artistic type," Steve mumbled.

Raising my voice, I said, "I'm sorry I dragged you here. Rita said I had to do penance for waking you up at two o'clock in the morning by taking you to the most romantic place in Boston. I thought this was it."

"The most romantic place in Boston is your bed," Steve said. "With you in it."

"That's not what the guidebooks say."

"Little do they know."

"Do you want to go home?"

He just smiled. Then he asked how my book was coming along. I remember talking mainly about Geraldine R. Dodge and her husband. I also remember how noisy the café was.

"Mr. Geraldine R. Dodge had money, too?" Steve asked.

"Lots. Not as much as she did, but he was still loaded. His grandfather was the head of Remington Arms and some other companies. The grandfather was Marcellus Hartley. His daughter Emma married a man named Norman White Dodge, and for a wedding present her father gave them a house right next to his. He lived on Madison Avenue. Anyway, Emma died in childbirth, and the grandfather raised the baby, his only grandson. And then when Marcellus Hartley Dodge was a junior in college, at Columbia, when he was only twenty, his grandfather suddenly died, and he inherited everything. He became the head of the family and the head of the companies and everything."

"Did he know about her when he married her?" Steve asked, meaning, of course, Geraldine R.

"I've wondered," I said. "Even then, she must have been a little, uh, eccentric. She was always crazy about animals. But she had other interests. She was a very important art collector. It's a miracle, when you think about it, that her paintings and things weren't chewed up by all those dogs, but lots of them were shepherds, and she was very fussy about temperament and training, so maybe they weren't destructive. And, of course, it wasn't as if her husband had had to pay for her, uh, extravagances. She had essentially unlimited funds. And they stayed married until he died."

Steve smiled. "She got another dog, and he died of apoplexy?"

"Actually, I don't know what he died of. I guess it could've been apoplexy." I paused to eat some salad. "What is apoplexy, anyway?"

"A stroke."

"Well, I can't imagine that another dog would've bothered him. He must've been used to it by then. Besides, they lived in separate houses. As far as I know, they were both perfectly happy with the arrangement. I mean, I do sort of assume that he was driven out by her dogs, but after that, I think maybe they had quite a happy marriage. I've wondered whether the death of their son might not have brought them together. He was their only child. It must have been a terrible loss for both of them. They donated lots of things in his memory. He went to Princeton. There's a gateway in his memory there, a great big monumental arch, and I think they both gave that. And the Madison, New Jersey, town hall. The entire building."

"What did she look like?"

"The *Times* called her 'outdoorsy.' Or something like that. Big. Heavy by today's standards. When I first saw her pictures, I thought she was homely, but the more I know about her, the more I see her as imposing. She looked powerful. And gracious."

To hear each other over the din of the crowded café, Steve and I had been leaning over our plates. Since we hadn't been discussing anything private, at least for a while, we hadn't been paying attention to whether we were overheard. Consequently, when I finished my lunch and casually looked around, I was surprised to find the art student at the next table regarding me with a piercing look I couldn't read. Anger? Suspicion? Something unpleasant. I couldn't imagine what I'd done to arouse his attention.

After we left the café, we went to the museum shop. There Steve bought me a beautiful guide to the treasures of Fenway Court. The covert message was, I guess, that I should read about museums instead of dragging him to them, but I was still grateful. I insisted that before we left, we had to go up to the third floor to see the museum's most famous painting, Titian's *Europa*. For some mysterious reason, the robbers had left it. Maybe it was too big for them. The canvas alone must be at least five feet by six feet. Or maybe no one had ordered it: One of the many hypotheses about the heist was that the robbers had arrived with a shopping list dictated by a nefarious mastermind who arranged to have particular works stolen on commission for wealthy collectors.

"If so," I said to Steve as we stood before the grand canvas, "you'd think that this would've topped the list."

What it shows is a plump nude woman riding a bull through the sea. The full title is *The Rape of Europa*. As my brand-new book informed me, Zeus, the father of the gods, stumbled across the beautiful Europa while she was strolling by the sea. To seduce her, he transformed himself into a gorgeous, tame white bull, and in that guise, lured her onto his back and then took off with her to Crete. Archaic date rape. As I recalled, Zeus was always running around with young women. You could hardly blame him, really. His wife, Hera, was a shrew, wasn't she? Also, wasn't she his sister? Anyway, the big painting was lush and, despite the rape theme, joyful. It actually got to Steve, who studied it for a few minutes and then suggested that I might want to gain a pound or two.

Since we found ourselves on the third floor, we wandered around, leaned over the open gallery to get a high view of the courtyard, then meandered into the room that contains the best-known portrait of Isabella Stewart Gardner. According to my guidebook, it was painted by John Singer Sargent in 1888, when Mr. Gardner was still alive. Although his wife was forty-seven at the time, the painting made her look about twenty years younger, and her husband apparently didn't like the halo around her head, the plunging neckline, or the loving portrayal of her alluring body, so he decided that the painting shouldn't be exhibited in public.

Maybe Mr. Gardner was right. On his knees before the John Singer Sargent portrait was the art student from the café. His head was tilted upward. His face wore an expression of unabashed adoration. He was kneeling not to examine the brushwork or the technique. He wasn't worshiping John Singer Sargent. No, he knelt in worshipful prayer before, perhaps even to, Saint Isabella Stewart Gardner.

Chapter Four

I **FOLLOWED THE NORMAL** morning routine of a hardworking freelance writer by drinking coffee and reading the paper. Among the death notices was the name MOTHERWAY—CHRISTINA (HEINCK), beloved wife of B. Robert, as the paper called her. She had died at home after a long illness. Funeral services and interment would take place at Mount Auburn Cemetery in Cambridge. Christina Motherway's death came as no surprise; Mr. Motherway had made it clear that his wife was dying. He'd been determined to keep her out of an institution. His desire had been granted; she had died at home.

Mount Auburn Cemetery was no surprise, either. It's so beautiful and so upper-crust that it almost seems a shame its permanent inhabitants are in no position to enjoy the verdant gentility of their surroundings, not to mention what would undoubtedly be the stimulating company of such famous and diverse neighbors as Mary Baker Eddy, Henry Wadsworth Longfellow, B. F. Skinner, Winslow Homer, and Isabella Stewart Gardner. It is also the final resting place of Rowdy's previous owner, Dr. Frank Stanton, whose grave I visit occasionally to deliver updates on Rowdy's accomplishments. When I take Rowdy to visit his former owner, I have to sneak him in, because Mount Auburn prohibits dogs. Live dogs, that is. Remains, too, I believe. Art, however, has achieved a symbolic triumph over the ban by populating the garden cemetery with splendid representations in stone of mastiffs, sheepdogs, and other noble canines, as illustrated in photographs and described in words by yours truly in a *Dog's Life* article people still compliment me on. Mount Auburn also forbids bicycling, skating, and picnicking, but actively encourages what Rita informs me is properly termed "birding", rather than "bird watching." To my initial astonishment—Rita is anything but outdoorsy—she had recently enrolled in an introductory course on the subject. My amazement faded when I discovered, first, that she was going on guided walks at Mount Auburn rather than plunging through wilderness and, second, that she found it impossible to do so much as glance at a house sparrow, never mind identify one, unless she was attired in one of a variety of fashionable new earth-toned outfits chosen, I suspected, more to attract the human male members of her birding group than to fool the avian population of Mount Auburn into mistaking a psychotherapist for a tree, a shrub, or some other natural entity.

So Christina Motherway had been close to death, and the move from the Motherways' aristocratic colonial house to the equally elite grounds of Mount Auburn was about as minimal a discontinuity as such transitions ever are. The surprise was this: According to the death notice, Christina Heinck Motherway, beloved wife of B. Robert, was also survived by her devoted son and daughter-in-law, Peter B. and Jocelyn Motherway, and a grandson, Christopher Motherway. The sullen kennel help? Peter. The silent maid? Jocelyn. Maybe I should have guessed. After all, Mr. Motherway hadn't said of Jocelyn, as employers do of maids, that she was just like one of the family.

Christina Motherway's funeral was scheduled for Wednesday. I had an appointment with her husband on Friday afternoon. He certainly wouldn't want to keep it; indeed, he'd probably forgotten it. Even so, soon after reading the death notice, I decided to call Mr. Motherway to cancel our meeting as well as to express my sympathy. Yet I found myself postponing the phone call.

The reason for my procrastination was clear: I felt as if I

should send flowers, but because I was working on the book about the Morris and Essex shows instead of generating income-producing articles, I was even more broke than usual. The kind of cheesy floral arrangement I could afford would be worse than no flowers at all, wouldn't it? Feeling like a tightwad, I wished that the death notice had requested donations in Mrs. Motherway's memory be sent to some charity that would inform her husband I had sent a check and would tactfully refrain from specifying that it had been for a measly amount. A phone call followed by a tasteful letter of condolence would be preferable to a shoddy little basket of dyed carnations and cheap ferns, wouldn't it? Putting off the call, I reminded myself that I had met Mr. Motherway only once, his late wife, never; there was no obligation to send flowers. Still, I felt ashamed of having no choice in the matter.

Having firmly reminded myself that Mr. Motherway was not going to cross-question me about whether I was sending an expensive wreath of rosebuds, I finally dialed his number. He answered himself. I'd somehow expected to hear Jocelyn's voice. I began by saying that I was very sorry to hear about his wife. As soon as I spoke, I felt foolish. I hadn't heard about her death; I'd read about it. The distinction was trivial. My self-consciousness gave it undue importance. Mr. Motherway didn't embarrass me by asking, for example, who had told me. He just thanked me.

Talking to the recently bereaved always makes me feel as if every word I utter should sound mournful. "We had an appointment on Friday." I spoke as if the world were coming to an end on Thursday night.

"We still do," Mr. Motherway said matter-of-factly. "Unless it's inconvenient for you?" He paused. "Car trouble?"

"No." I was suddenly more defensive than dolorous. People couldn't fail to notice that my Bronco was a disaster, but they should have the grace to keep their impressions to themselves. Recapturing my funeral tone, I said, "No, I just didn't want to intrude."

"Not at all!" That's not exactly what he said. He ran the *at all* together: *a-tall!* "Not a-tall!" he repeated. "It would be a pleasure. And I've come across a few snapshots that might be of minor interest to you. Nothing of Mrs. Dodge, I'm sorry to say. Still, they are from Morris and Essex, and they've revived a few old memories. One is of a dog of my stepfather's. There's another with a judge you might have heard of, Forstmeister Marquandt."

"I *have* heard of him! He was from Germany." Again, I felt foolish. Where else would someone named Forstmeister Marquandt have come from, for heaven's sake? Italy? Well, Austria, maybe. France. Lots of other countries. Still, I tried to redeem myself. "He was the president of the Dachshunde Club of Germany. That must have been in 1937."

Just as Isabella Stewart Gardner had brought European art to America, Mrs. Dodge had imported European dogs and European judges. In those days, it seemed to me, everything foreign had been more alluringly exotic than it was now. The names of some dog breeds had yet to be anglicized. Today's *samoyeds* had an extra *e* at the end: *samoyedes*. *Dachshunds* ended in an *e*, too: *dachshunde*. It was easy to imagine that those long-ago dogs had recognized themselves as other than ordinary American canines, and had flaunted their foreignness by barking in exotic tongues and gaiting across show rings with a stylishly international flair. In 1937, the Dachshunde Club of America held its national specialty, its annual all-dachshund show, in conjunction with Morris and Essex. The specialty began on the day before Morris and Essex, and continued on the day of the grand show. The dachshund had a bigger entry than any other breed.

"Marquandt. Delightful fellow," Mr. Motherway commented.

I was suitably impressed, which is to say, impressed with myself: Here I was chatting with someone who had not merely watched Forstmeister Marquandt judge dachshunds at Morris and Essex in 1937, but who had found the famous foreign judge a delightful fellow. I couldn't afford flowers. I drove an old car, or I did when the engine started, anyway. I hadn't even entered Rowdy in any of the upcoming summer shows because I couldn't swing the fee for his handler, and I couldn't count on the Bronco to transport him. So what? I was a step away from modestly declaring Forstmeister Marquandt a delightful fellow. Glory, glory. I could hardly wait to keep the Friday appointment.

I should have spent the intervening days working on the book and writing freelance articles. I might even have drafted my next column for *Dog's Life*. Instead, I devoted myself to what I rationalized as research. I surfed the Web and exchanged e-mail. Searching the Web for references to Geraldine R. Dodge produced an overwhelming number of Web sites that thanked the Geraldine R. Dodge Foundation for supporting activities Mrs. Dodge had cared nothing about. In 1955, Mrs. Dodge drafted a will leaving the bulk of her fortune to St. Hubert's Giralda, an animal shelter she had founded in 1938. In October of 1962, she signed a will stipulating that most of her estate be used to establish the Foundation, a charity with broad goals that have little to do with dogs. Seven months after signing that will, she was declared mentally incompetent. She was, too. If she'd been in her right mind, she'd have made sure that her money went where her heart had always been. A court battle raged after her death. Eventually, the second will was recognized as the valid one. Outrageous! A perversion of justice. Here was a woman who had devoted a long lifetime to worshiping dogs. Then, in a burst of dementia, she suddenly got the crazy idea of funding this ridiculous foundation. And did the court dismiss that second will as the product of a mind gone mad? No, it did not. Thus the zillions of Web sites thanking the Geraldine R. Dodge Foundation for supporting environmental causes, education, public television, National Public Radio, and other worthwhile endeavors about which she didn't give a damn.

That's not quite true. She did give a damn about some of the causes, and she didn't entirely disinherit animals. St. Hubert's Giralda ended up with a fair chunk of money. And during her lifetime, Mrs. Dodge collected art, supported the arts, and donated generously to civic and charitable activities in New Jersey. She collected both dog art and . . . I'm at a loss for words here. Normal art? In about 1931, she bought a marble bust of Benjamin Franklin by Jean-Antoine Houdon. After her death, the British Rail Pension Fund paid $310,000 for it. It subsequently cost the Philadelphia Museum of Art a whopping three million. And it wasn't a bust of a *dog* named Benjamin Franklin, either. In 1935, Mrs. Dodge presented Madison, New Jersey, with what is still its town hall, the Hartley Dodge Memorial Building, given, of course, in memory of her son. The original estimate of the cost of the town hall was $500,000. It ended up costing $800,000. Mrs. Dodge apparently didn't balk at coming up with an extra $300,000, and she paid for all the equipment and furnishings as well.

The Houdon bust was on the Web. So was the Geraldine R. Dodge Poetry Festival. I mentally drafted a frivolous submission:

I think that I shall never see
A hydrant lovely as a tree.
Hydrants are made by fools like thee,
But only God gave Dog the tree.

Doggerel! What could be more suitable? When I'd completed that phase of my research, I composed a lot of e-mail messages to individuals and to lists like Malamute-L, Showdogs-L, and Dogwriters-L in which I reminded people that Elizabeth Kublansky and I were doing a book about Morris and Essex, and were eager to hear from anyone who had information about the shows or about Mrs. Dodge. I modestly mentioned in passing that B. Robert Motherway, the well-known shepherd breeder and retired AKC judge, was sharing his memories of Morris and Essex with me. Friends of his might want to know that his wife had just died. I was sure he would be grateful to hear from people.

I felt only a little guilty about suggesting a closer relationship with Mr. Motherway than I really had.

Chapter Five

THE RICH EVEN HAVE better trash cans than the rest of us. Or so I reflected as I drove onto the gravel in front of the Motherways' barn. The four big barrels were larger than mine. What impressed me, though, was their color and design. They were made of heavy-duty plastic in the fashionable light-charcoal gray you see on upholstery in expensive cars. At least I assumed that the material was plastic. I didn't fondle it. Even Geraldine R. Dodge hadn't had genuine leather trash barrels. Or had she? The Motherways' barrels also distinguished themselves from ordinary trash receptacles by shunning the traditional barrel shape in favor of an angularity that made them look like tall, roomy storage boxes. They rode on sets of sturdy wheels. Their green lids were, I swear, the precise color of dollar bills. Hundred-dollar bills. The damn thing was that I'd never seen trash barrels like these before and wouldn't have had the slightest idea where to buy them. I sometimes think that there must be a Rich Person's Store, a sort of consumer version of Mensa, open only to shoppers with incomes over a million dollars a year. What it sells are elite versions of seemingly ordinary household objects: alien-looking curtain rods, doorbells and light switches of strange design, wonderfully peculiar garden hoses, and all kinds of other marvelous hardware kept secret from the hoi polloi.

A few yards from the elegant trash barrels, Jocelyn was arranging six or eight neatly sealed cardboard boxes and a sad collection of paraphernalia for invalids. A cane, an aluminum walker, and a wheelchair documented the late Mrs. Motherway's loss of mobility. One of the items was, I thought, a contraption designed to prevent falls in the bathtub. Another had adapted a toilet for her use. There seemed to me something obscene about exposing these private accoutrements to the clear sun of the May afternoon. It was almost as if the woman herself lay naked in public, her intimate vulnerability callously exhibited to revolted strangers.

With no preliminary greeting, unless you count the barking of the kenneled dogs, Jocelyn said, "They're going to some veterans' organization. You can't just throw them out. It wouldn't be right. They cost more than you might think. Someone else should get some use out of them." The rationalization seemed directed more to herself than to me. Her eyes were bloodshot, and even more than on my previous visit, she was bent with the burden of shouldering unwanted height. She wore what looked like a man's white dress shirt with a dowdy gray skirt, athletic socks, and running shoes. As before, a wide elastic band bound her hair to the nape of her neck.

"Yes," I said. "I guess you can't just throw them out."

As if I were a critical and reluctant representative of the charity to which the items were being donated, Jocelyn added, "They've been disinfected. Not that Christina had anything contagious. She had Alzheimer's. Senile dementia."

"I was very sorry to hear about her. I gathered she'd been sick for a long time."

"Yes and no." The sharp tone surprised me. "Oh well, I'd better tell him you're here."

I trailed after Jocelyn to the front door, which she opened with one of the keys on a ring she pulled from a pocket of the dreary gray skirt. She entered ahead of me. As she did, the black shepherd rose from his rug and growled at her. If he'd directed the behavior at me, the intruder, I'd have found it unacceptable. Dogs don't have to wag their tails, sing *woo-woos*, throw themselves at the feet of visitors, and roll over for tummy rubs the way Rowdy and Kimi do. But in my view, they damned well do have to mind their manners: If they don't have something pleasant to say, they should keep their mouths shut. But this fellow was committing a far worse breach of etiquette than making a visitor feel unwelcome; he was publicly expressing aggression toward a member of his own household.

Dutifully minding my own business, namely, dog behavior, I told Jocelyn, "There's no reason you should have to put up with that. It's intolerable! He shouldn't be allowed to get away with it."

You'd have thought I'd growled at her, too. She cringed. Then she repeated what she'd said on my previous visit: "He's not my dog." She paused. "And he has his good points. He's not a *bad* dog."

The subject of our discussion was once again lying on his rug. I was willing to bet that if I tried to take the rug from him, I'd lose an arm. If he'd been my dog, that rug would've immediately gone into one of the fancy trash barrels. I'd also have removed anything else he deemed his possession and not mine. "Has he ever bitten you?" I asked forcefully.

She hesitated.

"He's put his teeth on you," I guessed, "but he hasn't broken the skin."

Jocelyn nodded. As she was about to speak, Mr. Motherway appeared at the top of the stairs. Viewed from below, he looked even taller than he was. In advanced age, he was a handsome man. "About the dog," I murmured to Jocelyn. "I can help."

She looked skeptical.

"Jocelyn," said Mr. Motherway, when he'd descended the stairs, "we'll be in my office." Opening a door off the hall, he gestured to me to enter first. I did. The room had a brick fireplace, walls painted in an odd shade of pale green, yet more American primitive paintings, and the most beautiful desk I had ever seen. Mr. Motherway was a big, tall man. The desk could have accommodated someone twice his size. It was made of cherry, I think, and had shiny brass hardware. Upholstered chairs faced the fireplace. Except for Mr.

Motherway's framed college diploma—Princeton, 1930—the museum effect of the entire room was so pronounced that I half expected to see velvet ropes fastened across the chairs to prevent tourists from making themselves at home. And the whole house obviously had what the dogs and I would kill for: central air-conditioning. Mr. Motherway followed me into the room. The dog trailed at his heels. He was a long shepherd with the exaggerated rear angulation that produces a gait known as a "flying trot." That distinctive angulation, together with the resulting gait, is the hallmark of the German shepherd dog bred for the American show ring.

"What's the dog's name?" I asked.

"Wagner." He made the *W* sound like a *V*. The *a* was *ah*.

Smiling gently, he said, "My dear wife was fond of music."

"I'm very sorry." I meant to refer to her death. What else? Why offer condolences on the deceased's love of music? Or on an inoffensive dog name? Although Mr. Motherway couldn't have misunderstood me, I felt awkward. In less elevated social circumstances not involving a recent death, I'd probably have tried to turn my faux pas into an unfunny joke. Now, it seemed best to ignore it. "Are you sure I'm not intruding?" I asked.

"Certainly not." He directed me to one of the chairs by the fireplace and took a seat in the other. He didn't sit until I did. Neither did Wagner. He waited for Mr. Motherway, and then sank to the floor at his master's feet. Strange human manners: Remain standing until the lady is seated, but let her assume that your daughter-in-law is the maid. The growling, too: odd hospitality. "I believe in keeping busy," Mr. Motherway went on. "Resumption of normal activity and all that sort of thing. And this book of yours must, after all, have a deadline."

The word hung in the air: *deadline*. Then it reverberated in my ears: *dead, dead, deadline*. But Mr. Motherway's family line wasn't dead. Kennel help or not, Peter was his son, and there was also the grandson mentioned in the death notice, Christopher, presumably Peter and Jocelyn's son.

Still, the word unnerved me. I pulled a steno pad and a pen from my purse. "There is a deadline, but it's flexible."

Mr. Motherway rambled a bit about Morris and Essex. Like everyone else who'd ever described it, he kept saying that it was fabulous. I was getting tired of the word. I wanted details, not adjectives. But the man's wife had been dead for less than a week; this was no time to lean on him. If he wanted to ramble, I'd listen patiently. Eventually, I said, "You mentioned that you'd found some snapshots?" I wished that he'd come up with a menu instead.

He rose and went to the magnificent desk, where he rummaged and eventually found a couple of tattered, curling black-and-white photographs printed on old-fashioned paper with scalloped edges. They were just what he'd said, snapshots, and amateur ones at that; Elizabeth, my photographer coauthor, would have no use for them. In one, two men and a shepherd posed by a car with running boards. Both men were dressed in suits. The shorter, older-looking man had a substantial paunch. On his head was one of those felt hats that men wore back in the days when ladies wore white gloves. The other man, bareheaded and towheaded, was easily recognizable as the young B. Robert Motherway. The men and the dog wore serious expressions. They didn't seem to be having fun.

"Kaiser," Mr. Motherway said. "My stepfather's favorite dog. Judge never looked at him." His eyes looked distant. "That was 1929. My stepfather died before the year was out. He lost everything in the Crash. My mother couldn't live without him. She never adapted to this country. She was German. He met her there. She was a war widow. He was there doing some research. He was an art historian, too, in a way—had a modest collection, even had a little gallery. He brought us to this country. Adopted me."

I remembered the admonition not to ask Mr. Motherway about his sister, the one who'd died in Germany, the one he never talked about. "It sounds as if he was good to you," I said. "And he had a major impact on what you've done with your life." I meant, of course, art and dogs.

For no obvious reason, he looked startled. "With my wife?" he said sharply.

"With your *life*," I said distinctly. "He had a big impact on your life."

Mr. Motherway relaxed. As he was showing me another snapshot, a picture of himself with another shepherd posed near a big pot of flowers, the door opened and in walked, I swear, a clone of the B. Robert Motherway shown in the old photos from Morris and Essex. The newcomer was, I guessed, in his late twenties.

"Miss Winter," Mr. Motherway said, "may I present my grandson? Christopher, this is Holly Winter. Miss Winter is writing a book about the Morris and Essex shows."

"How do you do?" I said. The black shepherd, Wagner, didn't growl at Christopher. On the contrary, the dog's eyes brightened, and he thumped his tail on the floor.

Christopher nodded at me. I couldn't help staring. The resemblance between grandfather and grandson was almost comical. Allowing for shrinkage—Christopher was an inch or two taller than Mr. Motherway—the pair were virtually the same man two generations apart. They had the striking sameness of appearance you see in closely inebred dogs. The grandfather's hair was white, the grandson's pale blond. They had the same build, the same upright posture, and identical facial features. Each was as German-looking as the other. Age had not greatly faded those arresting blue eyes.

Approaching his grandfather, Christopher asked for a word. Mr. Motherway stood and excused himself. With no command or signal, Wagner quietly accompanied the grandfather and grandson. They held their private conference just outside the door, which, I might mention, was not equipped with a magical latch from The Rich Person's Store, but had an authentic Early American one that failed to catch and thus left the door slightly ajar. Several times, his grandfather told him to stop mumbling. I caught phrases and tones of voice. Christopher was lodging a complaint about his father, Peter. The discussion concerned someone named Gerhard, who I somehow gathered was a foreign student. Perhaps Christopher objected to the way Peter was treating Gerhard? I couldn't be sure. I had the sense that Mr. Motherway promised to correct whatever situation was troubling his grandson.

Mr. Motherway returned with Wagner but without Christopher. "You'll have to excuse me," he said. "Something's come up."

I thanked him for seeing me and agreed to a third meeting. I made it sound as if it had been my idea. It could have been, I suppose. I still hadn't seen a photo of Forstmeister Marquandt, and Mr. Motherway still hadn't told me much about Geraldine R. Dodge and her son, M. Hartley Dodge, Jr., the one who'd died young in a car accident in France.

Mr. Motherway saw me to the door. After he'd closed it, I fished in my purse for my car keys and furtively located one of the business cards I'd made with the new computer and printer my father had given me. As I approached my car, Jocelyn staggered out of the barn carrying another neatly sealed cardboard box. With the irrational sense of committing myself to serve as a secret agent in a dangerous conspiracy, I took deliberately casual steps toward her. Making a show of fiddling with my keys, I slipped her my card. "I don't want to see you get bitten by that dog," I said softly. "Call me. I can help."

Her pasty skin turned scarlet, but she seized my card and surreptitiously slipped it into a pocket of the dowdy gray skirt. She said nothing, not even good-bye.

As I drove home, I honestly did see the same car more than once, or I was pretty sure I did. I can't tell one make of car from another unless I'm close enough to read the lettering on the front or rear, or unless the car is something so distinctive that anyone would know what it was. This car was behind mine. I couldn't read anything written on it. It was definitely not a 1950s Cadillac with tail fins, an old Porsche, or a VW bug. It wasn't a station wagon or a four-by-four. But I know my colors; I went to kindergarten. The car was tan. I had the feeling it might not be American. But my primary feeling about the car had nothing to do with its size, color, model, or country of origin. Rather, I had the strong sense of being followed.

Chapter Six

ON SATURDAY MORNING, heavy rain pelted Cambridge. Deferring to Rowdy's hatred of water at any temperature above thirty-two degrees Fahrenheit, I left him at home and took Kimi for a three-mile run. After I'd returned, showered, and dressed, a glorious dog-training opportunity presented itself in the form of passing fire engines. With admirable presence of mind, instead of just seizing a clicker and treats to reinforce the dogs' howling, I grabbed my tape recorder and dashed out the front door to Concord Avenue. The neighbors are used to me. If I ran outside naked and started shrieking about alien spaceships, the people up and down the block would shrug their shoulders and agree that I was practicing another new and probably harmless method of training dogs. Anyway, no one had me locked up, and although the taped sirens proved less provocative than the live performance, the dogs were already revved up from the real thing, and we made gratifying progress—and all this at a more civilized hour than two A.M., I might note.

Then I checked my e-mail. I should perhaps explain that my office looks nothing like Mr. Motherway's. For one thing, if I'd ever owned an antique desk, upholstered chairs, and Early American paintings, they'd long ago have been destroyed by dogs and replaced with the makeshift desk and other cheap graduate-student furnishings I now have. I really do wonder just how Geraldine R. Dodge managed to protect her art collection. And what about Isabella Stewart Gardner? She was a dog lover, too, and *she* owned Rembrandts! They hung on the wall, of course. Even so, it galls me to think that Mrs. Dodge's and Mrs. Gardner's dogs may have been more civilized than mine. Anyway, the only expensive objects in my office are my computer and printer, so mine is a perfect example of the famous paperless office possessed by everyone enamored of technology, which is to say that it is a papery mess of first drafts, second drafts, final versions, photocopies, notebooks, legal pads, and Post-its, all containing information that I'm going to discard or put on the computer someday other than this one.

Instead of oil paintings of people, my walls display pictures of dogs and all sorts of other dog stuff, like a framed copy of Senator Vest's famous Eulogy ("faithfull and true even to death"), certificates from the American Kennel Club attesting to titles my dogs have earned, and a bulletin board heavy with snapshots sent by people who read my column. The office also holds zillions of dog books and magazines, urns containing the cremated remains of departed canine loved ones, ribbons and trophies from dog shows and obedience trials, and, anomalously, the ugliest cat I have ever seen. In an effort at what Rita calls "positive reframing," I named the cat after a famous Alaskan malamute, the late Ch. Kaila's Paw Print, called Tracker, who was as beautiful as my feline Tracker is homely. Tracker is, however, far better-looking than she'd be if Rowdy and Kimi got hold of her. For a start, she's alive. And yes, I am doing my damndest to train the dogs to accept Tracker. In the meantime, she and I share my office.

My newfound addiction to cyberspace has been a boon to Tracker. When I'd first adopted her, about three months earlier, she'd hissed and fled at the sight of me. These days, she still hisses when I move her off the mouse pad, but after that, she tolerates my presence and even hangs around in a more or less normal way, not that she does anything really normal and wonderful like bark, for example, or sing *woo-woo-woo* while wagging her tail in delight, but it has been a month since she's scratched or bitten me and a month since I've sworn at her, so we are beginning to make friends.

After politely asking Tracker to get off the mouse pad, I signed on—unlimited access, another gift from my father—and discovered a couple of replies to my inquiries about Mrs. Dodge and the Morris and Essex shows. The previous responses had been sparse, probably because most people who'd been active in the dog fancy in the late thirties were either dead or not on-line, which in the popular view these days means the same thing. The first reply was from Sheila, whose last name I should have remembered but didn't. She was on Dogwriters-L, the list for professional dog writers, of course. It read:

Hi, Holly!
Have you seen the Dog Fancy article on G. R. Dodge from a couple of years ago? Didn't know you knew Motherway.
Sheila and the Woofs

And the second:

Holly,
Have you checked the New York Times for coverage of Morris & Essex? There were long write-ups you shouldn't miss. Too bad shows don't get that coverage these days, huh?
I'd love to be a fly on the wall when you talk to Motherway. Or has the new cat got your tongue?
Harriet
Am/Can Ch. Firefly's Stand By Me, CD, JH, CGC

Harriet is not an American and Canadian champion, Companion Dog, Junior Hunter, and Canine Good Citizen, but she does belong to the Dog Writers Association of America and to numerous golden retriever clubs, including Yankee Golden Retriever Rescue. I know her through breed rescue. I help to find homes for homeless malamutes. Harriet lives in Connecticut. We see each other at shows and obedience events, and we exchange e-mail. E-mail saves on phone bills, but has its limitations. For instance, when someone says she'd love to be a fly on the wall and asks whether the cat's got your tongue, you can't instantly find out what she means. I sent an e-mail reply to ask just that.

I remained fretful for the rest of the weekend. Steve and I went out to dinner on Saturday night. For once I had trouble deciding what to order. On Sunday we took our four dogs to the Berkshires for a hike made memorable by ticks and black-flies. When we got home, my Internet provider informed me that I had no new mail. Nonsense! I always have e-mail!

I spent Monday morning rechecking my e-mail, surfing the Web, and otherwise pursuing my research. For example, while visiting a Web site devoted to generating anagrams, I discovered that the letters in *Geraldine* could be rearranged to spell, among other things, *Danger lie, Angel dire,* and *Alien dreg.* The yield from *Geraldine R. Dodge* included the sadly appropriate *Aging elder odder. Holly Winter* produced *Wholly inert.* Taking the anagram as a hint, I signed off. My snail mail brought an overdue notice from the electric company, a threat from the phone company, two kennel-supply catalogs from which I couldn't afford to order anything, and a plain white envelope with my name and address in block capitals, a postmark blurred to illegibility, and nothing in the upper-left-hand corner.

At first, I thought the envelope was empty. It wasn't. It contained a long, narrow strip of paper with a blob of dry glue on one end. The glue, I soon realized, had originally fastened the strip of paper to a bottle of pills. An anonymous someone, for reasons I couldn't fathom, had sent me a pharmaceutical company's informational material about Soloxine, a drug commonly prescribed to treat hypothyroidism in dogs. Although I already knew what Soloxine was, I read the little brochure, mainly because I had no idea what else to do with it. Soloxine—levothyroxine sodium tablets—was a trademark of Daniels Pharmaceuticals, Inc., St. Petersburg, Florida. I sure could have used an all-expenses-paid week under a palm tree, but the uninformative envelope was now empty. A picture of the structural formula of the drug told me nothing. As

I knew, Soloxine was indicated for thyroid-replacement therapy in dogs. Primary hypothyroidism, the common kind, was caused by atrophy of the thyroid gland. Hypothyroidism sometimes appeared in young large-breed dogs, but was more typically found in middle-aged and older dogs of all sizes. I'd read the characteristic signs of hypothyroidism dozens of times in articles in dog magazines. About half of the articles said that the condition was overdiagnosed; the other half claimed it was underdiagnosed. The classic picture was of an overweight, lethargic dog with a poor coat and a sad expression. The brochure didn't mention some of the relatively subtle behavioral signs of hypothyroidism. Some hypothyroid dogs hated to be brushed. Aggressive dogs sometimes sweetened up once hypothyroidism was diagnosed and treated. The pharmaceutical company dutifully listed contraindications, precautions, and adverse reactions, and went on to discuss dosage. The main point was to monitor thyroid levels in the blood and adjust the dosage accordingly. The big risk was thyrotoxicosis, in other words, thyroid poisoning, hyperthyroidism caused by an overdose.

Fine. But why me? I wasn't overweight or lethargic, and neither were my dogs. My hair wasn't styled like Rita's, but there was nothing pathological about it, and Rowdy and Kimi had beautiful coats. Tracker? Hypothyroidism is common in dogs, both purebreds and mixes, but the characteristic thyroid problem of cats is exactly the opposite, hyperthyroidism. Tracker was not hyperthyroid. If she had been, so what? She was a spayed pet. Furthermore, I'd adopted her recently. Most people didn't even know I owned a cat. And who cared about my hormones? Steve, of course, but if he'd thought there was something wrong with my libido, he wouldn't have responded by mailing me a brochure about Soloxine. Besides, I was a dog writer and a dog person. The cryptic message of the Soloxine leaflet simply had to have something to do with dogs.

Yes, but what? A possibility came to mind. It concerned Rowdy's and Kimi's successes in the show ring. As I knew, or in some cases merely suspected, there were exhibitors who administered small doses of thyroid medication in an effort to

EVIL BREEDING / 49

improve the dogs' coats. Like many other hairy breeds, Alaskan malamutes "blow coat," as it's said, about twice a year; all of a sudden, they shed massive amounts of undercoat and guard hair. Last month's perfect show dog becomes today's perfect fright. Furthermore, some dogs simply have showier coats than others, and an alarming number of malamute judges act as if they're hired to adjudicate at fluffiness contests. Consequently, a dog with a pretty coat and not much else sometimes takes the ribbons and the points from competitors with superior structure and movement. I had never tampered with Kimi's female hormones to prevent the unhappy effects of her heat cycles on her coat. Not for a million ribbons would I have dosed a dog with any of the toxic coat enhancers thrust down the throats of show dogs: not thyroid medication, not steroids, not human birth-control pills, not arsenic. Arsenic? An old favorite. My dogs' water gets run through a Brita filter. Meanwhile, I drink what comes straight out of the faucet. If I wouldn't jeopardize my dogs' health by giving them tap water, for heaven's sake, I wasn't about to fool around with thyroid medication. One of these shows, Kimi would finish her championship, but she was no big threat. Rowdy, however, was serious competition. What's more, genetic good fortune combined with robust health, excellent veterinary care, an ideal diet, and careful grooming had given him an outstanding stand-off coat. Was a jealous competitor attributing Rowdy's wins to Soloxine? If so, I couldn't imagine who.

A second, remote possibility concerned an agreement I'd made to let Rowdy's breeder use him at stud. Although the data aren't absolutely clear, hypothyroidism seems to be especially common in Northern-breed dogs. To complicate matters, there's disagreement about what should be considered normal thyroid levels in malamutes and their Arctic kin. One point of almost universal agreement, however, is that no ethical person knowingly uses a hypothyroid dog in breeding. Some people do it, of course. Rowdy's breeder was not among those people. Neither was I! Rowdy and his proposed mate had both been screened. But had the condition ever occurred in Rowdy's lines? Yes. Now and then, it cropped up in every malamute line I'd ever heard of, just as it did in other breeds and in random-bred dogs. Even so, maybe someone without the guts to ask direct questions was suggesting that Rowdy should not be bred.

Once again, I upended the envelope and shook it. Nothing fell out. I tore it fully open. It was completely empty. Nothing linked that leaflet to the death of Christina Motherway.

Chapter Seven

I HAD SEEN DOZENS of photos of Geraldine R. Dodge. Three were my favorites. The first showed her with Rin Tin Tin. She and the famous dog faced each other. Their eyes met. Both wore relaxed smiles. He was sitting up, forepaws in the air. She was kneeling. Her right hand was raised. Her index finger was pointing. At first glance, the gesture suggested that Mrs. Dodge had just told the shepherd to sit up and was now signaling him to keep on performing the trick. If you followed the direction of her finger, however, it became apparent that my soul mate, my kindred spirit, America's First Lady of Dogs, was pointing Upward with a capital *U*. What's more, close, emphatic study revealed that Mrs. Dodge was not kneeling in the ordinary, secular sense. Rather, with religious fervor akin to my own, she was genuflecting before God and Rin Tin Tin.

The second of my favorites must have been taken when Mrs. Dodge was very old. She sat outdoors. Tall trees and low shrubs rose in the background. To the right of her chair stood two of her beloved shepherds. Two more sat on her left, and, beyond them, another rested on the lawn. What drew me into the picture wasn't just the obvious health and happiness of the beautiful and well-loved dogs. All five dogs were smiling, I admit. So was Mrs. Dodge. But what reached out and seized me were those six startlingly identical pairs of eyes.

Mrs. Dodge had seen the world through the eyes of her joyful dogs. They, in turn, gazed with delight at the perfect world she had created for them. When Mrs. Dodge was in her early eighties, her court-appointed guardians applied for legal permission to reduce the amount of money allotted to feed her dogs. Why the guardians? She had been declared mentally incompetent. Her husband had died the previous December. Although she paid $90,000 a year in taxes on her Fifth Avenue mansion, the house was never used and had been boarded up. In terms of dog ownership, she had hit what must have been the low point of her adult life: She shared the five hundred acres of Giralda with a mere forty-nine dogs. Her guardians applied to have the dogs' annual food allotment drastically reduced from $50,000 to $14,000. On June 24, 1964, in Newark, New Jersey, Superior Court, Judge Ward J. Herbert ruled against the guardians. Mrs. Dodge's dogs, he decreed, were entitled "to live in the style to which she had allowed them to grow accustomed." That's what the *New York Times* said. Gee, no wonder her shepherds had happy eyes. *I* said that.

The third picture was the one that inspired me to buy the hat. It was printed in 1973 with one of the stories about the legal battle over her will. It was a studio portrait taken about 1940, a close-up of her head and shoulders. Her features were large and heavy. To her dogs, she must have looked beautiful. I, however, felt no desire to change faces with her. No, all I wanted was her hat, which was a cloche, I guess, worn at a jaunty angle, with the brim turned up. Fastened to it was a tiny pin that represented a dog. The original hat probably came from a smart Fifth Avenue shop. In the newsprint, the hat looked black. It might actually have been a dark shade of blue, green, purple, or crimson. Its material was anyone's guess. My guess was velvet. That's what I bought in a shop in Harvard Square: a black velvet hat with a brim. I put it on at that memorably jaunty angle. I turned up the brim. Although I had no tiny pin of a dog, I added Mrs. Dodge's strong smile and the bold expression of her dark eyes. The pin would come later. Hers had probably been gold or platinum. With unpaid bills sitting at home, I shouldn't have bought the hat. I would wait for the pin. Maybe one of Mrs. Dodge's dogs had won hers. Maybe Rowdy or Kimi would win one for me.

Having illustrated the intensity of my wishful identification with Geraldine R. Dodge, I will move on to reveal the disenchanting discovery I made late that Monday afternoon while fiddling around on the World Wide Web. I was using what are called "search engines," super-duper indexes that find things on the Web. Imagine that the Web is an old-fashioned library with thousands of books, newspapers, and periodicals. To find what you're looking for, you don't use a catalog that consists of file cards arranged alphabetically by author, title, and subject. Rather, you use a miraculous device that hunts through every word in every piece of printed matter in the library. Yes, you can search for authors, titles, and subjects by the trillion. You can also search for individual words and phrases, not just in titles, but anywhere in the text of anything in this astronomically gigantic library known as the World Wide Web.

Like many other miracles—birth, death—search engines are actually quite simple. One minute the baby's inside, the next she's out and breathing for herself. One minute the person is alive, the next she isn't. Okay? One minute, you're at your computer typing "Geraldine R. Dodge." The next, you're seeing a long list of Web sites—screens of information, Web pages—that have something to say about her. And all it takes to visit one of those sites is a click of the miraculous gadget known as the mouse.

As usual, I found dozens of bothersome references to grants from the Geraldine R. Dodge Foundation, and page after page about the Dodge Poetry Festival. The on-line catalog of The Outdoor Book Store was selling old auction catalogs from Sotheby's. For fifteen dollars, I could have ordered *Magnificent Jewelry and Gold Coins—The Collection of the Late Geraldine Rockefeller Dodge.* The jewelry and coins had been auctioned on October 15, 1976. I wondered whether the collection had included the hatpin. The catalog I longed for, however, was *The Contents of Giralda—From the Collection of the Late Geraldine Rockefeller Dodge.* That auction had lasted from October 7 through October 11, 1976, and had consisted of 1,804 lots. I'd have loved to own almost anything that had been hers. At twenty-three dollars, the catalog alone was beyond my means.

The American Kennel Club Library's page popped up. The library, at AKC headquarters on Madison Avenue in New York, has a tremendous collection of periodicals, newspapers, videos, and dog books, including special collections of famous dog people. Geraldine R. Dodge was one of them. So, I was pleased to see, was Alva Rosenberg, who was, according to everything I'd heard and read, the greatest dog-show judge of all time. In a world in which titles were almost exclusively canine, Alva Rosenberg was one of the few human beings to earn one; he was universally known as the Dean of American Judges. Rosenberg's influence was still evident: He was the mentor of some of today's best judges. Mrs. Dodge must have shared the esteem for him. She had repeatedly hired him to judge at Morris and Essex. I wanted nothing more than to don my black velvet hat, stand at ringside at Giralda, and watch the Dean, Alva Rosenberg, pick the best.

So it was that the Web pages about eugenics hit me hard. What I remembered about eugenics was a name, Francis Galton, and the vague sense that eugenics had been a naïve movement aimed at breeding better people. My memory of the name was correct. Sir Francis Galton, a cousin of Charles Darwin, invented the word *eugenics*. Galton and his successors had not, however, been concerned with the betterment of humankind in general; rather, Galton had wanted to improve "the inborn qualities of a race." Hitler and his followers, of course, loved the idea of what was called "racial hygiene." What I hadn't known was that Nazi compulsory-sterilization laws were modeled on U.S. sterilization laws passed in twenty-five states. Unconstitutional? In 1916 and in 1927, the U.S. Supreme Court had ruled that compulsory sterilization was legal. Between 1907 and the mid-1960s, more than 60,000 people in the United States were involuntarily yet legally sterilized. The idea behind the eugenics movement, especially so-called negative eugenics, was that bad genes caused mental deficiency, which in turn caused poverty, crime, and other social ills. Good genes, in contrast, made people smart and rich. Another phrase from college: oh yes, Social Darwinism. Tooth and claw, the fittest fight to the top of the economic heap! The stock-market Crash and the Depression had cast some doubt on the validity of the theory. Did the Crash that overnight turned paper millionaires to paupers simultaneously turn good genes to bad? Eugenics prospered nonetheless. The Nazi sterilization legislation adopted in Germany in July of 1933 was explicitly called an "American Model" law. It was a small step from eugenics to genocide.

Throughout the twenties and thirties, American and German eugenicists had traveled back and forth between the two countries, shared ideas, and supported one another's aims. Dog breeders had, of course, done the same. But who had belonged to the American Eugenics Society? John D. Rockefeller. John D. Rockefeller, Jr., a Patron of the society. Percy A. Rockefeller. Helen Hartley Jenkins had been a member of the Second International Congress of Eugenics that met in New York in 1921. From 1923 to 1930, she served on the Advisory Council of the American Eugenics Society. In 1929, she chaired its Finance Committee. Helen Hartley Jenkins was Marcellus Hartley Dodge's aunt.

Who else had been a member of the Eugenics Society of America? Geraldine Rockefeller Dodge. As deeply as anyone on earth, she'd been devoted to breeding better dogs. The step from eugenics to genocide? Had it been an equally small step from better dogs to better people?

Chapter Eight

ONE OF THE BOOKS I'd read about the Rockefeller family claimed that the death of M. Hartley Dodge, Jr., had impelled his heartbroken mother to seek solace in dogs. Nonsense! Mrs. Dodge was breeding and showing her Giralda Farms German shepherd dogs by 1923, seven years before the accident that killed her only child. She started with imports and continued to import German and Austrian breeding stock, including two famous bitches, Arna aus der Ehrenzelle, the 1926 Siegerin of Germany, and Pia von Haus Schutting, the Siegerin of Austria. *Siegerin*: the top female from the working class at the Sieger Show, which was and is the show of shows for the breed. *The Sieger show* is the one in Germany, but other countries may hold their own Sieger shows, too. In brief, Mrs. Dodge bought the top GSD females from Germany and Austria. Even today, some breeders fail to understand the need to start with the best females as well as the best males. In that respect, Mrs. Dodge was ahead of her time. I suppose I have to admit that she understood the eugenics of dog breeding.

For Morris and Essex, she imported people as well as dogs. Forstmeister Marquandt, who judged dachshunds in 1937, and Gustav Alisch, who judged the breed a year later, were both from Germany. But she'd been mad for dozens of breeds! One of her Dobermans, Ch. Ferry v. Rauhfelsen of

Giralda, won Westminster in 1939. Doberman. Okay. But Ch. Nancolleth Markable, a pointer also owned by Giralda Farms, won Westminster in 1932. Mrs. Dodge was the president of the English Cocker Spaniel Club of America. It was under her direction that the club conducted the research on cocker pedigrees that made it possible to separate American cocker lines from those of purely English descent. Oh, my. Purity. Racial purity. But her Morris and Essex judges came from countries other than Germany. Johnny Aarflot, who judged elkhounds in 1935, was from Norway. Some of her judges were from England, where the dog-show game started: William McDerment, Scotties, 1935, and Lady Kitty Ritson, shepherds and elkhounds, 1933.

In an era when international travel was slow and expensive, Geraldine R. Dodge had time and money. Now, because of the Internet, I had friends all over the world who shared my love of the Alaskan malamute. Before exchanging e-mail with a malamute fancier in a foreign country, did I send a preliminary questionnaire about the nation's politics and human-rights policies? Of course not. Mrs. Dodge couldn't be expected to have done the equivalent. As to her membership in a eugenics organization, I reminded myself of what I'd learned on the Web: Appalling though the thought was, eugenics had not been some fringe movement supported by a little coven of lunatics; rather, in the United States and in many other countries, it had been mainstream policy. My suspicions turned to Helen Hartley Jenkins, chair of the Finance Committee of the American Eugenics Society, Mrs. Dodge's aunt by marriage. Here we have this racist, eugenicist Jenkins woman in charge of raising money for her evil cause. To whom does she turn? To her nephew's rich wife, to the eccentric heiress too wrapped up in dogs to ask astute questions before writing a check.

What proved to be my final meeting with Mr. Motherway was set for the next morning, Tuesday. The last time we'd talked, I'd been unable to keep him focused on Morris and Essex or on Mrs. Dodge. I hadn't really tried. He'd buried his wife a few days earlier; he was entitled to talk about anything he pleased. I resolved that this time I'd take charge of the interview by focusing my questions and, with luck, his replies, on the presence of German judges at Morris and Essex and of German dogs at Giralda Farms. In the thirties, the *New York Times* had made a big deal of Mrs. Dodge's fancy foreign judges and fancy foreign dogs. If the *New York Times* then, why not Holly Winter now?

So Tuesday morning found me once again seated in an upholstered chair in B. Robert Motherway's study. When Jocelyn had answered the door, the black shepherd, Wagner, had been nowhere in sight. Neither she nor I had mentioned my offer to help with the dog's unfortunate habit of growling at her. The dog's absence had made me hope that Jocelyn had taken some initiative in the matter. Maybe she'd persuaded her father-in-law to keep the dog away from her. I doubted it. She had a touchingly downtrodden air. When she was alone with her father-in-law, he probably growled at her, too.

He didn't growl at me. He didn't exactly leap to obey my every command, either. I asked about Gustav Alisch and about a man named Sickinger who'd come from Germany to judge shepherds at Morris and Essex in 1935.

"Sickinger," Mr. Motherway repeated. "Rings a bell. I knew quite a few German breeders back then. I used to escort groups of students. In the summer, you know." Indeed, I did. He was repeating himself. I didn't say so. "Expose them to the Continent and so forth," he went on. "Museums, cities, the language. I'd take advantage of the opportunity to meet the breeders I'd corresponded with, take in a show or two when I could fit it in." And then, damn it, he was off on an almost interminable tangent about the past and present differences between the judging and breeding of shepherds in the United States and in Germany. I'll spare you the details, which, in the case of the German system, are very complicated. Among other things, the German championship system requires working titles, endurance testing, and hip and elbow X rays to evaluate soundness. It also involves the assessment of what shepherd people call "progeny groups," that is, offspring. In contrast, to register a litter of GSD puppies with the American Kennel Club, you need do nothing but breed two AKC-registered GSD parents. Period.

"Incomparably superior," pronounced Mr. Motherway, referring to the German system.

I nodded. Who could disagree? When it came to breeding dogs, most European countries practiced what I now thought of as canine eugenics. With good results, too. I was in no position to object; I wholeheartedly believed in that kind of planned reproduction. For dogs. But for people? Voluntary planning? Yes. Involuntary? Certainly not! There was, however, a point on which I wanted to challenge Mr. Motherway, one I'd ordinarily have raised. For decades, the man had served as an American Kennel Club judge. In that role, hadn't he felt like a hypocrite? I held myself back.

"Americans," Mr. Motherway continued, "are finally starting to add German dogs to their breeding programs. Long overdue. I've done it myself for years. Mrs. Dodge did, of course. From the beginning."

And during the Nazi era? I longed to ask. *Just what did Geraldine Rockefeller Dodge do and not do? Who were her friends in Germany in those days?* I do not raise sensitive topics with the recently bereaved. Mr. Motherway had been born in Germany to German parents. He'd had a sister who'd died in Germany, a sister he never spoke of. For all I knew, she'd perished in the Holocaust, a victim of Nazi eugenics. For all I knew, Geraldine R. Dodge had been oblivious to the rise of German fascism. Her tremendous wealth had bought a protected life. She had been deeply absorbed in her dogs, her horses, her art collection, her peaceful passions. I struggled to rationalize her membership in the American Eugenics Society, a group with strong ties to the German eugenics movement that culminated in the death camps. All her life, Mrs. Dodge had taken in stray animals. In 1938, she'd founded St. Hubert's Giralda, which to this day carries on her mission of sheltering homeless dogs and cats. She'd taken animals from that shelter into Giralda itself. The Lady of Giralda had been kindness personified. It was simply impossible that she'd been anything remotely like a Nazi sympathizer. But from the edge of consciousness, something gnawed at me, some jarring bit of information. I felt plagued by the sense that Mr.

Motherway could not only supply the information, but clarify and explain it.

He let me down. I let myself down: I supplied nothing. Our meeting ended.

He rose. We shook hands. "It has been a pleasure," he told me. He sounded sincere.

"I'm especially grateful to you for seeing me at this difficult time," I said.

"Distraction is the best medicine," he replied graciously. "Shall we get together again? In a few weeks, let's say?"

I mumbled a promise to call him. Then he escorted me to the door of his study.

"You don't need to show me out," I assured him. "Thank you again."

According to the controls on the dashboard, my old Bronco had air-conditioning. The controls lied. Because the weather had taken one of those ghastly New England leaps from mild spring to sweltering summer, I'd left the windows down and parked in the shade of the barn, closer to the kennel runs than the resident dogs had liked. As I approached the car, the dogs in the kennel runs began barking, and Peter Motherway came stomping toward me from around a corner of the barn.

"That look like the driveway to you?" he demanded.

The complaint was unfair. Yes, I'd pulled off the gravel, but the spot I'd chosen was on a roughly mown area, not on the lawn. To make myself heard over the din of the dogs, I had to shout. "I'm sorry. I didn't think anyone would mind. My air-conditioning doesn't work too well. I always try to park in the shade. I'm leaving right now."

With shamelessly bad manners, Peter shook a fist at me. "Good! And stay gone! In case you don't know, this is a family in mourning."

Blood rose to my face. I certainly did know that it was a family in mourning. The knowledge helped me to keep my mouth shut. As I was about to take a step toward my car, Christopher Motherway, Peter's son, B. Robert's look-alike grandson, threw open the front door of the house and took long, commanding steps toward his father. The resemblance between grandson and grandfather, I instantly realized, had as much to do with attitude and demeanor as it did with physical attributes. Indeed, although Peter was shorter than his father and his son, he shared their fair coloring, their blue eyes, and their even features. But he dressed like kennel help. Did clothes unmake the man? Mr. Motherway had worn a dark summer suit. Christopher looked like a model in a magazine ad for some trendy chain of expensive sportswear shops. His blond hair was carefully tousled, and he had on tan pants, a white shirt, and leather shoes with no socks. Peter, in heavy canvas dark-blue work pants and a matching work shirt, could have been costumed to play the role of a garbage collector. In inexplicably skipping a generation, the glitter of moneyed aristocracy had excluded Peter from the elite to which his father and his son had been born.

With the air of taking the hired help to task, Christopher glared at his father. As he shouted, the barking of the dogs seemed to echo him. "You are out of line. Grandfather was looking out the window. He saw what happened. He can guess the rest. He offers his apology to Miss Winter, who is his guest here. In case you've forgotten, guests park where it is convenient for them to park."

As if determined to top his son's rudeness, Peter replied, "Mind your fucking business, you lazy little shit!"

I wanted to disappear. If the battery didn't let me down, I had the means at hand. Quietly edging my way around the quarreling father and son, I made it to the driver's side door and slid in. Looking anywhere except at the ugly family scene, I found myself staring into the distance as I turned the ignition key. As the engine caught, the great size of the distant kennels registered on me. Just how many dogs did Mr. Motherway own? Outside the open passenger window, the shouting grew increasingly violent.

"And keep that goddamned crazy Gerhard the hell away from me!" Peter bellowed. "Or I'll break his fucking neck for him. And I know how!"

I shifted into reverse and backed out. My car backfired. The sound didn't embarrass me. Neither did the car's dents and scratches. I took a deep breath and savored the lingering aroma of dogs. I could hardly wait to get home to Rowdy, Kimi, and Tracker. Rowdy and Kimi had an air of nobility that the cat and I lacked. Tracker hissed and scratched out of fear, but at least she didn't scream obscenities in front of visitors, and the dogs literally fell to the floor at the feet of my guests. I made people feel welcome. I offered food and drink. Rowdy had the gracious habit of appearing before guests bearing toys he had carefully selected as tokens of friendship. Kimi occasionally pushed hospitality a bit far by merrily sailing into someone's lap. In the privacy of our little family, I sometimes informed the dogs that they were out of line, but when they offered their paws, I said thank you. And when I needed Tracker to get off the mouse pad, I often added the word *please*. If the scene I'd just witnessed represented the graciousness of the moneyed aristocracy, I'd take genteel poverty any day.

Chapter Nine

REMEMBER THAT MOUNT AUBURN *is a cemetery and not a public park and always act accordingly.* Considering Mount Auburn's popularity as a birding spot, I hesitate to call this injunction the cemetery's cardinal rule, but that's exactly what it is. A sign near the main entrance on Mount Auburn Street specifically stated that dogs were not allowed. I had no need to take Kimi to the cemetery. It was Rowdy who had to visit the grave of his previous owner, Dr. Frank Stanton.

After returning from Mr. Motherway's, I removed both dog crates from the back of the Bronco and placed a copy of Peterson's field guide in a prominent position on the dashboard. Raising the backseat and settling Rowdy in a downstay on the floor, I took pleasure in my ability to enrich the famous garden cemetery's canine population, which, in Rowdy's absence, consisted exclusively of marble and granite dogs. In memorializing Dr. Stanton's birthday as he would have wished, I was making a creative contribution to Mount Auburn.

The first time Rowdy visited Dr. Stanton's grave, he and Steve and I went on foot. In refining my technique, I'd switched to the car and explored alternatives to the main entrance. For a city cemetery, Mount Auburn is big—174 acres. It extends beyond Cambridge into Watertown and has more than ten miles of roads and paths. It started as a rural cemetery for Boston's elite dead. Just why do I have these facts at my nontouristic fingertips? Because in preparation for writing my article about the dog statues of Mount Auburn, I'd helped myself to free pamphlets available from a rack at the entrance gate. I'd also bought a map, a necessity for finding your way around as well as for plotting ways to sneak in a dog. As my map shows, the cemetery stretches from Mount Auburn Street all the way back to the intersection of Grove Street with Coolidge Avenue, which borders Mount Auburn on the east and southeast. To the west is a Roman Catholic cemetery. Now and then, the dogs and I walked along Coolidge Avenue on our way to the Charles River. Grove Street, which is semi-industrial, has what I had hoped would be a useful service entrance to Mount Auburn. I tried it a few times, but eventually settled on the main entrance, where my car was just one of many carrying birders, walkers, tourists, and, of course, mourners.

As I turned in at the main gate, I spoke a warning to Rowdy. "Down!" I reminded him. "Good boy! Stay!" I could hear his tail thump. He is not immune to the delights of forbidden pleasure. After bearing right and then left, I followed Spruce Avenue—green line, no parking—through the heart of the cemetery and eventually turned onto the narrow road that led to Dr. Stanton's grave.

"Now, be a good boy while I reconnoiter!" I told Rowdy. "Stay!"

Our adventure was not, admittedly, in a league with the Gardner heist. Even so, I didn't want to get caught. If our secret forays became known, the guards might watch for my license plate and stop us before we even entered. Nothing worse would happen, I thought. I did, however, *imagine* worse outcomes, for example, wanted posters of a guilty-looking woman and her innocent accomplice, a handsome gray-and-white malamute, plastered on tree trunks throughout the cemetery. So far, we had pursued our life of minor misdemeanor with impunity.

Leaving Rowdy in the car, I walked the few yards to Dr. Stanton's grave, which was marked by a plain granite stone that bore only his name and the dates of his birth and death. Sometimes I brought flowers, but only as a prop. Dr. Stanton would have traded every blossom in the Garden of Eden for one glimpse of Rowdy. Today, empty-handed, I pretended to read his stone while concentrating my attention on the periphery of my vision. I listened. From the low branch of a shrub, a catbird imitated Tracker. Any species I could identify was too common to attract a flock of skilled birders. The catbird wouldn't squeal on us. No one else was around.

I stepped back to the car, opened the door, picked up Rowdy's leash, and smacked my lips. "Here we go, pal!" I whispered. Rowdy knew the routine. He moved swiftly out of the car and toward Dr. Stanton's grave. Wagging his tail and tossing me a conspiratorial glance, he almost danced on the ground in front of the stone monument.

"Happy birthday," I said. "Thank you for my perfect dog."

Then Rowdy and I bolted for the car. After meandering along roads and avenues with names that sounded more suburban than mortuary, we neared the main gate. It's an area with a lot of foot traffic. People chain their bikes to the bike rack there, and there's a bus stop nearby. I'd been driving at a respectfully slow speed, but now I slowed to a crawl and watched carefully for pedestrians. I saw one, too, one I recognized almost immediately as the art student from the Gardner museum. I'd last seen him on his knees in prayer before what the papers always called the "controversial" John Singer Sargent portrait of Isabella Stewart Gardner. The thought crossed my mind that today, the art student might have been making a pilgrimage to her grave.

The incident would have remained just that, incidental, had it not been for the murder. I heard the story the next morning on WBUR, the National Public Radio station in Boston that broadcasts mainly news, commentaries, interviews, call-in shows, and many other features that have nothing to do with dogs, but are nonetheless generously and—in my dog-biased, Dodgian view—unjustly supported by grants from the Geraldine R. Dodge Foundation. I was idly sipping coffee, glancing through the paper, and listening to NPR out of the corner of my ear when I heard the word *Gardner* and caught a note of suppressed excitement in the announcer's voice. The body of an unidentified man had been found only minutes earlier in Mount Auburn Cemetery in Cambridge. A local bird-watching group had made the discovery. According to one member of the group, the body had been propped up against the Gardner family vault, the final resting place of Isabella Stewart Gardner.

During her lifetime, the flamboyant and eccentric Isabella Stewart Gardner was big news in Boston. She persuaded the zookeeper to let her walk a young lion on a leash. Her friends included Anna Pavlova and Nellie Melba. She wore a purple velvet robe copied after one owned by Marie Antoinette. The robbery had reawakened the legend. The Boston papers found frequent excuses for articles about Mrs. Gardner: the anniversary of the theft, the perpetration of a comparable crime anywhere, or the recovery of stolen art in some distant part of the world. The theme of these stories was always the same: We should remain hopeful! The stolen art might yet turn up, and the criminals might yet be identified. Federal and state statutes of limitations had expired, but the U.S. attorney could still charge the robbers if the art had crossed state lines within the past five years; the robbers might yet be punished.

Although the murder's only connection with the robbery was the finding of a body at the Gardner vault, a local NPR reporter launched into a mandatory recap of the facts of the heist: thieves disguised as Boston police officers, guards who'd disobeyed orders by opening the museum door, the loss of thirteen pieces, all uninsured, the probable value of the stolen Vermeer and the three Rembrandts, the five-million-dollar reward.

When I switched from radio to television, a photo of Vermeer's *The Concert* filled the screen. It vanished, to be replaced by the John Singer Sargent portrait of Mrs. Gardner. Then a live camera showed a slick-looking male reporter posed in front of a familiar scene: the main gate to Mount Auburn. "We have just been informed that the man whose body was found this morning here at Mount Auburn Cemetery in Cambridge has been identified." He spoke a name that startled me. "Authorities are working on the assumption that this was not, repeat not, a natural death." After a pause, he added, with a smug note of happy finality, "James McDougall reporting. Live at Mount Auburn Cemetery!"

A sudden flash of horror crossed the reporter's face as his closing words registered. Indeed, live at the cemetery. As Peter Motherway, among others, was not.

Chapter Ten

BESIDES BEING MY next-door neighbor and an anomalously beefy long-distance runner, Kevin Dennehy is a Cambridge police lieutenant. With no success, I tried to reach him at headquarters and at home. I toyed with the thought of searching for him at Mount Auburn, but decided that the area around the Gardner vault would be sealed off. The entire cemetery might be closed to the public. What about burials scheduled for today? Would they be postponed because of murder? Held anyway? If I costumed myself in black and attached myself to a funeral party, I might get stuck at a grave in the new part of the cemetery, far from the prestigious old neighborhood of family burial chambers. Is there class after death? There is at Mount Auburn. The Gardners rest eternally in an august private residence in a tiny, thus exclusive, valley on the shores of a miniature lake. Nearby dwell Mary Baker Eddy and Henry Cabot Lodge. New neighborhoods will age. Saplings will become old trees. But they haven't yet.

I phoned police headquarters again. This time, I left a message for Kevin, a gracious invitation to dinner that evening. I promised steak. Kevin lives with his mother, who is a Seventh-Day Adventist. A strict vegetarian, she allows no meat in her house. Kevin would turn up. I pay no attention to the old taboo on training with food.

The noon news on TV showed a photo of the Gardner vault, which was as I remembered it: a quaint little flat-roofed bungalow that sat, together with other equally darling cottages, near the shore of a lake. If I hadn't known who already lived in the houses, I'd have been eager to move in. As I'd forgotten, though, the Gardner family vault had one feature I disliked, a decorative frieze that ran just below the roof and looked something like an exterior version of a wallpaper border. The repeating motif was angular and, I am positive, Greek. Still, the pattern reminded me of swastikas.

According to the TV report, Peter Motherway had last been seen alive the previous evening at the cargo area of Logan Airport. The TV showed footage of the long, bleak road that leads to Logan's cargo terminals. According to the newscaster, the victim had worked in his family's dog-breeding business and had been at the airport to ship three puppies. After accepting the puppies for shipment, airline employees had seen Motherway leave the building. Sometime thereafter, he had been strangled. His body had been found by a bird-watching group soon after eight o'clock this morning. Authorities were pursuing their investigations.

I suppressed the uncharitable thought that if Peter Motherway had been as unpleasant to other people as he'd been to me, it was no wonder someone had strangled him. Instead, I mulled over the matter of the family dog-breeding business and the shipment of the three puppies. If there's one thing that's ethical, reputable dog breeding is *not*, it's a business. My friend and mentor, Janet Switzer, was the prototype of a good breeder. And not just in the sense that her kennel had produced Rowdy! Janet bred selectively and seldom, almost always when she wanted a puppy for herself. Before her retirement, she'd worked to support herself and her dogs. Once in a while she shipped a puppy to someone in another part of the country, but only to someone she knew: another careful breeder, for example, or someone who'd previously bought a puppy from her. I couldn't imagine circumstances in which Janet would ship *three* puppies. The conventional term for someone like Janet, or for that matter, for someone like my late mother, is "hobby breeder." Hobby? Dear God! A hobby is a leisure pursuit. Whittling. Playing the glocken-spiel. Making doll dresses out of pastel facial tissues. Tropi-cal fish might be a hobby, I guess. But dogs eat every second of what would otherwise be leisure time, and they devour your income as well. Geraldine R. Dodge was about the only person I could think of who'd easily been able to afford the "hobby."

The media might have been guilty of misrepresentation. Still, I couldn't rid myself of the image of those large kennel buildings separated from Mr. Motherway's house and barn by a long stretch of field. How many dogs did they hold? Geral-dine R. Dodge, I reminded myself, had luxurious kennel space for a hundred and fifty. For breakfast, her dogs ate oatmeal mixed with fresh eggs from Giralda chickens and fresh milk from Giralda cows. To maintain the manor house and kennels, Giralda Farms employed more than sixty people. By my standards, Mr. Motherway was loaded, but he was no Rockefeller. M. Hartley Dodge, Jr., had alarmed his mother by pursuing a passion for aviation; if he'd returned alive from that summer in Europe, he'd probably have joined his father's business. He certainly wouldn't have been drafted to serve as his mother's kennel help. I'd scrubbed and disinfected the family kennels. I'd exercised, groomed, and trained our dogs. But our visitors met me; no one assumed I was a hired hand.

Dog breeding as a true business takes several different forms. Wholesale commercial breeders, otherwise known as puppy-mill operators, mass-produce puppies sold to dog bro-kers for resale in pet shops. Puppy-mill operators and brokers are the scum of the world of purebred dogs. Equally scummy are operators of what are, in effect, direct-sales puppy mills. These breeders mass-produce puppies but eliminate the mid-dlemen by selling directly to buyers, any buyers at all, anyone willing to pay cash or produce a credit card. The back pages of the dog magazines are packed with ads for these kennels. Some reputable breeders advertise there, too. The situation is a consumer nightmare. But the ads for mass-production ken-nels are pretty easy to spot. The phrase *puppies always avail-able* should arouse suspicion. Never, ever does a reputable breeder have "puppies always available."

And B. Robert Motherway? Before I had a chance to check the ads in the dog magazines, Rowdy and Kimi announced the delivery of our mail in typical malamute fashion: They ran to the door, where they stood silently wagging their tails in happy ignorance of such human afflictions as overdue notices and threatening so-called reminders from banks. Today's onslaught announced that my subscriptions to two dog magazines would expire unless I immediately sent money I didn't have. I also received my second plain white envelope. Again, the upper-left corner was blank, and my name and address were printed in block capitals. This time, the postmark was legible: Boston. Opening the flap, I half expected to find another Soloxine leaflet. What I discovered was a hand-written letter dated March 1939. The writing paper might originally have been cream-colored. Or perhaps white had yellowed with age. The return address, handwritten, consisted of a single word that it took me a moment to decipher. When I succeeded, my heart pounded. The word was *Giralda*.

The ink was faded. The backhanded penmanship was almost illegible. Here is my best try at a rendering of the letter:

Dear Bro,

A brief note to report I am settled here in great happiness in a little room of my own with fresh yellow paint and flowers on the curtains.

The arrangement is as you were told. Outdoors there are large numbers of dogs and inside at this moment a dozen, which do as they please. They are sweet of temperament, and small wonder! The best of everything goes to the dogs. Their hair makes a mess. You see I find myself in a topsy-turvy world with the husband's own fine house far away. Here the dogs occupy His place of honour.

Your,
Eva

"Very strange," I remarked to Rowdy and Kimi, who were sniffing at the old letter. "Did this come from someone who has dogs? Is that what you're smelling? Or could it be''—I paused for dramatic effect and then lowered my voice—''the lingering scent of Giralda?'' The dogs consider me the reincarnation of Sarah Bernhardt. They also love my singing, which is unrecognizable as such by any other creatures on earth. In their eyes, I perform miracles: Impenetrable barriers open before me; I unlock doors. A mighty hunter am I, departing unarmed, yet returning with forty pounds of premium kibble. Amazing grace.

''Your faith in me is entirely unjustified,'' I said. ''I have no idea who Eva is or was, who sent this to me, or why.''

Malamutes ''talk,'' as it's said. Kimi is wonderfully vocal. She delivered herself of a lengthy reply that culminated in a question: *Rrrr-ah-rooo?*

''Hypothesis,'' I replied. ''This second mysterious missive has something to do with the first. Same kind of envelope, same block-cap printing. Soloxine, Giralda, the husband in one house, the dogs in his place in the other. So . . . ?'' Where thought should have been, I found a great void.

Chapter Eleven

"SO," SAID KEVIN DENNEHY, his big face suffused with self-congratulation, "they get this kid on the stand, Jeffrey, age fifteen, and they ask him why his big brother, Robert, wanted to kill the parents. And what's Jeffrey say?"

"Kevin, I saw that in the paper, too," I replied. "He testified that Robert didn't like their parents because they wouldn't get him everything he wanted. Robert asked for a cellular phone for Christmas, and he didn't get one. It's a good thing for the rest of us that these kids didn't shoot Santa instead."

Kevin ignored my frivolity. Although nothing makes him happier than a family murder, he expects his morbid interest to be taken seriously. The murder he was discussing took place in New Hampshire; Kevin had nothing to do with investigating it. Still, he followed the newspaper accounts and police scuttlebutt about it with interest and pride. Until Robert and Jeffrey evened the score, New England, sadly lacking its very own Menendez brothers, was one down on California. Kevin is not a ghoul; violence is not what makes him happy. On the contrary, he has a strong personal and professional commitment to preventing it. What delights him about family killing is his pleasure in being proven right. You can tell by looking at Kevin that there's nothing macabre about him;

with his red hair, blue eyes, and freckles, he presents an altogether wholesome, if overwhelmingly enormous and looming, appearance. If the murder of Peter Motherway led Kevin to visit the victim's father, I hoped Mr. Motherway had had the sense to protect the delicate antique chairs. My own kitchen chairs had withstood the test of Kevin's bulk. Now, as he sat across from me with his greasy, empty plate in front of him, his mammoth frame entirely obscured the chair, but the wood hadn't cracked under his weight.

"I've forgotten the last name of those kids," I said. "Dingbat?"

Kevin was not amused. "Dingman. Jeffrey shot both of the parents first, and then Robert took the gun and finished the job. But it was Robert's idea. Robert's eighteen. He conned the kid into it. The little one, Jeffrey, went along. Eighth-grader. Said his parents yelled at him a lot."

"You want another beer?" I asked unnecessarily. Kevin almost always wants another beer. Most of the beer in my refrigerator belonged to him, anyway.

Kevin said he'd get it himself. When he rose, the dogs did, too. They'd been patiently lying on the tile floor waiting for the chance to lick our plates. I cleared the table and let the dogs sanitize the dishes before I stacked them in the dishwasher. When I turned around, the dogs were posed expectantly, Rowdy on Kevin's left, Kimi on Kevin's right.

"Kevin," I said firmly, "you are to *stop* sneaking them beer!"

"Builds the blood," Kevin replied defiantly.

"The whole performance is beneath them," I said. "It's the setting that's déclassé. I know a malamute, Tazs, who went to Germany to do weight-pulling demos, and *he* learned to drink beer, but *that* was German beer! Out of a stein! He was toasting international friendship at a festival in Berlin. He wasn't guzzling Bud out of a can in a kitchen in Cambridge."

"Hey, hey!" Kevin protested. He caught the dogs' eyes. "What we've got here," he told them in dire tones, "is a saboteur hell-bent on breaking up an important meeting of the Irish-Alaskan Friendship League. We gonna stand for that?''

''Yes *we* are!'' I said. ''They're *my* dogs. No beer!''

Then I poured myself a glass of jug red wine and resettled myself at the table. ''So,'' I said, ''you want to hear everything about the Motherways?'' I'd already told Kevin that I knew Mr. Motherway and had met Peter and Jocelyn. In fact, the topic of the Motherways was what had led Kevin to the Dingman brothers.

''The wife is an odd duck,'' Kevin commented. It was, I thought, his way of beginning an indirect interrogation.

I supplied her name. ''Jocelyn. The first time I went there, I mistook her for a maid, or maybe the older Mrs. Motherway's nurse. That was Christina, B. Robert Motherway's wife. She just died.''

''Advanced arteriosclerosis. Alzheimer's.''

''Jocelyn took care of her. The family was determined that Christina would be allowed to die at home. Or her husband was, anyway. And she did. I think that Jocelyn was genuinely devoted to her.''

''Takes flowers to her grave,'' Kevin informed me.

''I didn't know that. She's buried at Mount Auburn. Is that . . . ?''

Kevin's beefy face broke into a grin. ''A *clue?*''

''Well, yes. Peter was killed where his recently deceased mother was buried. By coincidence?''

Kevin's head is about the size of a mastiff's. When he shakes it, I involuntarily flinch in expectation of being spattered with drool. ''He wasn't killed there. The body was moved.''

''Where *was* he killed? At Logan? Speaking of which, I have a lot to tell you about this puppy business of theirs. I really was very stupid. I thought Mr. Motherway was perfectly respectable. He'd been in shepherds forever, and he was an AKC judge, and he knew these important people. And I never questioned that. Until today. When I heard on the news that Peter had been shipping three puppies and that he was in the family's dog-breeding *business,* it made me wonder, so I did some checking. Kevin, these people are not who

I thought they were. Ages ago, Mr. Motherway, old Mr. Motherway, was respectable, but now they run what's basically a direct-sales puppy mill. They sell to absolutely anyone. They run ads in all the dog magazines. They breed tons of dogs.''

''So how come you didn't know?''

''If they'd had malamutes, I would've known. And now that I do know, I can see that people were giving me hints. Someone e-mailed me that she'd love to be a fly on the wall when I talked to Mr. Motherway. I couldn't understand what she meant. I asked, but I never got a reply. Now I realize that she expected me to give Mr. Motherway a lecture on responsible breeding. What a dope I am! I thought people were impressed that I knew Mr. Motherway. And, uh, I sort of overplayed the extent of my acquaintance with him, so naturally, people didn't come right out and say insulting things about someone they thought was a friend of mine.''

As I didn't bother telling Kevin, I now viewed the mysterious Soloxine leaflet as a hint I'd ignored. The point of sending it to me, I'd now decided, had been to suggest that Motherway was breeding hypothyroid dogs. Once my suspicions had been aroused, I'd checked the dog magazines and found big ads for Haus Motherway German Shepherd Dogs. Puppies, adults, and stud service were always available. There was even a toll-free number to call. In every magazine, the Motherway ad prominently displayed a professional photo of a black-and-tan male shepherd with an impressive number of German titles. A phone call to my friend Elise, who does shepherd rescue, gave me a piece of information omitted from the ad: The dog in the picture had been dead for twenty years. German Shepherd Rescue knew all about the Motherways. Elise said that no one was sure how many dogs the Motherways had. Guesses ranged from fifty to a hundred. The Motherways' puppies were notorious for health and temperament problems attributable to a lack of genetic screening compounded by repeated inbreeding: autoimmune disorders, hypothyroidism, hip dysplasia, elbow dysplasia, and everything from extreme shyness to outright viciousness.

''They just churn them out as fast as they can,'' Elise had

said, "and take no responsibility afterwards. When someone turns one of their dogs over to us, we don't even bother calling him. Motherway has never taken a dog back in his life. The reputable German breeders won't sell to him anymore. They're sorry they ever did. They think he's garbage."

Pouring a little more of the vinegary wine into my glass, I said to Kevin, "I should have known there was something fishy. Mr. Motherway came across as the gracious old gentleman, American antiques, European travel, the whole bit. The grandson, Christopher, looks exactly like him. Christopher struck me as sort of arrogant. 'Entitled,' Rita would say. And Peter was definitely unpleasant. Sullen. But the strange thing was that it was as if Christopher, the grandson, was Mr. Motherway's son, and Peter was some serf who worked for both of them. Except that Peter didn't exactly play that role gracefully. He obviously didn't get along with his father or his son, and he sort of went around radiating resentment. His wife, Jocelyn, is the original doormat. They have this dog, this big black shepherd, Wagner, that tags along with Mr. Motherway, and even the dog realizes that Jocelyn is at the bottom of the hierarchy. The dog growls at her, and no one interferes, and she just kind of takes it as her due. It's pitiful. But there's something likable about Jocelyn. I offered to help her with the dog, but I guess she wasn't interested."

Kevin was sipping his beer from the can. Although I knew he was listening, his eyes were on Rowdy and Kimi. Rowdy lay in almost comatose bliss on his side as Kimi leaned over him and energetically scoured his face with her maternal pink tongue. She licked repeatedly at one of his ears, moved to the other, then ministered to his eyes, which he was forced to close to avoid having his eyeballs groomed. After that, she apparently meant to give herself a break, but Rowdy stirred. Gently and tenderly, he poked her in the chest with one of his big forepaws. *More!* As if she were glad to know that he appreciated her efforts, she resumed her task. The sight of Kimi playing dental hygienist with her tongue was too much for Kevin. He looked back at me.

"Quiet type." Kevin's tone was ominous.

"Kimi? Kevin, I'd hardly call her the——"

"The widow. Jocelyn. Sometimes it's the mousy ones that—".

"That what? Turn out to be bubbling with murderous rage that finally comes spewing out? Kevin, Jocelyn Motherway is not some sleeping volcano. I've met her. She just isn't."

Stretching his gorilla-like arms in an immense shrug, Kevin said lugubriously, "Marriage. It'll do that to a person." Kevin's prejudice against the institution is not based on personal experience, unless you count his experience with his mother and his late father, who died a natural death, at least as far as I know. Rather, according to Kevin, he merely possesses a professional understanding of the risks of marriage and parenthood. For as long as I've known him, his view has been that if your spouse doesn't kill you, your parents, your siblings, or your children will.

I hoped Kevin wouldn't launch into statistics. He did. Forty-five percent of murder victims were killed by people they knew. Twenty-six percent of female murder victims were done in by a husband or boyfriend. When women committed murder, in thirty-one point four percent of the cases, the victim was the husband. *Mate homicide* is a phrase he savors.

"Kevin, I don't remember numbers the way you do, but I seem to recall from one of our previous discussions that the great majority of murderers *and* victims are men. Violence is a predominantly *male* phenomenon. It is in dogs. The typical dog that bites someone is an intact male.

Kevin turned red.

"But," I added, "does that mean that Rowdy is going to bite someone? No. And all the statistics going do not mean that this particular murder is a mate homicide. Since most murderers are male, the raw probability is that Peter was killed by a man."

"Never said otherwise." With a look that falsely suggested a change of subject, Kevin asked, "You read about that guy in Watertown?"

Watertown is west of Cambridge. I'd assumed until now that Kevin had been too busy to follow the latest local example of what was definitely a family murder. This one was especially gory and dramatic. At five-thirty in the evening on

EVIL BREEDING / 79

a quiet street of small houses, a thirty-six-year-old man cut his sixty-seven-year-old father's throat. The father got up and ran. Neighbors tried to intervene, but the son caught the father and stabbed him to death.

"Yes," I admitted, "and if you know any details that weren't in the paper, I don't want to hear them, and in particular, considering that we have both just eaten a big meal, including steak, it would be nice of you to refrain from quoting the autopsy report." I particularly hate hearing post-mortem incisions compared to letters of the alphabet. I *like* the alphabet. I don't want to think of its letters in terms of shapes incised in dead bodies. "Peter Motherway wasn't stabbed, was he? I thought he was strangled."

"Garroted. Strangled with a thin length of wire." He got himself another beer.

"What makes you think he wasn't killed at Mount Auburn?"

Kevin was succinct. "Everything. M.E. says so. And Motherway's vehicle was left at Logan, probably right where he parked it. Poor bastard probably never got back into it. Eight forty-five P.M. Comes out of the cargo terminal, proceeds to his vehicle, perp moves in from behind, wire around his neck—"

"Well, you can probably rule out old Mr. Motherway. He's in great shape for his age, but I'm far from sure he's strong enough. And Jocelyn doesn't have the gumption. Christopher?"

"Out to dinner with Granddad. Got to the restaurant—French place in Acton—at seven-thirty. Left at ten. Service must've been awful. Stopped for gas on the way home. Verified." Acton is west of Boston, nowhere near Logan airport or Mount Auburn Cemetery.

"Jocelyn wasn't with them," I said.

"Home alone," Kevin replied. "Big, brawny woman. A lot of muscles from lifting the old lady." He paused. "Home alone."

Chapter Twelve

LET ME INTRODUCE Althea Battlefield, BSI, as she likes to be presented. Instead of boldly stating that Althea was born in the year before Marcellus Hartley Dodge and Ethel Geraldine Rockefeller became man and wife, I'll explain that the letters after Althea's name proclaim her membership in the Baker Street Irregulars. I can best explain the organization in terms of my own native language and subculture: The Baker Street Irregulars is *the* elite, by-invitation-only kennel club for fanciers of Sherlock Holmes.

Just as the American Kennel Club long refused to allow women to serve as delegates, so the BSI persisted in barring women from membership. The AKC was established in 1884. One of its founders was William Rockefeller, father of you know who. Not until 1973 did the AKC make the dramatic announcement that it would permit women to serve as delegates. Geraldine R. Dodge died the same year—not of surprise. So far as I know, the events were unconnected. Founded in 1934, the BSI waited until 1991 to admit women. Before that, Althea was stuck in the ladies' auxiliary, known, incredibly, as the Adventuresses of Sherlock Holmes.

Althea? An *adventuress*? The word has licentious connotations. The other Adventuresses may, I suppose, have sashayed around madly contracting scandalous liaisons. Althea, however, is in all respects a thoroughly upright person. She uses a wheelchair, but she sits up straight in it with her extremely long legs stretched ahead of her and her large feet resting on the floor. Everything about her is lengthy: her arms, her hands, her torso. She has a large, bony head. Althea's memory, too, is immense. She remembers everything about the many years she has lived through. That's why I consulted her about the eugenics movement in the twenties and thirties. I was counting on her to exonerate Mrs. Dodge.

I'd met Althea the previous January, when she lived at the Gateway, a nursing home where Rowdy and I still do therapy-dog visits. Most people in nursing homes move only to the same final destination, but almost everyone dreams of leaving as Althea did, which is to say, alive. Not that the Gateway is a terrible place; on the contrary, it is cheerful, busy, and attentive. Even so, Althea was far happier sharing a house with her sister, Ceci, than she'd been at the Gateway. There, Althea's living space had consisted of half a shared room. Although she'd tried to surround herself with Sherlockian artifacts, she'd had space on her nightstand and windowsill for only a few treasured volumes and a handful of carefully chosen objects. Meanwhile, her sister, Ceci, a wealthy widow, had lived all by herself in a big, beautiful house on Norwood Hill in the suburb of Newton.

Althea's room in the house on Norwood Hill had originally been the library. It was a large, sunny room with a fireplace. The built-in shelves that lined the walls held hundreds, perhaps thousands, of books about Sherlock Holmes, and displayed pipes, Persian slippers, deerstalker hats, statuettes, and zillions of other Holmesian icons. The collection was especially large because Ceci's late husband, Ellis, another Sherlockian, had maintained the library as a shrine to Baker Street. The addition of the items Althea had had at the Gateway and those she'd kept in storage had turned the room into a little museum. The only non-Holmesian object was Althea's bed, although it, too, may have slyly alluded to the Canon in a way that escaped me. One of the advantages of Althea's new Sherlockian quarters was, I thought, that she wasn't confined to them. The library-bedroom was right next to the living room, which was where Rowdy and I often found her on what were no longer therapy-dog visits, but calls of friendship.

On Thursday morning at ten, I rang the bell of the big white house on Norwood Hill. One of Althea's nurses, Ginny, answered the door and led Rowdy and me to the far end of the living room, where a plant-filled alcove formed a miniature conservatory. The French doors of the alcove gave a view of the terrace and the spacious backyard. The alcove had a tile floor and was crowded with potted palms and rattan furniture. Althea's wheelchair had been positioned to bake her in the sort of solar oven that people in their nineties often enjoy. The skin on her face had passed beyond wrinkles to translucent purity. Her white hair was so thin that it revealed her pale scalp and the skull beneath; she could have modeled for a phrenologist. Although Althea had lost most of her vision, her faded eyes retained an unmistakable look of sharp intelligence. She wore a pink silk dress.

"Good morning, Holly!" Althea is one of the few friends I have who greet me first. "Rowdy, good morning to you, too."

The big boy was on his best therapy-dog behavior. He did not chomp on the palms and then deposit half-digested leaves on some prominent spot on the living room rug. Instead of dropping to the tile to beg for a tummy rub, he sat close enough to Althea to let her reach his head. Then he raised a massive paw and rested it on the arm of her chair. Posed together with the palm fronds in the background, the two looked like figures in a sentimental Victorian oil painting.

Taking a seat in one of the thickly cushioned rattan chairs, I said, "Althea, I need to ask you something that isn't about Sherlock Holmes."

She chortled. "If pressed, Holly, I am capable of limited small talk on one or two other subjects."

"Eugenics," I said abruptly. "I need to know about the eugenics movement: who supported it, what it meant, how people felt about it." I hesitated. Althea's age was no secret, and she was ferociously proud of her memory. Even so . . .

"In the thirties," she said with a knowing little smile.

"Yes," I replied gratefully. I leaned forward in my chair.

"I have the impression that, at least for some people, eugenics meant different things before and after the Holocaust. That in the late twenties maybe . . ." I stumbled. "Or in the early thirties." I took a breath. "That *some* people, some decent people, saw it just as a way to improve social conditions, end poverty, and so forth."

"Revisionist nonsense!" Althea decreed. "Eugenics was as evil then as it is now. Breeding better people, indeed! Ridding the gene pool of unfit stock! Elitist, racist, anti-Semitic, pseudoscientific palaver! People are not show dogs, and that's that."

"But why would . . ." I began again. "Why would a kind, decent person have supported it?"

"Stupidity?" Althea suggested. "Naïveté. And people who are kind and decent in some respects may still harbor delusions of their own superiority. Vanity plays a role. It isn't flattering to be told that we're all created equal, is it? Ah, but to be told that by virtue of nothing more than birth, one is an Aryan superman? The appeal to vanity was as effective as it was dangerous."

"A lot of Americans were taken in, at least temporarily," I pointed out. "They had German friends. They visited Germany in the thirties. Just the way they do now. Althea, Americans visit Germany all the time. American dogs do!" Mindful of the beer lecture I'd delivered to Kevin, I said, "I have a friend, Delores Lieske, whose malamute, Tazs, went to Berlin, for heaven's sake, to celebrate the reunification of Germany. This was for the German-American Volksfest. Tazs was specially invited. All expenses paid! He gave weight-pulling demonstrations, and he visited with people. Paws across the water. He's very charming. Among other things, he purrs and moans when you pat him, and he turns somersaults. Or he did then." I hesitated. "He's a little old for somersaults. Now he corkscrews. Anyway, in the thirties, most of the visits back and forth between Germany and the U.S. were probably just like that! Innocent! Americans went there, and they didn't see——"

Althea jabbed a bony fist in the air. She seemed almost to be mocking the Nazi salute. "*Then*, in the thirties, there was evil to be seen. And if people didn't see, it was only because they were fooling themselves. I ask you! What kind of person is taken in by *goose-steipping*? Flashy uniforms, braggadocio, national self-aggrandizement, tirades of *hate*! Your friend's dog wouldn't have been deceived! My dear, from the beginning, the evil of the Third Reich was visible, audible, and palpable. The essence of that evil was, of course, the death of compassion.'' Althea paused. ''Holly, if I may ask, is there someone in particular you have in mind? Besides a somersaulting dog?''

I told Althea about Geraldine R. Dodge. I gave the short version. ''She'd had friends in Germany since the early twenties,'' I finally said, ''if not earlier. These were other dog people, breeders, important dog-show judges. I can't believe that they were any more political than dog people are in this country right now.''

Althea corrected me. ''Here, in this country, we enjoy the luxury of choosing whether to be political. Or perhaps the luxury of imagining that we are not. In Germany in the Nazi era, that choice did not exist.''

''Althea, I just cannot see Mrs. Dodge as someone who wanted to kill off the poor or sterilize people against their will, and I cannot see her as a Nazi sympathizer. But . . .''

''Yes?''

''She had German judges at her shows in the thirties, and not just in the early thirties.''

''And?''

''And I just found, on the Web—''

Althea came close to snorting. One of her Sherlockian friends, a man named Hugh, is a computer type from way back who is hooked on the World Wide Web and persists in futile efforts to introduce Althea to its wonders. But she does know what the Web is.

''Well, I did find it on the Web!'' I insisted. ''And I must have known this before, but maybe I'd forgotten. The point is that when the Nazis took over, they took over *everything*, including, believe it or not, dog clubs. They disbanded every breed club and every training club, every dog organization throughout Germany, and they nationalized all dog activities and events under the control of one government-run organization. And Mrs. Dodge absolutely must have known that. So when Mrs. Dodge invited German judges to her shows in the mid- and late thirties, they didn't just come here as individuals. These people arrived with *Nazi blessings.* Otherwise, they wouldn't have been here."

"You are shocked that the Nazis took over a part of *your* world? And sent it here?"

"Yes, I am."

Althea's expression was slightly cynical, but her tone was kind. "Holly, have you ever heard the word *totalitarian?*"

"Of course," I replied.

"Well, my dear, what did you think it meant?"

Chapter Thirteen

THE STAR OF DOG TRAINING that Thursday evening was, for once, a human being, a woman named Sherry who'd joined the Cambridge Dog Training Club about six months earlier. Sherry's dog, Bandit, was a bright, eager Aussie—Australian shepherd—who harbored a prejudice against Rowdy and Kimi, whom he apparently saw as a threat to sheep. I didn't hold Bandit's opinion against him. I thought he was right. To avoid arousing Bandit's sheep-protective instincts, I usually kept my dogs away from him. Consequently, I hardly knew Sherry. Tonight I risked Bandit's wrath by easing Rowdy into the little crowd that surrounded Sherry, who, it turned out, lived within a half mile of the Motherways. What's more, Sherry's best friend had gone to high school with Jocelyn.

The Motherways were already the main subject of talk in the advanced class when Rowdy and I arrived at the Cambridge Armory, which is on Concord Avenue within easy walking distance of my house. At the end of the hall close to the entrance, the big beginners' class was laboring over such rudiments of civilization as sit and stay, but at the far end of the room, Roz, our advanced instructor, was working individually with a single dog-handler team at a time. At the moment, Ray Metcalf and one of his Clumber spaniels had all Roz's attention. Everyone else was clustered around Sherry, a plump woman with short, gray-blond curls. At a guess, she was fifty, about Jocelyn Motherway's age. Age was the only thing the women had in common, I thought, age and, as I soon learned, the friend who'd gone to high school with Jocelyn. In particular, Sherry had the self-confidence and animation that Jocelyn sorely lacked.

"Ask anyone!" Sherry exclaimed. "The old man was always, always stinking mean to Peter, who was, believe me, no sweetheart, but you have to ask yourself, If you'd been raised like that, what would you be like?" Bandit, sitting squarely at Sherry's left side, kept his eyes fastened on her face and listened with anticipatory interest, almost as if he expected her to order him to go fetch Mr. Motherway and shape him up. "When Jocelyn and Peter got married," Sherry continued, "it was just awful. Peter's father had a fit—and for the stupidest reason, which was that Jocelyn was adopted. Peter's father figured she wasn't good enough for his son because she didn't know who her parents were, like it matters. And it wasn't like Peter was some great catch, either. He flunked out of the academy, where his father taught, and then he got kicked out of another prep school, and he ended up in high school, and he barely graduated. And then he got sent to Vietnam, and when he got back, he moved in where they live now, in this little house, like a cottage, on his parents' property, and he did odd jobs around town, but mainly he just did stuff there for his father. Sandra, my best friend, the one who went to school with Jocelyn, says the only reason Jocelyn ever got mixed up with him, Peter, to begin with was *low self-esteem*." Sherry made it sound as if the rest of us had never encountered the phrase before. After letting the idea sink in, she lowered her voice. "But about getting married, Jocelyn didn't have a lot of choice. Things were different back then."

To my annoyance, Roz interrupted. "Sherry? You and Bandit are next." Really! What, after all, is the purpose of dog training? Gossip? Or just training dogs?

While Sherry and Bandit worked with Roz, I got Rowdy's cheese cubes and roast beef from my little insulated bag, filled my pockets, and warmed him up with some heeling.

But as soon as Sherry's turn was over, I felt compelled to rejoin the group.

"What was Mrs. Motherway like?" I asked. "Peter's mother, Christina. The one who just died."

"Oh, she tried to be nice to Jocelyn, but she'd spoiled Peter rotten, and it was too late to fix that. When Peter was a kid, his father'd make him do this awful stuff, and Peter'd go running to his mother, and she'd give him whatever he wanted. And then his father'd call him a sissy."

"What awful stuff?" I asked.

Ron, who is my plumber as well as my dog-training buddy, said in my ear, "Holly, you don't want to hear. She was telling us before you got here."

"I *do* want to hear," I told him.

"It's gross. Take it from me. You don't want to hear."

I should have listened to Ron. A dog-training plumber is, by definition, a person who understands how things work. I persisted. "What awful stuff?" I asked Ron.

Unfortunately, he told me. "The old man used to make the son, Peter, kill the puppies there was something wrong with. He made him drown them. Sherry says he made the grandson do the same thing. When they were just little kids."

Ray Metcalf was listening in. "The Nazis used to do that," he commented. Ray is old enough to remember the era. He served in World War II. "Training for the Third Reich. They'd give a soldier a dog to raise, and then make him strangle it with his own hands."

"Ron is *right*," I said vehemently. "I really don't want to hear this." My stomach was turning. To settle myself, I stroked Rowdy's soft ears, but when our time with Roz finally arrived, I still felt queasy. By concentrating on Rowdy and on the exercises, I managed to escape from myself, but as soon as our turn was over, the nasty feeling returned. For once, I was glad to leave the armory.

Walking home up Concord Avenue, I tried to blot out the ugly images by focusing on Rowdy's pleasure in the cool of the evening, his wholesome happiness in trotting briskly over familiar pavement, and his earthy satisfaction in marking trees, shrubs, and utility poles he'd claimed as his own many times before. Terrible, unspeakable things, I reminded myself, had happened and would happen to millions of people. The perversion of the human-canine bond that Ray had mentioned was simply a form of dehumanization I hadn't happened to hear of before. If Mrs. Dodge had known of this or any of the other horrors perpetrated by the Third Reich, she'd have had nothing at all to do with anyone even remotely connected with the Nazis.

But what of B. Robert Motherway? In referring to his travels in Germany in the thirties, he'd said not a word about Hitler. Had he been a Nazi sympathizer? The notion seemed fantastic. Then I realized with a jolt that he'd had the perfect cover: He'd been an art history teacher who spent his summers leading American students on tours of Europe. If his German was good? His field was art history; of course his German was good. And he didn't have a German name. *Robert* was innocently English. *Motherway*, I realized for the first time, must have been the name of B. Robert's stepfather, the American who'd married a German bride, adopted her son, and cultivated the boy's interest in art and in dogs.

With a second jolt, it hit me that Mr. Motherway hadn't been the only character in this drama with the perfect cover. Those famous foreign judges? The experts Mrs. Dodge had imported to officiate at Morris and Essex? Mrs. Dodge's German judges had visited Giralda with the blessing of the Third Reich. Those judges had returned to Nazi Germany. No one would have suspected a bunch of harmless dog nuts. How suspicious had the U.S. government been in the thirties, anyway? Not nearly suspicious enough, it seemed in retrospect.

Geraldine R. Dodge could *not* have sympathized with the Nazis, I reminded myself. Her support of the eugenics movement, I told myself, must represent a hideously naïve lapse of judgment. But it was just possible that she had been used: It was remotely possible that my book about the Morris and Essex shows would require a chapter about German spies.

Chapter Fourteen

ON FRIDAY MORNING at ten-thirty when Rowdy and I arrived at the Gateway for our weekly therapy-dog visit, I found a note from the director of social services pinned next to my volunteer's badge and sign-in sheet on the cork bulletin board in the nursing home's office. "Maida Garabedian," the note said. "Room 416. Likes dogs."

The characterization proved to be an understatement. After moving upward through the nursing home to visit Rowdy's regular customers, we took the elevator from the fifth and top floor to the fourth, and made our way to 416, which was a private room at the end of a corridor. A new-looking plastic plaque near the door frame read M. GARABEDIAN. Before I had a chance to poke my head through the open doorway to make sure we'd be welcome, the tiny, dark, and ancient woman in 416 caught sight of Rowdy and burst forth in a high-pitched peal of glee. Experience at the Gateway had taught me the wisdom of double-checking my reading of every initial response, no matter how enthusiastic it appeared. A few residents were so heavily medicated that they greeted everyone and everything with a calm, bland smile that could swiftly turn to a grimace of terror when a big dog suddenly loomed. Some of our regulars found Rowdy's size and wolflike appearance so overwhelming that they preferred to admire him from a distance. Others longed for the primary, primitive contact of touching the soft hair on his ears and digging fingers into the depths of his thick coat. Several real dog people wanted nothing more than to have their faces scoured by his clean pink tongue. The universal friendliness that made Rowdy a natural therapy dog sometimes led him to overestimate people's eagerness for close contact. I always held Rowdy back until I'd asked, "Do you like dogs?"

In response to my question, Maida Garabedian clapped her tiny, gnarled hands together and then patted her lap invitingly with her open palms. When I let Rowdy take a few steps toward her, her face vanished in a mass of grinning wrinkles. "This is Rowdy," I told her. "I'm Holly." She had eyes only for him. As she stared at Rowdy and made smacking sounds with her lips, my task became clear: I was going to have to prevent Maida Garabedian from enticing Rowdy to leap into her lap. She'd have to settle for cradling his head; the weight of the whole dog would have crushed her frail bones to powder. "Easy does it," I cautioned Rowdy.

We spent about ten minutes with Maida, who caught Rowdy's name and addressed him by it again and again, but gave no sign of understanding anything else I said. At first, I tried out a few topics of conversation. "Maida is such a pretty name. Do you remember the children's books about Maida? *Maida's Little House? Maida's Little Zoo?*"

My childhood reading was heavily concentrated on dog books. What now struck me as the absurd premise of the Maida series had, however, taken my fancy. Maida was a little invalid whose widowed father, Jerome Westabrook, a Boston financier, cured his daughter's loneliness and, eventually, her limp, by recruiting poor children to live on his fabulous estate. Each book was devoted to a new and yet more extravagant project that Mr. Westabrook arranged for his indulged daughter and the fortunate young objects of his beneficence: Maida's little house, little shop, little houseboat, little island, little theater, and any other obscenely expensive little thing Maida craved, I guess.

Maida Garabedian, however, hadn't read the series, had forgotten it, or had lost her capacity to chat about it. What took her fancy was feeding treats to Rowdy one at a time from her open hand. "Like a horse!" I instructed, in what was probably an unnecessarily loud voice. Although Rowdy is gentle, it's risky to offer him a tiny bit of food pinched between a finger and thumb, unless, of course, you happen to have taken a violent dislike to the tips of your digits. Maida had no trouble in mastering the correct technique. Every time Rowdy's tongue swept a bit of dog cookie off her hand, she burst into laughter, then offered me her palm for a refill. Playing my limited role, I found myself thinking that, damn it all, locked somewhere in Maida's brain cells were vivid sensory memories of the era just before World War II, the days of the great Morris and Essex shows, shows that this woman who was now feeding my dog had had the glorious opportunity to attend. Had she availed herself of it? I didn't even know whether she'd ever owned a dog or gone to a dog show in her entire and exceedingly long life, never mind made the pilgrimage to Giralda. For a moment, I envied Rowdy's animal capacity to link with her. Had I been able to do the same, I'd have tapped her recollections. And found . . . ?

Unexpectedly, the question led to a sort of negative epiphany. Is there such a thing? Yes. I had one. For all I knew, this Maida's experience of the thirties had less to do with the foreign judges, the top dogs, and the sterling silver trophies of a lavish dog show than with the breadlines of the Great Depression. What came to me as I longed for a direct line to Maida Garabedian's memory was an image from my own recent memory, an image in a photograph I'd looked at only a few days earlier. There'd been a dog in the picture, a shepherd that had belonged to Mrs. Dodge. It wasn't the dog that bothered me. It was the vehicle in which he rode. While people by the thousands, including some of the people I now visited at the Gateway, had stood in breadlines, voted for FDR, and labored for the WPA, the lucky dogs of Geraldine R. Dodge had traveled in comfort and style. These days, exhibitors either drive their dogs from show to show on superhighways or ship them rapidly by air. In the twenties and thirties, dogs and people alike poked along on slow roads or traveled by rail. Unwilling to subject her dogs to the discomforts endured by plebeian canines, Mrs. Dodge commissioned a Cadillac touring car, a maroon stretch limo that took three men more than three years to custom-build. It had eight doors and carried as many as a dozen dogs. Wide-eyed, I'd studied the photo of this wonder. Now, fed by the reality of people at the Gateway who'd survived the Depression, nurtured by the chance association of a name, Maida, the image assailed me. Belatedly, the photo spoke of decadence. Or maybe it sang the theme song of the Depression: "Brother, Can You Spare a Dime?"

As Rowdy and I drove home from the Gateway, I found myself taking pride and pleasure in everything that was wrong with my old car. Instead of cursing the windshield wipers for senselessly leaping to life whenever I signaled a turn, I interpreted the malfunction as proof that no matter how well my dogs lived, no one could accuse me of decadence when I was at the wheel of so blatantly proletarian a clunker. Arriving home, I reminded myself that in 1937, the Dodges' country estate had covered seven thousand acres, making it larger than my lot at the corner of Appleton and Concord in Cambridge by more than 6,999 acres. Furthermore, in contrast to the Dodges, who had lived in separate mansions, I rented out my upstairs apartments. Rowdy, Kimi, Tracker, and I occupied only the first floor, I did most of the repairs and maintenance myself, and if I'd been fortunate enough to own another house, I wouldn't have let it become an eyesore like Mrs. Dodge's neglected town house at 800 Fifth Avenue. The premise of the Maida books wasn't so ludicrous after all,' I decided. What had Isabella Stewart Gardner really done with her inheritance from her stinking-rich father? What had Geraldine R. Dodge done with hers? *Maida's Little Museum*, I thought. *Maida's Great Big Dog Show.* And if Geraldine R. Dodge was me with money, just what did that make me?

A lucky person, I decided. Yes, Mrs. Dodge and I shared a passion, but she had the means to carry that passion to excess. I didn't. In pursuing the love without the money, I was doubly blessed.

With the peculiar sense of having clarified and deepened

my relationship with the long-dead Mrs. Dodge, I felt free to work on the book, perhaps because I'd overcome a lingering fear of discovering facts I didn't want to know. Liberated, I made myself a cup of strong coffee and settled at the kitchen table with both dogs snoozing at my feet. The material I'd been avoiding consisted of *New York Times* articles that I'd hastily copied from microfiche and deposited largely unread in a manila folder labeled "Wartime Hiatus." Because the book was supposed to focus on the Morris and Essex shows held before World War II, I'd had a handy rationalization for poring over the *Times* articles from that era while neglecting the contents of the folder I now opened. Still, in the time I'd frittered away exchanging e-mail and surfing the Web in search of anything whatever about Mrs. Dodge, I could practically have memorized the articles about the wartime cancellation of Morris and Essex. After all, how much had there been to report about shows that hadn't been held? One sentence a year would've been adequate: "The Morris and Essex Kennel Club has announced the cancellation of its annual show." End of story. But the real articles didn't stop there. As I remembered from the skimming I'd done before copying the articles from microfiche, the *New York Times* went on to express a low opinion of the cancellations; between the lines, the paper blamed Mrs. Dodge.

The first of the hiatus articles, as I thought of them, had been published on January 28, 1942. Mrs. M. Hartley Dodge, president of the Morris and Essex Kennel Club of Madison, New Jersey, had announced the cancellation of the organization's annual all-breed dog show because of war conditions. The unanimous decision, based on the recommendation of Mrs. Dodge, had been made at the club's yearly meeting at Giralda Farms. The *Times* described the club's action as the "first major break in the big show circuit ascribed to war conditions." The article went on: "Both the United States and England in the first world war found that sports contributed to sustaining army and civilian morale. Great Britain, despite terrific bombing, has continued to carry on in sports as far as possible. Many organizations all over the United States have voted to continue." The final paragraph noted a "sharp contrast" between this cancellation and the determination of other kennel clubs in the United States to hold their shows as planned. The implication was clear: Whereas the Westminster Kennel Club, the Eastern Dog Club, and other major dog organizations were patriotically following the British example of carrying on, Morris and Essex was letting our side down. Furthermore, since Mrs. Dodge practically *was* Morris and Essex, the failure was her fault.

In a letter to the *Times* published on February 2, 1942, a patriotic dog fancier took Mrs. Dodge and her club to task for delivering a "body blow." According to the writer, instead of following the weak example set by Mrs. Dodge and the Morris and Essex Club, other dog people and other clubs should boldly carry on and rally round in the inspiring fashion of the British. As I interpreted the letter, it went on to accuse Mrs. Dodge of weakness, cowardice, and stupidity. She must have read the letter, too. It had not changed the club's decision.

As sharp as the contrast between Morris and Essex's caving in and the struggle of other dog clubs to charge ahead was the contrast between the tone of *Times* articles before and after the '42 cancellation. From 1928 on, as Mrs. Dodge's shows grew larger and grander, the coverage in the *Times* grew increasingly extensive and laudatory. Separate articles, most under the byline of Henry R. Ilsley, announced plans for the show, oohed and ahed about the judges, reported on the number of entries expected, and raved about the trophies and prizes. Year after year, the *Times* heralded Morris and Essex with a long article about elaborate preparations and glorious expectations, and the next day, reported with wild enthusiasm on the excitement and splendor of the event. In 1936 the show was "one of the most notable sporting pageants ever staged." The next year it was "the greatest outdoor canine exhibition ever to be staged in any land." The show was "an institution" the fame of which had "spread to the ends of the canine world." It was "a pre-eminent pageant as well, unrivaled in the beauty and color of its environment, unsurpassed in the perfection of its staging." In 1939 this "fixture," Morris and Essex, was "the greatest dog show of all time." In 1941 it was "the world's greatest canine congress." Interestingly enough, in those years, Mrs. Dodge was always the "president" of Morris and Essex; after the war, when the shows resumed on a limited scale, she was the show's "sponsor." Furthermore, those who assisted her, the other officers of the club and the men who managed her kennels, became her "lieutenants." Was I making much of nothing? Possibly so. Beginning in 1946, when Morris and Essex resumed, a new byline appeared, that of John Rendel, who likened the show to a country fair, a carnival, and a circus, steps down, it seemed to me, from Ilsley's metaphors. But maybe Rendel was less extravagant than Ilsley; maybe the new tone reflected nothing more than a change in the correspondent who covered the event. And, of course, after the war, the show, in fact, never recaptured its prewar size and splendor.

But of the tone during the hiatus, during the war, I had no doubt, especially because the byline was consistently Henry Ilsley's. In 1943, according to Ilsley, exhibitors were "hungry for shows," and many dog clubs, including Westminster and Eastern, met the demand, whereas Morris and Essex did not. The difficulties were considerable. Gas rationing, for example, impeded travel to shows. Indeed, Morris and Essex was not the only club to cancel, and small-time exhibitors, the "little fellows," as the Times called them, sometimes found it impossible to show. In 1943 there were thirty-four fewer dog shows than there'd been the year before, and the number of entries dropped as well. Furthermore, a ruling of the War Committee on Conventions limiting shows to exhibitors and dogs from local areas directly conflicted with an established rule of the American Kennel Club stating that if entries were restricted, no championship points could be awarded. In 1945 the AKC lifted that rule for the duration of the war; as the Times proclaimed, dog shows were thus "saved."

Some things never change; I knew exactly how dog people had felt. From the viewpoint of the hard-core dog-show person, the aficionado, the distinction between the salvation of dog shows and the salvation of Western civilization had been nonexistent. What was freedom for, anyway? Life, liberty, and the pursuit of championship points!

And how had Geraldine R. Dodge contributed to the effort

to make the world safe for dog shows? And for the other hallmarks of peace? The answer was plain: Just when her grand show, Morris and Essex, was needed as a morale-boosting model of bold opposition to the forces of evil, she had, in effect, rolled belly up to the enemy and remained belly up for the duration of the war.

And before the war, had she done worse than that? Morris and Essex had, I thought, offered the opportunity for agents of the Third Reich to slip back and forth between Nazi Germany and the United States in the guise of innocent dog people. But had that potential become a reality? I couldn't believe that Mrs. Dodge had been knowingly complicitous in treason. Had she been an unknowing accomplice?

In cultivating suspicions about Nazi infiltrators, I had, at a minimum, caught the national paranoia of the wartime years. That anti-Dodge letter to the *Times*? February 2, 1942. Printed next to it was a letter reporting the removal, presumably by vandals, of the signs marking the first three miles of the Doodletown Ski Trail on Bear Mountain, New York. Park authorities would now have to replace the signs. Would the *Times* remind its readers to leave the new signs alone? Honestly, if you want to caution vandals against repeating their misdeeds, why address the civilized, well-behaved readers of the *New York Times*? But what interested me was the editorial note that appeared after the letter. "It sounds like sabotage on the Doodletown trail," wrote the *Times*. "Watch out for fifth columnists on skis."

"And if on skis," I said to Rowdy and Kimi, "why not in the show ring? If on skis, why not behind a judge's badge? Why not on the wrong end of a leash?"

Chapter Fifteen

"**I AM SHOCKED!**" Rita thumped her wineglass on my coffee table. We were, for once, sitting in my living room instead of at the kitchen table. "Holly, I have a cousin who *went* to Elmira College!"

"It's no reflection on your family," I assured Rita. "Besides, it happened a long time ago. Elmira College has probably shaped up by now."

The incident was this: On July 2, 1964, when Mrs. Dodge was in her eighties, Elmira College, located in upstate New York, sued her guardians for ownership of her art collection. According to Elmira, in 1958 Mrs. Dodge had agreed to give the college her paintings, tapestries, jades, bronzes, and other items in her collection at Giralda and in her Fifth Avenue town house. Here's the sneaky part: The objects were to become Elmira's when Mrs. Dodge "could no longer continue to enjoy them."

"Listen to this!" Rita brandished the copies of the articles from the *Times* as if representatives of the college had materialized in my living room and were about to be whacked across their greedy faces with the evidence of their misconduct. "Listen!" She read, " 'On the strength of the agreement, a large estate in Elmira was purchased, to be named the Geraldine R. Dodge Center.' It goes on. I can't believe it. 'Mrs. Dodge, who became a trustee of the college in 1961, gave two hundred thousand dollars toward a two-hundred-fifty-thousand-dollar pledge for the purchase and maintenance of the center, and gifts of porcelains and bronzes valued at about a hundred and twenty thousand dollars.' The nerve of those people! She'd given them three hundred and twenty thousand dollars, and they couldn't wait until she was dead to get their hands on more!''

"A lot more,'' I said. "The stuff they were after was valued at a hundred and seventy-five million. And at first, the court went along with that. But in the end, they got what they deserved. The New Jersey Supreme Court really let them have it. Did you read that part?'' I took the photocopies from Rita. "Here,'' I said. "Here's what the court said. 'Her age, loneliness, insidiously progressive arteriosclerotic disease, and the loss of her trusted advisor'—that means her husband—'made her respond with friendship and confidence to the synthetically effusive attention and appearance of friendship pressed upon her by representatives of the college.' ''

"It really is a sad story,'' Rita said. "And that a *college* would have tried to pull something like that! The poor woman.'' She paused. "Well, the unfortunate woman, anyway.''

"More wine?'' I offered.

"I'm going to nurse this,'' she answered. "Thanks. I don't want to look tipsy when he gets here.''

The he who was due to arrive any minute was the leader of Rita's birding group. His name was Artie Spicer, he lived on Belmont Hill—fancy!—he owned a company that manufactured paper products—money?—and, obviously, he watched birds. Oh, and he was an outdoor type. If topics like hiking, backpacking, canoeing, and snowshoeing arose, Steve and I were not to give even the slightest hint that Rita was other than an outdoor type, too. Steve, who actually is an outdoor type, was also supposed to arrive soon.

"Now, remember—'' Rita began.

"What you liked best about the summit of Everest was the lack of oxygen,'' I said. "When you did the Appalachian Trail, I mailed freeze-dried food to you at designated points on the route. There's no one I'd rather have along on a wilderness adventure in winter camping, provided that there are facilities for a hot shower every morning and that we pack a generator so you can use your electric blanket."

Rita lifted her chin. "I am not asking you to *lie*. I just don't want a lot of smirking if the topic comes up."

"I'll behave! So will Steve."

"Of course he will. It's you I'm worried about."

"Relax. Steve and I know the rules. No dog talk or almost none. No jokes about you and the outdoors. No disgusting details about animal illnesses. Nothing about bird hunting. Really, we'll be good."

"Artie is not very psychological," Rita said, as if confiding that the new man in her life spent his spare time dressing in garter belts, black stockings, and stiletto heels.

"Neither is Steve. They can talk about . . . oh, raptors, I guess. Parakeets. Canaries. Parrots. Steve knows a lot about cage birds."

"I'm not sure Artie . . ."

"Well, what are we allowed to talk about? Books?"

"He isn't very intellectual," Rita confessed.

"That's why you picked us. You knew we wouldn't scare him off. But we can't just sit there chewing in silence until the dessert arrives. Am I allowed to ask him if he has a key to Mount Auburn?" According to a persistent Cambridge rumor, certain dedicated birders had keys to the cemetery that enabled their fortunate bearers to observe birds at dawn, listen for night fowl, and otherwise pursue feathers and cheeps when Mount Auburn was closed to the public.

"Don't ask him that!" Rita was adamant. "What if he doesn't? I think it's only important birders who have keys. I don't know whether he's that important. He might be embarrassed to say so." She paused. "Maybe this whole thing is a mistake."

"No, it isn't. Really, Rita, it will be all right. No dog talk, no veterinary talk, nothing psychological, no keys." With the kind of smirk Rita feared, I added, "We'll just be ourselves."

When Artie Spicer arrived, he wasn't at all what I expected. I'd imagined him as tall and hawklike, with a small head and long arms spread like wings. I guess I was afraid he'd make a predatory swoop at Rita. In fact, he was of medium height and had a burly build and a round face. His neatly trimmed full beard blended into his short, curly hair. The conventional way to describe the color of both would be salt-and-pepper. To my eye, however, his hair and whiskers were a reassuringly familiar dark wolf gray.

In agonizing over the choice of a restaurant, Rita had been determined to avoid anything "too Cambridge," whatever that meant. Balsamic vinegar? Anything "too ethnic" was out. Despite his name, Artie Spicer might not like Thai peppers or authentic curries. High prices could scare him off. Dives and greasy spoons, however, were unacceptable. She finally settled on an upscale Japanese restaurant within the city limits, yet somehow not "too Cambridge," and in Rita's view not "too ethnic," either. It was actually a good choice. Rita had made a reservation for the traditional section, so we had to take off our shoes and sit with our stocking feet in a little pit under the low table. The need to remove pieces of clothing and then wiggle into seats on the floor created an informal, almost intimate, atmosphere. Steve, who sat next to me, was probably uncomfortable; his legs were long for the small space. As usual, though, he was a good sport. He and Rita enthusiastically ordered sushi. Instead of embarrassing Rita by announcing that I'd just as soon swallow live goldfish as let bits of raw tuna and, oh yuck, eel—snake! raw snake!—pass my lips, I quietly asked for miso soup and shrimp tempura. Looking relieved, Artie Spicer, who sat across from me, gave me a conspiratorial little smile and did the same.

Because the birding group at Mount Auburn was what Rita and Artie had in common, the talk started there and soon moved to the murder of Peter Motherway. By then, the soup and appetizers had arrived. The death by garroting of a man whose body had been left in a cemetery didn't hit me as any more tasteful than the topics Rita had banned, but she didn't glare at me or kick me under the table, and Artie did look the same.

"Are people allowed near the Gardner vault again?" I asked. "Or do the police have it sealed off?"

Rita and Artie exchanged a glance. He answered. "I didn't see any sign of the police this morning."

"Neither did I," Rita agreed. "Everything looked back to normal."

"What's not clear to me," Artie said, "is how anyone got in. Must've been in the night, Tuesday night. I'd've thought the guards would be around. I asked one of them. All he said was they didn't see anything, and they can't be everywhere at once. It's a big place. Anyone have any idea why he picked the Gardner vault?"

"I keep thinking about the robbery," Rita said. "But I don't know what connection there could be."

"I met Peter Motherway," I told Artie. Heavily censoring references to dogs, I outlined the circumstances. "The house is like a museum, but it's nothing like the Gardner Museum. It's all Early American. Paintings. Furniture. Silver." In deference to Rita, I refrained from mentioning what seemed to me the odd absence of any kind of dog art. The colonists didn't like dogs, I reminded myself; in their art, dogs appeared only in the occasional family portrait. If Motherway had collected Egyptian art, the absence of dogs would've been strange; in his collection, it made sense. "And Peter didn't strike me as a museum type," I added. "But I didn't really know him. It's possible that the murderer didn't even know it was the Gardner vault. He could've just picked any vault, anything that looked like a house."

"It's an out-of-the-way spot," Artie observed.

Unwittingly picking one of the forbidden words, I said, "Yes, down in a depression." I corrected myself. "In a little valley by that tiny lake. At night you wouldn't see anything going on there unless you were close to the vault."

A young woman in a kimono appeared with our main courses. By the time she was done, meat was sizzling on a stone above tiny flames, and the whole table was covered with dishes and bowls of all sizes.

"Well," Artie said jovially, "here we are gathered around the campfire."

I coughed up a bit of shrimp. Steve didn't choke on anything. He just turned silently red. "Rita tells me you're a backpacker," he ventured.

There followed one of those interminable conversations about the Sierras, preferred brands of hiking boots, the merits of various tents, and other matters about which I knew almost nothing and Rita knew not a single thing. I decided that salvation lay in letting the males bond. Deliberately addressing only Rita, I said, "Do you read German?"

"What?"

"The language spoken in Berlin. Do you read it?"

"Why?" Her expression was suspicious. She probably thought I wanted her to translate a book with *Hunde* in the title.

"I got something odd in the mail today. There are a couple of things in German. At least I think it's German."

"This isn't about . . . ?"

"No," I assured her. "It has something to do with Mrs. Dodge." When Rita first heard about Geraldine R. Dodge and the book, she was thrilled that I was writing about someone whose name was frequently mentioned on public radio and public television. I suppose she thought that my career was turning toward respectability, which is to say, away from dogs.

After chewing and swallowing what seemed to be a slice of yam, I said, "It was really very strange. I got a sort of little package addressed in block capitals, no return address. Inside was an old photograph. I'll show it to you when we get home. It seems to be a group of servants. Maids with frilly aprons and caps. A couple of men. A butler, maybe. Footmen. I don't know. But I think it must have been taken at Giralda, Mrs. Dodge's estate. The people are all standing outside on a staircase, sort of formally posed. And there were also three letters. The one in English is a letter of reference written by Geraldine Dodge for someone named Eva Kappe. She was apparently a housemaid I guess she's one of the women in the picture."

"What does the letter say?"

"Eva was industrious, tidy, and trustworthy. It's dated June 1939. I'm only guessing, but I think the others, the letters in German, are more or less the same." I may as well leap ahead by revealing that the letters were, in fact, in German, that Rita translated them, and that they were indeed similar to the one written by Mrs. Dodge. But back to the present. "The letters are dated 1938, and the same name is in them, Eva Kappe."

"German name," Rita remarked.

"My hunch is that this Eva Kappe came to America with these two letters of recommendation from people in Germany. Then she worked for Mrs. Dodge. And when she left, Mrs. Dodge wrote her this letter." I went on to tell Rita about the mysterious envelopes I'd received previously, including the letter to Bro from Eva written from Giralda.

"This is quite bizarre," Rita said.

"Why do you think I'm telling it to a shrink? It's weird. I mean, by now a lot of people know I'm writing this book and I'm interested in Mrs. Dodge, but why send me this stuff? I mean, a picture of her"—I dropped my voice to a whisper—"kennel help might be relevant." I resumed my normal volume. "But why send anything anonymously? And what am I supposed to do with bits and pieces about a housemaid?"

Chapter Sixteen

B EFORE RITA, ARTIE, STEVE, and I had left for the restaurant, I had performed the usual dog person's predeparture safety survey. The procedure bears a superficial resemblance to normal home security precautions like fire and burglary prevention, but is, in fact, exclusively aimed at making sure that the dogs don't die of smoke inhalation or get kicked, poisoned, or stolen by thieves. I'd made sure that the stove was off and that the front door and the door to the side yard were locked. I'd also cleared the coffee table of the remains of the drinks and appetizers I'd served to my guests. Rowdy and Kimi, agile creatures that they are, probably wouldn't have knocked over the drinking glasses or plates, but I didn't want to risk shards in their stomachs or in the pads of their feet. The cheese board could have triggered a dogfight, and the winner might have gnawed the wood and ended up with splinters requiring canine dentistry. Not to mention knives! I'd washed the cheese board and loaded the dishwasher. But having once read about someone whose dogs had died in a fire caused by a major appliance that she'd left running when she'd gone out, I'd left the dishes dirty. As usual, I'd checked the closet where I keep the dry dog food; if the dogs had found the door unlatched, they'd have torn into each other squabbling over the food and might have gorged themselves and bloated. I had definitely made sure that Tracker was in protective custody behind the firmly closed door of my study.

But when the four of us returned from the restaurant for what was supposed to be coffee at my place, the cat was perched on top of the refrigerator, and the dogs were prancing gleefully around. My first thought was that one of the dogs, probably Kimi, had opened the study door and gone after Tracker. Artie couldn't understand my alarm.

"It's a miracle she's alive," I explained. "These dogs were not raised with cats, and they aren't good with them." Actually, Tracker looked fine, at least for Tracker. Everything wrong with her was nothing new. She'd already lost most of one ear when I'd adopted her, and she has a birthmark on her face that's the shape and color of a festering wound. From the head down, though, she's a good-looking little plain black cat. I didn't see any traces of blood. Steve had reached up to the top of the refrigerator and was patting her. She was purring. She hisses at me, but she loves Steve. "Steve, check her for puncture wounds, would you?" I asked. "I'll get the dogs out of the way."

After I shut Rowdy and Kimi in my bedroom, it occurred to me to glance at my study to find out whether Kimi had left evidence of what I was sure was her crime. I did, indeed, find a crime scene. The meaning of the dogs' happy excitement was suddenly clear. *In your absence, they'd exclaimed, we've had a visitor! There's nothing we love more than unexpected company! Hurray!*

My computer was as I'd left it, still on. The printer, too, was as I'd left it: off. Neither piece of equipment had been damaged. A few books that had been shelved lay on the floor. Most of the mess consisted of loose paper pulled from the drawers of my filing cabinets and from plastic file boxes I use to store material on topics of interest to me: the Byrd expeditions, Alaska, Morris and Essex. The floor was also strewn with letters from people who read my column, newspaper and magazine clippings, sheets from a yellow legal pad, hard copy of pages from the World Wide Web, and the contents of my latest mysterious envelope: the letters of reference for Eva Kappe and the old photograph of Mrs. Dodge's servants.

The room reeked of Tracker's litter, which was strewn everywhere. The dogs, I felt sure, had made a postburglary raid on the cat box. The presence of the litter box explained the ease with which the burglar had entered. Although I changed the litter frequently, cat odor built up when the room was sealed. Consequently, I'd left one window half open. It was now open wide. The screen that kept Tracker in and flies out had been cut around its edges. After a few moments of paralyzed silence, I started to swear. Tracker was a disagreeable, ugly cat, goddamn it, but she was my disagreeable, ugly cat, and if she'd escaped through that window, she could've been killed within minutes in the traffic on Concord Avenue. If the dogs had followed her through the window? They could have hurt themselves leaping to the ground, but at least they'd have landed in my fenced yard.

Rita, followed by Artie, came rushing into the study. I pointed to the screen, which hung from the open window. "Damn it!" I kept yelling. "Damn it, damn it, damn it!" Then I came to my senses. "Oh, God. Rita, maybe there's more. We'd better check the rest of the building. You have things worth stealing, and so does Cecily." Cecily and her husband rent my third-floor apartment. "Oh my God! Is she home? We better make sure——"

"They're on the Cape for the weekend," Rita said.

"My kitchen door was locked," I said. "So was the outside back door. But we better check your place anyway."

Artie shook his head. "He could still be up there. Would you like me to call the police? Or do you want to do it?"

"Willie isn't barking," I said. "Rita's Scottie," I added for Artie's benefit. A tough, scrappy character, Willie will yap over nothing. He flies at the ankles of people he knows. He always goes after mine. He has eyes of fire.

Rita panicked. "He's dead! If he's quiet, he's dead!" She bolted out of my study, dashed through the hall and kitchen, flung open the door, and vanished up the stairs. Artie ran after her.

Still in shock, I wandered into the kitchen, where Steve was placidly holding Tracker in his arms and stroking her.

"No wounds that I can find," he reported. "Where do you want me to put her?"

"Anywhere. Uh, just hold her. Someone's been here. Someone broke in. Everything's a mess. I need to go up to Rita's, and I need to call the——"

A cacophony of terrier barking bit its way down through the ceiling. That's Willie's standard greeting. I hoped Artie had on thick socks and sturdy hiking boots, the kind meant to protect the ankles. Steve and I exchanged smiles. I felt suddenly better. "I guess Willie's all right," I said.

"Yes," agreed Steve, "but is Artie?"

"He wasn't supposed to meet Willie. That's why we had drinks here instead of at Rita's."

"He was all right with your dogs."

"They didn't bite him," I pointed out. On the contrary, they'd knocked themselves out to charm Artie. Kimi had dropped to the floor at his feet and wiggled her legs in the air in delight. Rowdy had presented Artie with a toy, a stuffed dinosaur lightly coated with dog saliva. The dogs had probably treated the burglar to an identical welcome.

"There is that," Steve said. "Are you all right?"

"Yes, I really am now. The worst was just realizing that someone had broken in." I took a deep breath. "The animals are all right. Nothing else really matters. But the window's open in my office. The burglar cut the screen. Tracker could have gotten out. I can't believe that the dogs didn't kill her. She went to the top of the refrigerator. I've been trying to teach her that it's her place."

"Your new computer?" Steve asked.

"Still here. Nothing's missing that I can see. It's just a total mess. I really do need to call the police."

By the time the cruiser arrived, I'd verified that my TV and VCR were still in the living room. My camera sat in plain sight on a bookshelf, and my handgun, a present from my father, remained in its case in the bedroom closet. There'd been no cash in the house and no jewelry worth more than about five dollars. A sheaf of notes by the kitchen telephone looked somehow different from the way I'd left it. That slight rearrangement was the only indication that the intruder had gone anywhere except my office. I reluctantly used my landlady key to enter the third-floor apartment. It showed no sign of forced entry, and nothing seemed to be missing. Rita reported that her possessions were where they belonged.

The police were diligent, but breaking and entering with no harm done was a dull crime; my house isn't exactly the Gardner Museum, and scattered papers sprinkled with cat litter weren't exactly stolen masterpieces. Playing the beam of her flashlight over the ground in the side yard, one of the officers, a young African-American woman, discovered shallow ruts left by the legs of my park bench, which had been hauled beneath the window of my study and subsequently dragged back to its original position. She seemed a little annoyed that I couldn't remember whether the gate between the yard and the driveway had been locked or unlocked. When I told her that I kept the study window open for ventilation, she shook her head ruefully and told me to buy an air purifier.

Neighbors stopped by to ask what the trouble was. The female officer asked whether anyone had seen any odd characters hanging around. Cambridge being the diverse community of eccentrics that it is, my neighbors understood the question perfectly. Some of them remembered Miss Whitehead, a Cambridge legend who habitually strolled through Harvard Square with a large parrot perched on her shoulder. She was almost as famous as her father, Alfred North Whitehead, the great philosopher. Miss Whitehead was before my time. I wish I'd known her, but like everyone else here, I take civic pride in the contribution she made to our community and in the daily appearances of her spiritual descendants.

Odd characters? My neighbors shook their heads. It had been a typical Cambridge evening: There hadn't been an ordinary person in sight.

Chapter Seventeen

PETER MOTHERWAY'S DEATH NOTICE appeared rather belatedly in Saturday morning's paper. A graveside service would be held that same afternoon at Mount Auburn Cemetery. Burial, too, I assumed. Why hold a service by an open grave and then traipse off elsewhere to dispose of the body?

When I'd finished reading the paper, I tidied the kitchen, made the bed, took a shower, put the dogs in the yard, and hurled myself into the nasty task of cleaning my study. After the police had left, I'd made the room decent for Tracker by sweeping up the spilled cat litter. Now I needed to vacuum thoroughly. Rebelling against the dirty sense that my home had been violated, I also resolved to sort through the files the intruder had tossed on the floor and to throw out everything I was never going to look at again anyway. Steve was scheduled to work all day. There was a dog show in Rhode Island, but I'd been too broke to enter, and in any case I didn't trust my car to get us there and back. As an inducement to endure the boredom of housework and filing, I promised myself some time on the Web and a session of clicker-training the dogs.

As I was getting the vacuum out of the kitchen closet, the phone rang. After I'd said hello, a patrician voice said,

"Christopher Motherway here. You had made an appointment with my grandfather."

Had made an appointment? What was this *had*? The pluperfect of death?

"Has something happened to him?" I blurted out.

"You seem to have forgotten that there have been two deaths in the family."

"Your grandfather," I said firmly, "suggested another meeting, but we did not make an appointment. If you've called to cancel, there is nothing to cancel."

"A future meeting would be . . ." Christopher paused. "Further *dates* would be inappropriate." From Christopher's tone, you'd have assumed I was some floozy who'd been wiggling her hips at his elderly grandfather. I'd interviewed the senior Mr. Motherway in his own home, for heaven's sake; I hadn't lured him away on a spree of barhopping. The idea was ridiculous. Could the octogenarian Mr. Motherway be the victim of unrequited attraction? He had, after all, been eager to see me almost immediately after the death of his wife. He had subsequently suggested an additional interview for which I saw no need. Christopher knew his grandfather better than I did; maybe the elderly Mr. Motherway did, indeed, have *designs* on me. If so, Christopher should be speaking to his grandfather, not to me. I felt insulted. *I* was no adventuress!

The conversation ended with curt good-byes. Twenty minutes later, as I was straightening the mess in my study, I finally remembered that I had neglected to offer condolences to Christopher on his father's death. The son's snottiness was no excuse. Neither was the emotional aftermath of the break-in. I made a mental note to write a sympathy letter to Peter's widow, Jocelyn.

By one o'clock, my study was clean. Tracker had vanished when I'd started the vacuum cleaner, but as I'd sorted, filed, and discarded paper, she'd reappeared and installed herself on the mouse pad to supervise me with the disdain of a wealthy employer who finds it utterly impossible to hire good help these days. With Tracker securely settled in her tidy abode, I treated myself and the dogs to clicker training. Having had less success than I'd hoped in encouraging Rowdy and Kimi to howl, I took the radical step of following the advice of clicker-training experts instead of relying on the wisdom of a certain know-it-all who'd decided that she and her brilliant dogs were the exceptions to the rules of operant conditioning. That is, I trained the dogs separately. Working on her own, Kimi rapidly began to vocalize. In subsequent sessions, I'd click and treat only when she emitted an approximation of a howl. Rowdy made stupendous progress, especially because a fire engine happened to pass during his session.

With satisfaction and self-confidence, I planted myself in front of my computer and made a list of the names of people connected to Geraldine Rockefeller Dodge, the Morris and Essex shows, and the Motherway family. If I could tame the wild howl of the malamute, what couldn't I bring to heel? Short answer: It's dogs that heel, not Microsoft mice and certainly not the spiders that spin the World Wide Web. The number of Web sites about the Dodge Foundation and the Dodge Poetry Festival had exploded in the short time since I'd last checked. Unless I was careful, *Dodge* swamped me with information about used cars and dealerships. A woman named Roberta Motherway-Simpson was an evidently successful jazz singer from Calgary. Visiting the anagram Web page, I found that the letters in *B. Robert Motherway* could be scrambled to spell *Robber-worthy team*. Gee, whiz. *Peter Motherway* yielded the rather touching *Empty heart wore.*

As usual, searches for names yielded zillions of bothersome genealogy pages and the Web sites of alumni associations planning reunions and seeking lost members of classes. According to Christina Motherway's death notice, her maiden name was Heinck. A genealogy page showed a girl named Christina Heinck who'd died in Westford, Massachusetts, in 1914 at the age of two. A relative? Or no connection? B. Robert Motherway had failed to stay in touch with his Princeton, New Jersey, high school. I didn't snitch on him. If anything, it was his public high school that snitched; the aristocratic Mr. Motherway wasn't quite so blue-blooded as he presented himself. The presumed buddy of M. Hartley Dodge, Jr., B. Robert Motherway had graduated from Princeton University; I'd seen his framed diploma. He'd gone to high school, however, in the other Princeton, the New Jersey town; at the university, the young Motherway had been a local boy. If the young Dodge, the heir to two fortunes, had befriended a townie, he'd been far more egalitarian than I'd ever have supposed. Turning from my list of names to a topic I hoped to research, I looked for information about Nazi activities in the United States in the years preceding World War II. Again I was deluged, this time with a zillion sites about neo-Nazis in the present day.

Having imposed chaos on order, I signed off. As if to continue the Web's job of flooding me with information, my snail mail brought another mysterious packet from my anonymous friend. Enemy? By now, the block capitals were familiar. Depositing the big brown envelope unopened on the kitchen table, I spoke aloud. No one heard me but the dogs. "Déjà vu all over again," I said. As I didn't bother explaining to the dogs, what I had in mind was a wish-you-were-here postcard from Acapulco that I'd received a few months earlier. On one side was a photo of turquoise ocean bordered by a gorgeous beach. The other side bore Mexican stamps as well as my name and address, and a friendly message that actually did include the phrase "wish you were here." The card was signed by someone named Linda. The handwriting was as legible as it was unfamiliar. Besides wishing I were there, Linda was having a wonderful time, or so she wrote. I had no idea who she was. I have never found out.

So, déjà vu all over again. I opened the brown envelope and slid its contents onto the table. One item was a repeat: the same old Soloxine leaflet. "Someone uses a lot of this stuff," I informed the dogs. "Or works for a vet?"

This time, however, the leaflet about the thyroid supplement was stapled to another document. The attachment was, of all things, the program from Christina Motherway's funeral. Program? Is that the right word? Handout? Flier? Circular? I hope not. Even brochure strikes me as an unsuitably commercial term for the folded piece of expensive-looking cream-colored paper headed IN MEMORIAM, with Christina Motherway's name engraved underneath. *Engraved underneath.* A pun? No, a morbid turn of thought. A minister had conducted the service, which seemed to have been arranged by someone with all the imagination of Linda from Acapulco, who'd been having a wonderful time and wished I were there. Funerals, though, like men's suits, were probably places where imagination was in bad taste. Mrs. Motherway's funeral had opened with an opening prayer and closed with a closing prayer. The minister had delivered the eulogy. If family members or friends had spoken, their names hadn't made it into print. I somehow had the feeling that B. Robert Motherway and his grandson, Christopher, had dressed unobtrusively in dark suits, whereas Peter had shown up for his mother's funeral in an ill-fitting sport coat, tawdry trousers, shoes of the wrong color, and an unmatched pair of socks.

Did I miss the point? No. It was neither the Soloxine leaflet nor the funeral program, but the conjunction of the two: thyroid medication *and* the death of Christina Motherway. The most intriguing item from the brown envelope was, however, a third piece of paper, a recent-looking photocopy of an old birth certificate issued by the town of Westford, Massachusetts, for a female infant born in 1912. The baby's name? Christina Heinck. The implication was murder: thyrotoxicosis, poisoning, death by thyroid storm. The unnatural death of a woman who had assumed the name of a long-dead child? I avoid funerals. Still, if I hurried, I could get to Mount Auburn Cemetery in time for Peter Motherway's.

Chapter Eighteen

I HAVE NOTHING AGAINST eulogies, prayers, hymns, memories, or tears. What bothers me about funerals is the presence of a dead body. Consequently, I didn't exactly attend the service for Peter Motherway. Instead, I observed it through Rita's binoculars while pretending to scan for migrating warblers. Rita made me borrow a tan hat that she considered fashionable for birding. On me, it looked stupid. She also insisted on accompanying me. "Birding is a companionable activity," she informed me. "Birds of a feather! You'll be more credible if there are two of us."

"I'll be more credible if I go alone. Plenty of novice birders go to Mount Auburn," I countered. "You, for example. I just don't want the Motherways to notice me. I don't want to look as if I'm spying on the funeral."

It was Rita's fault that we arrived ten minutes late. She had to change into one of her khaki outfits. In case the Motherways recognized my car, we took hers. After we drove through the main gate, I took a guess about the location of the grave. I directed Rita to the right, then the left until we were on the hill that overlooks the new part of the cemetery. In the few minutes since we'd left home, the sky had darkened. Pausing by a tree with a gnarled trunk, I trained the binoculars up into its leafy canopy and then downhill to the small group of people assembled for Peter Motherway's service and burial.

"Kevin's there," I reported to Rita. "He looks exactly like what you see in movies when cops go to a funeral. He's even wearing a trench coat."

"We should have, too. It's probably going to rain," Rita said. "If it does, that's it. I don't want my binoculars getting ruined."

Like everything else Rita owned, the binoculars were not only expensive but worth the money they'd cost. If a bird had landed on the shoulder of a mourner or a mortician, it would have appeared before my eyes in sharp focus. The only plumage in sight, however, consisted of the dark suits worn by the father and the son of the deceased; B. Robert and Christopher Motherway were disconcertingly dressed exactly as I'd envisioned in imagining Christina Motherway's funeral. Peter Motherway's widow looked, as usual, more like an employee than like a member of the family. Jocelyn's navy blue suit and white blouse would have done so nicely as a nanny's uniform that I had to quell the impulse to check for a toddler at her side. Her face was as expressionless as if the body in the shiny casket had been a stranger's. A remarkably young man with white-blond hair read from a small black book. He seemed too young to be a minister, but his reversed collar and his obviously central role in the ceremony said otherwise.

"Let me look," Rita demanded.

I handed over the binoculars, which were, after all, hers. "Kevin does look like a cop in a movie," she conceded after a few seconds. "Maybe he's seen *The Thomas Crown Affair* too many times."

Steve McQueen, Faye Dunaway? But the real star was Mount Auburn Cemetery. I hadn't seen the movie for years. It wasn't possible, was it, that half of it had been filmed at Mount Auburn? But that's how I remembered it.

"The tall men who look so much alike are Peter's father and son," I informed Rita. "B. Robert Motherway and Christopher."

"Distinguished," Rita commented.

"The woman is Peter's wife. Widow." There was no need

to describe Jocelyn. She *was* the only woman there. The group was pitifully small: Peter's father, his son, his widow, Kevin Dennehy, the minister, a few men who radiated the professionally glum dignity of undertakers. And one more man.

"Rita, let me take another look."

Peering again, I rested the index finger of my right hand on the little wheel of the binoculars and forced the anomalous face in and out of focus. "The art student," I said aloud. "What?"

"I don't know what he's doing here," I said more to myself than to Rita. "Steve and I saw him at the Gardner. First in the restaurant. Then upstairs. He was acting odd. He was in front of the John Singer Sargent portrait of Mrs. Gardner. He was on his knees in front of it. He seemed to be praying."

"How bizarre." Rita, I remind you, is a clinical psychologist. When she says *bizarre,* that's exactly what she means.

"It was," I agreed. "I also saw him here. At Mount Auburn. He was acting normal then, I guess. He was just walking along." I paused. "He has a strange tattoo on his arm. We noticed it in the restaurant. I couldn't tell what it was supposed to be. Steve couldn't either. It was very ornate."

Two days later, on Monday, I repeated the phrase. "It was very ornate," I said to Kevin Dennehy. "With curlicues, I think. I couldn't tell what it was supposed to be."

"Heart with 'Mother,'" Kevin ventured.

"That's exactly what it wasn't," I said.

Chapter Nineteen

"I T WASN'T AN ANCHOR, either," I told Kevin. "Or a dolphin. It certainly wasn't a portrait of a dog. I'm pretty sure there weren't any letters or words. I think it was an object, a fancy object I couldn't recognize. Or that's what I thought at the time. Kevin, who is he? And what was he doing at Peter Motherway's funeral?"

"We weren't introduced," Kevin said rather resentfully.

"I wasn't invited back to the house." He added, with a trace of smirk, "I wouldn't make too much of that genuflecting. A lot of people are nuts on the subject, and the *Globe* and the *Herald* fan the flames. Sells papers. You see that crazy letter in the *Globe*? Typical case in point."

"Today's *Globe*?" I always read the letters, but this morning, Monday, I'd made myself skip the paper entirely. I hadn't done any housework, either, and I hadn't trained the dogs, returned phone calls, or even checked my e-mail. Instead, I'd frittered away my time drafting and polishing my column. Question frequently asked of freelance writers: *What do you do when you don't feel inspired?* Answer: *Write anyway.* The payment for my column wouldn't buy me a third dog, but it would help to feed the two I already had. Hey, F. Scott Fitzgerald wrote for money. The key issue for him, as I understand it, wasn't feeling artistically inspired; no, no, it was feeling desperately broke. Of course, writing about new approaches to the ancient problem of flea control isn't exactly a literary achievement on the order of *The Great Gatsby*. I do understand that. My goals are modest. But by comparison with F. Scott's, so are my needs. By comparison, Rowdy and Kimi are a bargain. Which would you rather support? Yourself and two dogs? Or Scott and Zelda?

Anyway, I'd spent Sunday and most of Monday at home with my column. By the time I'd finally finished the column and sent it as a file attached to my e-mail to my editor at *Dog's Life*, it was five o'clock. After taking a glance at my incoming e-mail—just a quick hit, really, I swear, just enough to take the edge off the craving and stave off incipient delirium tremens—I fed Tracker and the dogs, washed my face, brushed my teeth, and remembered that, gee whiz, there was a whole World Wide World *outside* my computer, one that, among other things, smelled good to dogs and wouldn't short-circuit if they lifted their legs on it. Yes, Kimi as well as Rowdy. Hey, Zelda was female, too. And right out in public, she did a lot worse.

Returning home from walking my nondigital dogs in the highly nondigital streets of Cambridge, I noticed that some vandal had defaced my property by jamming a bundle of hard copy into the quaintly decorative object fastened next to the front door of my house. Having inadvertently wandered into a time warp, the dogs and I had been transported back to the paper-polluted days of snail mail. In addition to an extremely inconsiderate missive from the electric company and the premium list for a show I couldn't afford to enter, the litterer had left yet another of what I had come to think of as my Soloxine packets. This time, instead of mulling over its contents, I did the sensible thing: I called the police. Literally. I stuck my head out the back door of my house and called to Kevin Dennehy, who had wandered back to the time warp, the dogs and I had just getting out of his car.

Is everything in neat, linear, chronological order now? It's Monday. I have finished my column, sent it to my editor, fed my animals, walked the dogs, belatedly taken in my mail, opened what proved to be the last of the mysterious Soloxine packets, and called out to Kevin Dennehy, who has made a fast-food run and is now sitting at my kitchen table. Kevin has devoured one of three quarter-pound cheeseburgers with bacon and half of a large order of fries that he has painted with squiggles of ketchup. Idly wondering whether the Jackson Pollock effect is deliberate, I am chewing a bite of what is supposed to be a fish sandwich, but is obviously a fried fillet of rawhide chew toy. I am suctioning a chocolate milk shake through a straw. Kevin is drinking beer out of a can. Rowdy and Kimi are stationed on either side of Kevin. A droplet of saliva plummets from Kimi's mouth and hits the floor. A string of drool as fine as a spider web hangs from Rowdy's lips. Instead of answering my reasonable question about the identity of the tattooed art student I'd first seen at the Gardner Museum and lately noticed at Peter Motherway's funeral, Kevin has just asked whether I saw a crazy letter to the editor evidently published in today's paper.

"Lunatic," pronounces Kevin. When it comes to diagnosing mental illness, he always speaks with clinical authority that Rita, the psychologist, would envy. For good reason. As a cop, he probably has more experience with the extremes of looniness than she does. Rita's clients, after all, have voluntarily sought psychotherapy. In contrast, a lot of the people who end up in Kevin's office haven't exactly made appointments in the hope of finding help and understanding. Of course, his services are free, more or less. Except to the taxpayers.

"What was it about?" I asked, meaning the letter.

"You still got the paper?"

I obediently retrieved it and found the editorial page. "The one about Mrs. Gardner?" I skimmed the letter. "Honestly, this is ridiculous! They must have printed it because it's so foolish. I'm surprised they published it at all."

The letter was a response to a short article about the Gardner heist published during the previous week. Both Boston papers were always issuing optimistic updates about hopes for the recovery of the stolen art. The latest one had caught my eye mainly because it had described the FBI as "confident." The word had tickled me. As I understood matters, a lack of self-confidence wasn't the Bureau's most notable problem, or so Kevin always said. The letter in today's paper, however, had nothing to do with the FBI. In a sentence or two I'd forgotten, the article had apparently provided readers with background on the robbery, the museum, and its founder. The irate writer of the letter objected to two phrases the *Globe* had used to sum up Isabella Stewart Gardner. According to everything I'd ever read, the *Globe* was justified in calling her "an eccentric." Furthermore, there was universal agreement that she had been "no beauty." Or so I had supposed.

Just who do you think you are, demanded the writer, *to go around insulting the lady Mrs. Isabella Stewart Gardner who did more for the City of Boston and the World of Art than all of the rest of you combined? You think you know what she looked like better than the great artist John S. Sargent? If she and him was alive today, you wouldn't have the nerve!!! From now on keep your ignorant opinions to yourself. Some people don't want to hear them. Me for example. If I ever pick up your paper and read that garbage again I'm not sub-scribing which I don't anyway.*

The letter was unsigned. A sentence stated that the name was being withheld at the request of the writer. "Which I don't anyway!" I exclaimed. "It must be here for comic relief. Anyway, you're right. People do go nuts about Isabella Stewart Gardner."

"Half the City of Boston."

"Especially about the robbery. You know, Kevin, that really was a very personal crime. It wasn't like having a bank get robbed. My mother used to take me to the Gardner and tell me about how it used to be Mrs. Gardner's house, and now it was everyone's because she gave it to us. After the heist, lots of people felt as if they'd been robbed of things that belonged to *them*. The letter is silly, but it's true that Mrs. Gardner gave her house and her art to the public in a direct, personal way. Geraldine R. Dodge did the same thing when she gave dog shows. She gave them as personal gifts." Need I mention that I'd told Kevin about Mrs. Dodge? Of course I had. I went on. "Maybe the papers really should express some gratitude by saying that Mrs. Gardner was gorgeous. What does it matter now?" I sipped my melted milk shake. "Kevin, have you ever been there?"

"Where?"

"The Gardner Museum."

"Me?"

"Well, you should go. It's beautiful."

Kevin had almost demolished the third cheeseburger. He rolled his eyes, swallowed, and changed the subject. "What else you know about these Motherways?"

"That's what I wanted to tell you about. Actually, it's going to be show-and-tell."

Five minutes later, the fast-food debris was in the trash, the table was covered with everything sent to me in the mystery mailings, and I'd filled Kevin in on what Soloxine was. "I was beginning to think it was Peter Motherway who was sending this stuff," I said. "Or I wondered, anyway. Obviously, it wasn't." I tapped a finger on the most recent material, which consisted of a snapshot of Wagner, the growly black shepherd, a photocopy of Christina Motherway's death notice, yet another Soloxine leaflet, and a newspaper clipping about Peter Motherway's murder. "Peter," I said unnecessarily, "was in no position to send this. I don't know who did. Possibly Jocelyn, his wife. Possibly someone else, including someone I don't even know."

Kevin grunted.

"The implication," I continued, "as I see it, is that Christina Motherway was murdered. The recurring item is this leaflet about Soloxine. Thyroid medication for hypothyroid dogs. Sent to *me*. So at first I naturally assumed that in a cryptic way someone was telling me something about dogs. In a way that's true, but what I think now is that the real message, from the beginning, was about Mrs. Motherway, Christina. The message I didn't get was that she'd died of thyrotoxicosis. The Motherways have a lot of dogs. What I didn't know at first, but what I've heard since, is that there's a lot of hypothyroidism in those lines: a lot of dogs, a lot of Soloxine, a lot of brochures." I hesitated. "And when I put that together, I thought maybe it had been more or less a mercy killing, although I'm far from sure that that kind of death is merciful. Anyway, that's what I thought. Christina was dying, and the family really wanted her to be able to die at home, not in an institution. I could sympathize with that. I know you disagree, Kevin, but in some circumstances, I don't see that as murder.''

Kevin named a doctor and made a slanderous accusation.

''Many doctors,'' I insisted, ''would have sympathized with a family that decided to speed the death of a woman who was dying anyway, and dying confused and in pain, at least in psychic pain. Besides, there wasn't necessarily anything to arouse suspicion. Christina was terminally ill. The whole idea was to let her die at home. And then she did. A person who was disoriented to begin with, a person with advanced Alzheimer's, got to die in familiar surroundings. Good! She died at home. What could be more natural? Why ask questions? Or maybe you wonder about them in private, but why ask them in public?''

''Why ask you?'' Kevin demanded. ''No doctor's going to ask you.''

''I know that. What does seem possible is that the family didn't do this together. Someone ended Christina's life. Someone else knew that and didn't consider it mercy killing. But in that case, the logical thing would be to go to Christina's doctor and start asking questions. Or go to the police. I mean, why send mysterious collections of hints to someone who's writing a book about famous old dog shows? Believe me, Kevin, it doesn't make any more sense to me than it does to you. But what's solid, what's not just speculation, is that Peter Motherway *was* murdered. And this strange collection of stuff that's been sent to me *is* about Christina's death and, as of what arrived today, Peter's murder. *That's* why I'm showing it to you. It's your business, not mine. For all I know, someone knew we were friends and sent this stuff to me on the assumption that I'd do exactly what I'm doing right now.''

Chapter Twenty

AT NINE O'CLOCK the next morning, the wail of sirens on Concord Avenue set off sympathetic vibrations in my dogs' vocal cords. With all the free will of the crystal shattering in response to the power of a high soprano note, I snatched a little yellow-and-white noisemaker and a handful of cheese cubes and began to click and treat. The scenario serves as a handy paradigm. An environmental stimulus triggers a response in dogs that itself acts as a stimulus for a human behavior. This neat behavioral chain is what we in the profession succinctly refer to as "dog training." I am happy to report that a mastery of the fundamentals of this sport enables the trainer to generalize her skills to the modification of human behavior.

Consider, for example, my success in letting Kevin Dennehy elicit a ton of homicide-relevant behavior from me while supplying me with hardly any information. What had I learned from Kevin? That Peter had not been murdered at Mount Auburn. That the murder weapon had been a length of wire. That B. Robert Motherway and his look-alike grandson, Christopher, alibied each other for the time of Peter Motherway's demise, and that Jocelyn claimed to have been home alone. So what? I already knew that the elderly Mr. Motherway lacked the physical strength to have garroted Peter or to have moved the body to the Gardner vault. Although Christopher was young and powerful, what motive could he have had to kill his father? Although he was B. Robert's biological grandson, Christopher was, in effect, his grandfather's favorite son. Why do in a rival he had already defeated?

And the unalibied Jocelyn? I continued to see her as the victim, not the victimizer. This was, after all, a woman who couldn't even stand up to an ill-mannered dog. In desperation, she might have lashed out at her husband. But Peter had been intercepted at Logan Airport, not killed at home, and he'd been garroted. The murderer must have prepared the garrote in advance. And the method was gruesome. Kevin might be right that murder was often a family affair. But murder by garroting? Women shot their husbands and lovers, didn't they? They poisoned them. Or stabbed them with kitchen knives. If I decided to murder someone, I'd choose a weapon I at least knew how to use. A length of wire: How long? With handles fastened to the ends? Handles? What kind? Fastened how? Then wrap it around the victim's neck. But what if the victim resisted? Even if he didn't, then what? Yank hard? Once? Repeatedly? Twist the weapon? Or not? Pull and keep pulling? For how long? I couldn't possibly garrote anyone. Even if I were that kind of person, I wouldn't know how. And Jocelyn? Even if she had the specialized knowledge I lacked, did she have the requisite force of will?

But let me return to the application of the principles of dog training to the shaping of human behavior in everyday life. After making great progress in using the click-and-treat method with the dogs, I settled in front of my computer and retrieved my e-mail, which included a message from my co-author, Elizabeth Kublansky. "IMHO," she wrote in e-mail jargon—*in my humble opinion*—"if you cannot get it together to turn out straightforward text in your usual orderly fashion, you should just say so, and I'll find someone who can. I don't know about you, but I need the second half of our pitiful advance. My part of this book is done. Where's yours?"

With one click of the mouse, I deleted Elizabeth's message. The treat was the Web. Having resolved to obey Elizabeth's sensible command by writing publishable sentences to accompany her photographs instead of continuing to amass increasing amounts of useless information, I rewarded myself with what was supposed to be a minute or two on-line to search for anything about Eva Kappe, the housemaid recommended by Mrs. Dodge, the writer of the 1939 letter from Giralda. There wouldn't be anything. Why would there? In five minutes, after finding nothing, I'd be off-line and dutifully double-clicking the icon for the first chapter of the book, and otherwise clicking and treating the computer instead of letting it act like an untrained dog that dragged me around and dropped me where it pleased.

A scant thirty minutes later, I was revisiting the Web site devoted to the alumni of the Princeton, New Jersey, high school attended by B. Robert Motherway. As I'd previously discovered, Mr. Motherway had failed to stay in touch with the class of 1926. I didn't wonder a lot about whether he'd been more loyal to Princeton than to his public high school. Which diploma hung on his wall? Anyway, the same high school's class of 1930, I now saw, was searching for a member, Eva Kappe, who did not graduate, but left at the end of her sophomore year.

Chronology of the life of Eva Kappe: Due to graduate from high school in 1930? At age eighteen? So, she is born in about 1912. In 1928, she lives in Princeton, New Jersey, where she is a high school sophomore. At the end of the year, she leaves the school. By the thirties, she is working as a maid in Germany; she receives letters of reference from her employers. Rita had translated the letters for me; the recommendations were strong. In 1939, Eva Kappe is back in New Jersey. This time, she is in Madison, at Giralda, where she works as a housemaid for Geraldine R. Dodge. From Giralda, she writes a short note to Bro, whoever he is. She poses for a group photograph of Mrs. Dodge's household help. She leaves with a recommendation from Mrs. Dodge.

From New Jersey in the late twenties to Germany in the thirties. In the late thirties, back to New Jersey. She speaks enough English to attend an American high school, enough

German to work in Germany. Back and forth. A go-between? Yes, my mysterious mailings were about the death of Christina Motherway and, as of yesterday, about the murder of her son, Peter. But the odd collection of items included the photograph of servants at Giralda, the note written from there, and Eva Kappe's recommendations from German employers and from Mrs. Dodge. Could my cryptic messages have a double or triple meaning? Christina's death. Her murder? Peter's murder. *And* treasonous activity at Mrs. Dodge's estate.

Ah yes, Mrs. Dodge, Giralda, the Morris and Essex shows. My book. Our book. Elizabeth's justified ire. My unpaid bills. *Web:* silky net spun by predatory arachnids to trap prey. My love of animals, I reminded myself, did not extend to spiders. As a useful high-tech aid to the professional writer, the computer ranked somewhere below the stylus.

Fresh out of styluses, I settled for a pen, yellow legal pad, and the manila folders containing copies of articles culled from old microfilmed issues of the *New York Times.* Sitting at the kitchen table instead of at the computer, I would go through the reports on the Morris and Essex shows, and I'd study stories about the Dodges. Today, now, damn it, I would go through these folders for the last time, taking notes on articles that were gratifyingly unavailable in cyberspace. My notes, I resolved, would consist exclusively of information directly relevant to the book.

And so it went. For two scribbled pages. Then I happened on a little three-paragraph, three-sentence article published in the financial section of the *New York Times* on July 5, 1928. It read, in its entirety:

H. DODGE JR. RIDES STEER
John D. Rockefeller's Nephew Wins
Applause at Montana Rodeo

LIVINGSTON, Mont., July 4 (AP)—Hartley Dodge Jr. of New York, a nephew of John D. Rockefeller, has won his spurs in range fashion.

The youth of 19 thrilled spectators at a

rodeo here yesterday when he rode a wild steer "to a finish."

Dodge is visiting here with a party from New York, including his father, head of the Remington Arms Company, and his mother.

Hold it! I'd heard this story before, and certainly not from the lips of M. Hartley Dodge, Jr., who had died in France only two years after riding that wild steer to a finish. The storyteller had been B. Robert Motherway. A teller of tales he'd been! In his version, who was the youth who had won the applause at that Montana rodeo? Who had won his spurs by riding a wild steer to the finish?

It was remotely possible that B. Robert Motherway had been among the party that accompanied Mr. and Mrs. M. H. Dodge and their son to Montana that summer. If the nephew of John D. Rockefeller, the son of the head of Remington Arms, rode a wild steer, the feat deserved mention in the financial section of the *New York Times*. Not so the equally daring accomplishment of a townie classmate. But if the young B. Robert Motherway had, in fact, traveled to Montana as a guest of the Dodges, the elderly Mr. Motherway would undoubtedly have exercised brag rights by telling me so. Furthermore, he'd have used his own words instead of precisely the phrases printed in the *New York Times*.

Charitably speaking, B. Robert Motherway had borrowed an episode from the life of the young Hartley Dodge. Uncharitably speaking? B. Robert Motherway was a damned liar.

Chapter Twenty-one

ALTHEA BATTLEFIELD is given to quotation. Her fanatical devotion to Sherlock Holmes means that her source is almost invariably the Sacred Writings. Today, however, she produced a line of verse that had not been penned by Sir Arthur Conan Doyle. "Oh, what a tangled web we weave," declaimed Althea, "when first we practice to deceive!' Sir Walter Scott.'

"Web," I repeated gratefully. "A tangled *Web.* Exactly. You see, Althea? I knew you were the right person to consult." I thanked her as she likes to be thanked. "'The tidiest and most orderly brain,'" I quoted, "'with the greatest capacity for storing facts of any man'—or woman—'living.'" I had touched up the Great Detective's famous description of his brother, Mycroft Holmes.

"Tampering with the Canon!" Althea scolded. "Shame on you!"

"If Sherlock Holmes had known you," I insisted, "he'd have had to update his views. You are the 'central exchange.' You are the 'clearinghouse.' Your 'specialism is omniscience.'"

"*Your* specialism," countered Althea, "is brazen flattery."

It was Wednesday morning. When Rowdy and I visited Althea, we usually sat in front of the fireplace in the living room or in the sunbathed alcove packed with rattan furniture and potted palms. Today, Althea and I were at her dining room table. Rowdy snoozed under it. The polished mahogany top was covered with manila folders and stacks of paper. In making sense of the plethora of information, Althea had a triple advantage over me. Her limited vision meant she couldn't read most of what was printed on the material I'd spread before her; she was drown-proofed against the deluge. Because of her great age, she reserved her energy for marching directly to the point. Most important, her tidy, orderly brain enabled her not only to absorb great amounts of information, but to distinguish between the useful and the useless, to ignore the irrelevant, and to sort what remained into meaningful patterns. Forced to organize and summarize for Althea, I found myself infected by her contagious intelligence. Or maybe all this blather is simply a way of saying that Althea was a retired teacher, a martinet, I suspected, in whose presence I felt compelled to *think*.

The dining room of the house on Norwood Hill, I might mention, provided a suitably Holmesian setting for the one-act play in which Althea took the role of the brainy Mycroft Holmes, the archetypal armchair detective, who, except in the extraordinary case of the Bruce-Partington plans, walked from his rooms in Pall Mall around the corner into Whitehall, and was seen nowhere else but at the Diogenes Club, conveniently located opposite his lodgings. Indeed, with its wood-paneled walls, mahogany sideboard, ornate silver, and heavy crystal, the suburban American dining room could have passed for the Stranger's Room, the only place at the Diogenes Club where talking was allowed. Heavy crimson velvet swathed the windows. Oil paintings hung on the walls. One showed two sailing ships about to capsize in deep swells underneath a dark sky. In the other, a pair of scrawny kittens took shelter from a rainstorm under an umbrella apparently made of skin as thin and translucent as Althea's. The maudlin pictures were favorites of Althea's sister, Ceci, whose mentality was as mushy and gushy as Althea's was logical and sparse. It was certainly Ceci who'd chosen the frilly white summer dress and white lace shawl Althea wore today, Ceci who'd lovingly daubed Althea's prominent cheekbones with powdery pink blusher and glossed Althea's age-thinned lips in rose. Fortunately, cosmetology had offered Ceci the means neither to reduce Althea's great height by six or eight inches nor to shrink Althea's amazonian feet to a girlish size six. Althea's hair had, however, been becomingly trimmed, moussed, curled, and fluffed. Its white aura hovered around her pink scalp as if emanating from the electrochemical whoosh and crackle of logical thought beneath.

"Bro," said Althea, impatiently tapping long, bony fingers on the table.

I'd finished summarizing facts and speculations about the Motherway family, Christina's death, Peter's murder, the background of Mrs. Dodge and the Morris and Essex shows, and the material I'd received in the mysterious mailings. Before presenting and subsequently surrendering the material to Kevin Dennehy, I'd made high-quality photocopies of everything, including the photographs. Donning eyeglasses with inch-thick lenses, Althea had peered at the picture of the servants at Giralda. At her request, I had just read aloud the note from Eva to the unknown Bro.

"Bro," she repeated. "Brother? Our cast of characters offers only one, does it not? We are told that the senior Mr. Motherway's sister died in Germany. Therefore, she lived or visited there for at least part of her life. The biological father of this same Mr. Motherway was German. The surname is not. The relationship between the stepfather and stepson was close. The stepfather passed along his interest in dogs, in antiques, in art. His name, too?"

"I wish my memory were better," I said. "I think that Mr. Motherway actually said he'd been adopted, that his stepfather had adopted him."

"Two children," Althea said. "Brother and sister. Your Mr. Motherway, if I may call him that, was adopted by the stepfather, who did not necessarily adopt the sister as well. Therefore, the sister and brother may have had different last names. Hers, presumably, was German. Her first name, too."

What came to mind was Brunhild. I had the sense to keep quiet.

"Many of what one thinks of as American first names," Althea continued, "are, of course, of German origin or are common to both countries. But let us broaden our focus to include other items in these mysterious packets, which are not, on reflection, all that mysterious after all. What are these mailings about? The Motherway family. Specifically, Christina Motherway. Her funeral. Therefore, her death. The murder of her son, Peter. Nothing cryptic there. If some items, why not all? Letters of reference from German employers for a certain Eva Kappe. *Eva*. An ordinary American name, an ordinary German name. Eva's connection to the Motherways? As you have cleverly discovered, a certain Eva Kappe attended the same New Jersey high school also attended by our unique brother, so to speak. An informal note from Eva to Bro. Eva Kappe to her brother. Bro? Oh my, yes. Yes, of course! Our only brother."

"Bro," I said. "Short for *B. Robert*. Short for *brother*. Althea, what Motherway wanted to paint for me was a picture of a patrician background. Princeton, tours of Europe, showing at Morris and Essex. He likes low-key name-dropping. Mrs. Dodge. Her son. Foreign judges. Even if he'd talked about his sister, he'd never have said that she was anyone's maid."

"My energy is beginning to run low." Althea does not complain. Rather, she reports. Now, she could have been a laptop issuing a low-battery warning. "Perhaps a cup of tea would help. Would you mind asking Mary? And a treat for Rowdy, too. We can't leave him out."

Roused by the sound of his name, Rowdy arose and did his debonair act, which consists of dancing around with the grace of Fred Astaire before seating himself next to a lady and proffering his outstretched paw. If his victim cooperates, he kisses her hand. Althea objects to saliva. Rowdy compromises by resting his chin on her knee or on the arm of her chair while training eyes of adoration on her ancient face. His posture and expression suggest that he is summoning the courage to propose marriage. What's interesting about the courtship behavior of Rowdy the Debonair is the contrast between the actual and the potential. In actuality, he suavely and gently pays tribute to an elderly friend. The potential is readily observable: the incisors, the canines, the premolars, and the molars of this or any other Alaskan malamute. Ponder the crushing power of those jaws. The dog could maim or kill in seconds. He could, yet he does not and will not; the distinction between the actual and the potential is strong and trustworthy. But it's always there, isn't it? There's nothing specifically canine about the distinction, of course. All of us could go around knifing, shooting, poisoning, and garroting one another. We could, yet most of us do not and will not. Still, the potential is always there.

For instance, Ceci and Althea's housekeeper, Mary, could have slipped a toxin into the tea that Althea and I were soon sipping. Before leaving to have her hair done, Ceci could have tampered with the lemon wafers Mary innocently served us on a bone-china plate patterned with delicate violets. Even so, I drank my tea and nibbled the wafers with the same sense of relaxation I felt in watching Althea happily violate my taboo on feeding a dog at the table by treating Rowdy to lemon wafers. Proof of my trust: If I'd harbored the slightest doubt about the wholesomeness of those wafers, I might have risked a taste myself, but I wouldn't have let a lemony crumb pass Rowdy's lips. Had Christina Motherway felt a hint of suspicion when she'd eaten her last meal, taken her last drink, or swallowed her last medication? Leaving the cargo terminal at Logan Airport, had Peter Motherway glanced suspiciously around in fearful search of a would-be attacker? Christina Motherway had had Alzheimer's. Perhaps she had suffered for years from the delusion that her loved ones meant her harm. For all I knew, her son, Peter, had been chronically plagued by the lunatic conviction that someone was trying to kill him.

"Caffeine," Althea said with satisfaction. "Of all the drugs that age has forced upon me, it is by far the most effective. Yes, B. Robert, Bro, brother. The brother of Eva Kappe, who attended high school in Princeton, left at the end of her sophomore year, worked as a maid in Germany, returned to this country by 1939, and joined the staff of Geraldine R. Dodge at Giralda. At Giralda, Eva had her photograph taken. She wrote a note to her brother. She evidently gave satisfaction. She left, apparently of her own accord, with a good reference."

"And returned to Germany?" I wondered aloud. "And was killed in the war."

Althea's lips pursed in disapproval. "She returned to the economic disaster of the Third Reich while leaving behind three strong letters of reference? Or she took them with her, only to have them sent to the U.S. after she was killed, perhaps, in the firebombing of Dresden? Or after her death in a concentration camp?"

"Sorry," I said, "I see what you mean."

Althea tilted her head upward toward the chandelier above the table. It was on. She can see light. "On *this* side of the Atlantic," she said censoriously, "Bro, if we may call him that, your Mr. Motherway, receives a note from his sister, a note that he does not destroy."

"He keeps it," I contributed.

Althea sighed. "He does not tear it up. He does not burn it. He does not throw it out. Indeed, it survives to this day. In whose possession we do *not* know. And who does know?"

The question was not rhetorical. "Mr. Motherway, presumably," I answered. "Christina might have known. Peter might have. Christopher? Jocelyn? Jocelyn does the housework. Maybe there are cleaning people who come in, but she does at least some of the housework. Jocelyn would be likely to know what was where."

"The location of family memorabilia," Althea said with approval. "Photographs, letters, documents. Birth certificates, for example."

"Christina Heinck's," I supplied. "Christina Heinck Motherway's."

"A woman," exclaimed Althea, "who was not who she seemed!" Now and then, Althea succumbs to the Holmesian devotion to melodrama.

"I think she assumed the name of a child," I said, "a child who died young."

Althea slowly raised her teacup to her lips. Her hands trembled lightly, but she drank without slurping or spilling. Then she slowly lowered the cup and placed it neatly in her saucer. "And all of this information," she said, "is sent to *you*. By whom? By someone with access to it. By a member of the Motherway household. Moreover, by a surviving member of the Motherway household. The elder Mr. Motherway, Bro, B. Robert, has no conceivable reason. The grandson, it seems, dislikes and mistrusts you. There remains the daughter-in-law. Jocelyn."

"She took care of Christina," I said, "so Christina wouldn't end up in an institution. She was in a position to know how Christina died. She acts browbeaten. Timid."

"Has she any reason to trust you? To approach you as, shall we say, a woman of action?"

"Yes! Yes, she does. Well, it may seem strange, but I offered to help her. I gave her my card, and I told her to get in touch, but it was about a dog, not about . . . One of the Motherways' dogs lives in the house, a big black shepherd, Wagner. And twice when I was there, the dog growled at Jocelyn. What bothered me was that no one did anything. Jocelyn just took that nasty behavior for granted. She didn't like it. She was afraid. Appropriately, I thought. I didn't trust the dog. But it didn't seem to occur to her that she could *do* anything about the dog. She sort of crept around hoping Wagner wouldn't notice her and hoping she wouldn't get bitten. And I thought that was outrageous." I paused. "He isn't really a bad dog," I added.

Althea crowed.

"There are some! Really, there are," I protested. "A few. Hardly any. But this situation was as unfair to the dog as it was to Jocelyn. A dog has a right to know what's civilized and what isn't, and no one had taken the time to inform this poor dog that aggression toward a family member is absolutely, unconditionally unacceptable. And no one had told Jocelyn that she didn't have to take it! Until I did. I told her it was unnecessary. I said that if she wanted help, she should call me. I gave her my card."

"Before you received the first of these mailings," Althea said.

"Yes. Before."

"And she did not call you. She lacked the gumption. You, however, demonstrably did not lack gumption. Faced with a large, menacing dog, you did not cower. Quite the reverse! You bravely offered to intervene."

"It wasn't gumption. It was common sense."

"Perhaps you could call her," Althea suggested. "A simple phone call might produce interesting consequences."

Althea looked exhausted. I started to gather the material spread on the table. She stopped me. "Could you leave that with me? Ceci is illiterate in matters concerning the Canon, but she is generous about sharing her eyes. Something is eluding me. I want to reconsider after I have recovered my forces."

I agreed, of course. Rowdy and I made a swift departure. Just before we left, Althea said, "Altruism. That's what it is! It's the altruism that I don't entirely trust. And something else. What can it be? I have the odd sensation that it has something to do with a *dog*."

Chapter Twenty-two

"**T**HANK YOU FOR CALLING *Haus Motherway German Shepherd Dogs,*" announced Peter Motherway's voice, "*proudly bred by geneticists for protection and devotion.*"

I'd dialed the toll-free number given in the ads in the dog magazines. The posthumous thanks reminded me of the urban myth about Mary Baker Eddy, the founder of Christian Science, whose monument at Mount Auburn is big enough for a few hundred bodies or one gigantic ego. Anyway, according to Boston legend, Mary Baker Eddy had been buried with a telephone in her coffin. So, in Mary Baker Eddy fashion, Peter Motherway continued: "*We offer world-class puppies and adults from outstanding German and American bloodlines. Stud service is available. For free information, including photos and pedigrees, leave your name and address at the sound of the beep. To order your beautiful Haus Motherway German shepherd puppy or adult, leave your phone number, and we will return your call as soon as possible. Please speak clearly and spell any unfamiliar words. And remember! If it isn't a Haus Motherway shepherd, it isn't a real dog.*"

Who needs to spell out *bullshit*? But after obediently waiting for the beep, I left a neutral message carefully phrased for the ears of B. Robert, Christopher, or Jocelyn. I had a hunch that Jocelyn got stuck with the clerical work as well as the housework, but in case I was wrong, I didn't want to alert the grandfather or grandson. Without actually trying to disguise my voice, I adopted the eager tone of a puppy buyer. "I'm interested in the material you sent," I gushed, "especially the picture of the black male. Could you call me?" I left only my phone number.

Althea had predicted that one simple call might produce interesting consequences. I left the message at about twelve-thirty. The consequence arrived at three o'clock in what I diagnosed as an advanced state of true panic. When I opened the door, Jocelyn's eyes darted left and right over her hunched shoulders as if she expected to see a knife-wielding hand poised to stab her in the back. Finding none, she bolted inside, only to flatten herself against the wall in a futile attempt to evade Rowdy and Kimi.

I launched briefly into my usual reassurances. The dogs were friendly, I showed them in obedience, they were Canine Good Citizens, Rowdy was a certified therapy dog, we visited a nursing home, yak, yak, yak, yak. I abandoned the tactic when it became obvious that Jocelyn was about to faint. The little color she had in her face drained visibly. Even with the support of the wall, she wobbled.

"Bend over!" I ordered her. "Get your head between your knees! I'll put the dogs away. I'll be right back."

Five minutes later, the dogs were behind the closed door of my bedroom and Jocelyn was seated at my kitchen table drinking a mug of heavily sugared microwave tea. After making sure that she wasn't going to pass out, I'd calmly issued instructions about taking slow, deep breaths and exhaling completely. It's thanks to my extensive experience in the relaxing, devil-may-care sport of dog obedience that I've become such an expert at recognizing and treating panic and associated symptoms such as trembling, sweating, violent gastrointestinal attacks, tachycardia, hyperventilation, and loss of consciousness. Every form of athletic recreation puts participants at risk of certain injuries. Runners get Achilles tendinitis. Weight trainers strain muscles. Downhill skiers break bones. After decades of nursing myself and other equally happy-go-lucky dog-obedience competitors through bouts of our very own sport-induced affliction, I could run an anxiety-disorders clinic.

"Maybe you should try breathing in and out of a paper bag," I suggested to Jocelyn. "If you're hyperventilating, it helps a lot. And go easy on the tea. Too much caffeine isn't a good idea."

The temperature in my house was a comfortable seventy degrees or so. The June day was sunny and mild. My kitchen windows were open to admit a warm breeze. Jocelyn wore a thick, shabby, cowl-necked gray cardigan over a light-blue, threadbare, button-down oxford-cloth shirt and a long blue-denim skirt. Although she was a tall, heavy-boned woman, the clothing was too big for her. The sweater and shirt looked like a man's discards. I wondered whether they were hand-me-downs from her late husband, Peter, or from B. Robert or Christopher. Inside the wool sweater, she shivered, but her face had gone from greenish-white to flushed red. Beads of moisture had formed on her forehead and nose. If I'm ever actually in charge of a panic clinic, I'm going to make sure that we stock a product I've needed now and then myself in the obedience ring, namely, a facial antiperspirant.

My ministrations had, I regret to say, done nothing more than prevent Jocelyn from collapsing. "I have to go," she insisted, warming her hands on the mug of tea. "I have to get back. Just give me the things. It was a terrible mistake. I must have been out of my mind. If he finds out, he'll kill me! I have to get back! You have to pretend it never happened!" With a hint of resolution, she repeated, "It *never* happened. Promise me! It never happened!" Seized by a new bout of panic, she demanded, "You didn't show anything to anyone, did you? You didn't tell anyone?"

The woman, I swear, was frantic.

"Of course not," I dismissed the possibility as calmly as I'd have done if I'd been telling the truth. "Why would I have shown it to anyone?"

"I need all of it back right now. Everything. I have to get back. I have to leave right now."

"Unfortunately," I said, "I took it all to my office. I left it there." The closest I have to an office is my study, in other words, Tracker's room.

The pupils of Jocelyn's eyes shrank in alarm. "Where? Where's your office?"

I hate to lie. "In another part of Cambridge." True! A nearby room wasn't exactly a distant part of Cambridge, but it certainly was *another* part. What was I supposed to say? *The police have everything?* "I'll run over and get it, and I'll return it to you. I'll drive out with it."

"NO!" So much for my future at the clinic. I was afraid she'd have a heart attack. "They'll see you. They'll find out. I, uh, have to get back. Christ! Meet me at . . . Can you meet me later? Meet me at . . . You know where Mount Auburn Cemetery is?"

I said that I did.

"Meet me there. Can you meet me there?" Her speech was rapid and driven. "I take flowers there all the time. That's where my mother-in-law—" Her voice broke like a teenage boy's. She took a breath. As if praying for the dead woman's salvation, Jocelyn added, in fervent defense of the unaccused, "Christina never meant anyone any harm in her whole life, you know. She was the only person like that I ever knew. I take flowers to her grave. I can, uh, I can do that. I do it all the time. I can be there at, uh, five-thirty. Five-thirty?"

I nodded.

Jocelyn's directions to Christina Motherway's grave were hurried and jumbled. I kept bobbing my head and saying that yes, yes, I understood. I did, of course. The directions to Christina's grave were also directions to Peter's, and I knew exactly where his was.

"Five-thirty," I said when she'd finished. "I'll be there. Are you sure you can drive? Can you make it home? And back? Are you sure you . . . ?"

Her sudden, bitter laugh startled me. The volume and strength were frightening. "If I'm killed in a car accident, it'll be a stroke of luck. It'd be a nice way to go.'' In parting, she added, as if savoring a tempting possibility, ''There'd be nothing personal about it. Not like if someone did it to you. Or if you had the guts to do it yourself.''

Her face wore a freakish smile.

Chapter Twenty-three

JOCELYN'S SMILE LINGERED on the periphery of my consciousness. Her words rang in my ears: *"the guts to do it yourself."* Her voice had caressed the phrase. Falsely believing that I could return everything she'd sent to me, she'd spoken fondly of her own death. I remembered the night at dog training when Sherry, whose best friend knew Jocelyn, had traced Jocelyn's problems to low self-esteem. Rita would have said, as Rita always did, that everything was more complicated than that. For Jocelyn, however, suicide would be a simple solution to the simplicity of low self-esteem and to whatever unknown complexities had landed her in her present situation. And she had the means. The Soloxine leaflets had been removed from the lids of bottles. Inside those bottles were deadly little pills.

I cursed myself for having given the photographs, the leaflets, the note from Giralda, the birth certificate, and the other original materials to Kevin Dennehy. Only a few of the photocopies I'd left with Althea would pass as originals. But they would have to do; they were all I had. When I kept my appointment with Jocelyn at Christina's grave, I could not arrive empty-handed. I would give her a sealed packet. It would not, however, be all I had to offer. Jocelyn had sent me the material to me because she'd seen me as a source of help. She hadn't been entirely wrong. Getting low scores in the obedience ring because you're docked points for handler errors? I can fix that. And I really could have helped with Wagner the Growling Shepherd. Then there's Alaskan Malamute Rescue. I am not merely an active member of Alaskan Malamute Rescue of New England, but an ardent proselytizer. Interested in adopting a homeless malamute? Call me! Better yet, visit our Web site at http://www.amrone.org.

See? I'm a proselytizer. But what I do is *Malamute* Rescue. People Rescue is Rita's job. I intended to enlist her help. Jocelyn's husband had just been murdered. Her mother-in-law had died under suspicious circumstances. Jocelyn could be the next murder victim. She was terrified. Once she discovered the absence of the documents she'd sent me, she might become suicidal. Rita would know. Rita knew about women's shelters. She knew about women! People! Clinics, hospitals, resources. My task, then, was to talk Jocelyn into returning home with me. I was meeting her at five-thirty. Rita was usually back by seven-fifteen, sometimes earlier. She would see Jocelyn's terror for herself. She would make phone calls. She and I would drive Jocelyn to a haven, a sanctuary, a safe house. If I failed to convince Jocelyn? At least she'd have the photocopies. For all I knew, the copies would serve whatever purpose she had in mind. They'd have to!

It was now three-thirty. I could zip out to Newton, retrieve the things I'd left with Althea, and be back in plenty of time to meet Jocelyn. When I politely called Althea to say I'd be stopping in, I got stuck in a prolonged conversation with Ceci, who can take longer to say nothing than anyone else I've ever met. Then I scribbled a note to my cousin Leah, who handles Kimi in breed and obedience. Leah was due at my house at four to train Kimi. She wouldn't need my help, and she had a key. I'd probably be back soon after she arrived. My note said so. I signed it in the manner of a real dog person, which is to say, someone who has a hard time remembering not to add the names of her dogs when she endorses a check. I wrote, "Love, Holly and Rowdy."

When I pulled up in front of Ceci's big white colonial, I left the engine running and didn't take Rowdy with me as I dashed to the front door. Unfortunately, it was Ceci who answered the bell. Even more unfortunately, instead of listening to what I'd said on the phone, namely, that I was popping in for a few seconds, she'd not only decided that I was coming for tea, but had announced my visit to Althea. Ten years younger than Althea, Ceci looks like a tiny, pretty version of her rawboned older sister, but has spent her whole life cultivating an air of scatterbrained girlishness that contrasts radically with Althea's rationality.

"Althea was so thrilled to hear that you were coming for tea," Ceci gushed. "She simply loves to *entertain*." Lowering her voice, she confided, "It's such a welcome change from that *institution* she was in, where she was unable to offer her visitors anything even remotely like *hospitality*. I should never, ever have left her in that place, so it gives her particular pleasure, as it does me, too, of course, I'm always delighted to see you, and your beautiful dogs, too, as goes without saying, doesn't it? Speaking of which, where are they? Would they like a nice run in the yard while we have our tea? Mary has fixed us a strawberry shortcake, she left ten minutes ago, I do wish she'd live in, but she refuses, and the water is boiling. You do like Earl Grey, don't you? Oh they are perfectly welcome to join us. As you know, dogs are always more than welcome in my home. . . ." Ceci continued in this fashion for what felt like an hour before drifting back to the topic of her sister, who, she said, "was dying, simply dying, well, not *dying*, of course, in the literal sense, there's nothing wrong with her health except the usual, but filled with *ideas* she is eager to share with you"—she made ideas sound like foreign entities—"*ideas* about all these bewildering documents she's had me reading to her until I practically have no voice left!"

If only, I thought. Althea claimed that as an infant, Ceci had gone by the baby name Leather Lungs. I should add that I have always liked Ceci. Her blather is heartfelt. And she really wants to make reparation for having left Althea in a nursing home, even an excellent one. Today, the coffee table in front of the fireplace in the living room held a silver tea service, delicate cups and saucers, and the promised strawberry shortcake, as well as an elaborate cut-glass contraption that suggested a three-story apartment building inhabited by tiny sandwiches with the crusts cut off. From her wheelchair next to the coffee table, Althea gave me a little wave. "Two visits in one day! We are honored."

What could I do? I went back to the old Bronco, killed the engine, and got Rowdy, to whom I delivered a brief, stern talking-to about shortcake, sandwiches, and the social graces expected of a civilized dog. It was now four-fifteen. I absolutely, positively had to be on my way back to Cambridge by five o'clock, as I immediately and apologetically warned Ceci and Althea.

"I have an appointment with Jocelyn," I explained to Althea. "At five-thirty. If I'm a minute late, she may take off."

"We understand completely," said Althea, directing an authoritative look at Ceci.

Responding perhaps to Althea's schoolmistress tone, Rowdy remained on a down-stay at my feet, and Ceci devoted herself to pouring tea and passing plates of goodies. The strawberry shortcake was made with real shortcake, not store-bought sponge cake, and had a generous ratio of fresh berries and whipped cream to carbohydrates. Consequently, I had something better to do with my mouth than interrupt Althea, who went directly and enthusiastically to the point.

"The final packet you received," Althea pronounced, "consists of the following items: a photograph of a black male German shepherd, a newspaper clipping about the murder of Peter Motherway, a second clipping, this one about the death of Christina Motherway, and an informational brochure for a drug with the capacity to induce thyrotoxicosis." She paused for a sip of tea. "Holly, you *do* know what a rebus is?"

I'd taken a larger mouthful of shortcake than my mother would have liked. I chewed and swallowed. "A puzzle."

"A puzzle with pictures," Althea informed me. "The pictures spell out syllables or words. A picture of an eye, for example"—she raised a hand to one of her own faded blue eyes—"conventionally represents the first-person-singular pronoun, nominative case, *I*, as in *I myself*."

"Yes," I agreed.

"Consider the dog," Althea said. Hearing herself, she burbled in glee. "As you so often do! But in this case, consider the photograph as a rebus."

"A shepherd? A German shepherd dog. German?"

"But your time is short. I will stop playing games. Regardless of the breed, a black male dog. Black. Male."

It occurred to me that if Althea had been my English teacher, I might have understood *Ulysses*. Or at least finished reading it. "Blackmail," I said.

"Indeed. Blackmail. What has been missing, of course, in questions surrounding the murder of Peter Motherway, is a motive, other than the obvious and universal in such circumstances, which was, of course, that someone wanted him dead. Our correspondent supplies a more specific motive than that by means of a rebus. Blackmail. Shall I translate? Peter was blackmailing his murderer, who had used Soloxine to kill Peter's mother, Christina Motherway. Or so it seems to me."

"If so," I said, "Peter would have been blackmailing—"

"A member of the household," Althea finished. "A member of his own family, which is to say, someone with access to Christina, access to this dog medicine, and the opportunity to administer it to her. And a motive, too, of course."

"Mercy killing?" I suggested.

"Hah! Mercy!" Althea was, well, merciless. "The object was to keep her out of an institution."

Ceci fussed nervously with the teapot. "Holly, may I offer you . . . ?"

"Ceci, hush," Althea ordered. "All that is forgotten. And we are not discussing ourselves. Holly's time and my energy are limited. We must press onward. So, why this apparently altruistic determination to spare a demented woman, a woman almost certainly lost in the past, oblivious to the present, the supposed horrors of a medical facility? Where, in my experience, far from enduring pain, the poor thing would have been doped to the gills with analgesics and antidepressants?"

"Now, Althea," Ceci began, "the Gateway was not, of course, a suitable home for you, but during the unfortunate period when you, uh, resided there, you were perfectly *com-*

pos mentis, although the same cannot, alas, be said of your roommate, Helen What's-her-name, who perhaps *was* doped to the gills, now that you mention it, and where on earth did you of all people ever pick up that vulgar phrase? I cannot—"

"The point," Althea continued firmly, "was to prevent the woman from talking to sympathetic strangers. To prevent her from speaking of the past."

"But—" I began.

"Forgive me for interrupting. I have a bit more to cover, and we have little time. We need to turn to the matter of Geraldine R. Dodge. Please take what I am about to say in the spirit in which it is intended, Holly. Each of us is inevitably locked in her own perspective. I, in mine. Sherlock Holmes. Puzzles. Cryptic messages! A touch of the dramatic. You in yours. Dogs."

"Guilty," I admitted. "But no more than Mrs. Dodge was guilty on the same count."

Althea folded her hands in her lap. "From an *objective* viewpoint," she said, "the central fact of Mrs. Dodge's life was *not* her passion for show dogs. Nor was it her apparently transitory membership in a eugenics society. Nor was it her acquaintance with dog experts who had the misfortune to live in Nazi Germany. Rather, it was her extraordinary wealth, the wealth that allowed her to pursue her passion for art."

"Art," I said. "Well, yes, she did collect art. She was . . . Well, I like to think of her as the Isabella Stewart Gardner of dogs. Among other things, she commissioned, oh, I don't know how many portraits of her dogs. Now, a lot of people don't exactly think of dog art as *art*, but—"

Althea shook her head. "Holly, when Elmira College tried to take advantage of this unfortunate woman's mental failings, the object of the shameful episode was not to lay claim to dog pictures."

"No. No, I see what you mean. Mrs. Dodge collected bronzes. Paintings. Gold coins. Jewelry. I get the point. She owned Houdon's bust of Benjamin Franklin."

"A marble bust," said Althea, "a bit over twenty inches high depicting, you will recall, Franklin and Franklin only,

unaccompanied by a canine companion. The work now belongs to the Philadelphia Museum of Art, which according to
one of these, uh, Web pages you left with me, paid three
million dollars for the work.''

"Althea, I never said that dogs were the only thing she
spent her money on. I mean, she had a lot of it to spend. The
Dodge Gateway at Princeton, in memory of her son. She and
her husband donated that. The Madison, New Jersey, town
hall. In memory of her son. Sometime in the forties, she
bought a house in the East Sixties, in Manhattan, from some
woman named Pratt. The house was rented, I think, by the
Soviet Consulate General. I don't know why Mrs. Dodge
bought it, but she did. She paid two hundred thousand dollars
for it. I *have* wondered about the Russian connection there, of
course.''

"There is no hint in the material you have presented,"
Althea said sternly, "that Mrs. Dodge had any interest whatever in politics, left, right, or center. There is overwhelming
evidence, however, that she was an avid collector of extremely valuable art. And *that* is the point you have over-
looked. Only connect! You observed an odd character at the
Gardner Museum and subsequently at Peter Motherway's funeral. Where was Peter Motherway's body placed after the
murder? *At the Gardner vault.* Just what did B. Robert
Motherway teach? *Art history.* His stepfather, the presumed
Mr. Motherway, collected, you tell me, in a small way. Your
Mr. Motherway, too, collects art. He collects Early American
furniture and paintings. On the income of a prep-school
teacher? I was one! And I have no such collection. In the
thirties, this man led student tours of Europe. Tours of dog
kennels? Of course not! Museum tours. Art tours. Art, again.
Everywhere. Art. *Valuable art.*''

Chapter Twenty-four

I'VE NEVER BEEN much of a science-fiction fan, mainly because I see parallel universes all the time in the here-and-now. To take a randomly chosen example, consider the world of purebred dog fancy, a so-called subculture that mirrors the supposed mainstream in more ways than you would dream possible unless you happen to belong to it. Speaking from the inside, let me assure you that if a phenomenon exists, it exists in the world of dogs, a proposition that is true of everything from nail polish to politics to social class to madness to undying love.

The principal difference between these parallel universes is that the dog equivalent costs ten times as much or is ten times as intense as the human version. You can get a hair dryer for yourself at any discount drugstore by plunking down just about exactly one tenth the price you have to pay for the sturdy forced-air blower you need for a show dog. To trim your own nails, you need a file or an emery board. For a dog, you need either manual nail clippers, costing maybe ten dollars, or an electric nail grinder, say, fifty dollars. On my own hair, I use a comb and brush. On Rowdy and Kimi, I use undercoat rakes, wire slicker brushes, natural boar-bristle brushes, finishing brushes with stainless-steel pins, and a variety of combs specially designed not to damage the dogs' hair. The dogs absolutely require a grooming table. I stand on the bathroom floor. The same goes for everything else: ten times as expensive, ten times as intense. Dog politics? The jockeying for power within the American Kennel Club makes the Knesset look like a Buddhist monastery occupied by a lone monk who's taken a vow of silence. Madness? You haven't met a lunatic until you've met a real dog nut. As to social class, why *breeding* is what it's all about, my dears.

To demonstrate the omnipresence of parallel universes, let me add a couple of examples that have nothing to do with dogs, namely, head lice and human mortality. The proposition we're considering is, I remind you, that if something exists in one universe, it exists in others. So, on to politics in the world of head lice. The National Pediculosis Association is now, as we speak (as we itch and scratch?), vying publicly with a rival head-lice organization that has obviously won the first round of the battle for America's scalps by discreetly calling itself Sawyer Mac Productions, instead of, say, The American Louse and Nit Foundation. Imagine the graphics on the letterhead stationery. Anyway, it's easy to see that just as national political parties divide themselves into conservatives and liberals, so, too, do external human parasitic parties. Truly, the National Pediculosis platform calls for the traditional, conservative reliance on a fine-tooth comb, supplemented in emergency cases of all-out war by the pesticide-shampoo defense, whereas the liberal Sawyer Mac agenda demands immediate, global comb and pesticide disarmament and proposes instead the near-pacifist policy of dousing louse-ridden heads in olive oil.

Human mortality. Delicacy, compounded by a profound and blissful ignorance of exactly what undertakers do to dead bodies, restrains me from pointing out what I am sure are exact parallels between the preparation of show dogs for the ring and the grooming of deceased human beings for open-casket viewings, but I am sure that the parallels are there. Ah, but politics? Cremation versus burial? Funeral services: In the conservative approach, a member of the clergy says flattering things about someone who may have been a total stranger. The liberal preference is for spontaneous eulogies delivered by family and friends, who are encouraged to celebrate the life of the departed by relating cheerful anecdotes of generous deeds, amusing pranks, revealing witticisms, and lovable quirks. A strength of the conservative approach is that the clergyperson usually admits aloud that the subject of the eulogy is dead.

Have I digressed? No. Parallel universes. If it exists, it exists in nations, dogs, lice, and human mortality. Politics. Grooming. Social rank. Art! Dog art. The art of head lice? Indeed. The *letterhead* stationery? And mortuary art, as is evident at Mount Auburn Cemetery, where the alert visitor may admire everything from immense stone edifices like the Mary Baker Eddy Monument, to quaint, homey cottages like the Gardner family vault, to intricately carved angels, crosses, and sheepdogs, to unadorned granite slabs. Old money rests peacefully in or under, as the case may be, the vaults and statuary on the artificial hillsides and next to the miniature man-made lakes of Mount Auburn's grand neighborhoods. Mature trees of exotic species soften the landscape. The section occupied by deceased parvenus suffers by comparison. With its skimpy, adolescent trees, its newly paved streets, and its unadorned slabs of rock, each barely distinguishable from all others on the block, it is the tract housing of death. There lay Christina Motherway and her son, Peter.

When I pulled up near the Motherway plot and parked behind a battered black Ford pickup truck, Jocelyn was kneeling by the brand-new headstone of her mother-in-law, and, to my surprise, of her father-in-law, too. The stone was a thick, substantial double model reminiscent of twin beds shoved together to form a king. Christina slept on the left, at least according to the name carved there. B. Robert's name had already been carved on the right. His late wife's headboard had two dates: birth and death. His had no date at all. The omission seemed odd. He didn't know exactly when he was going to die, but his birth date wasn't going to change, was it? If something is figuratively carved in stone, why balk at the literal? In contrast to his mother's grave and his father's grave-to-be, Peter Motherway's final resting place had no stone. I assumed it hadn't been delivered yet. Although Mount Auburn must have strict zoning codes to ban the headstone equivalent of hovels, I had the feeling that Peter's grave marker would be a thin and vaguely shoddy single-bed slab. I toyed with the idea that if Jocelyn were buried in the same plot, she wouldn't get so much as half a gravestone for herself. She might not even get a separate grave. Rather, Peter's would be opened, and his wife would be laid to rest directly above him. I imagined Jocelyn's posthumous astonishment at the radical transformation in her conjugal relationship. In life, I suspected, she'd never been on top.

Delayed by trouble in starting my car and then by commuter traffic between Newton and Cambridge, I'd taken a shortcut by turning off Greenough Boulevard, zipping uphill, and going straight ahead on Grove Street until reaching the gate that served as the cemetery's back door. Since I'd had no time to take Rowdy home, he was in his crate in the back of the Bronco instead of in his usual sneaking-into-Mount Auburn position flat on the floor, but no one stopped me to enforce the no-dogs rule. Maybe a dog crated in a car was perfectly welcome.

Before leaving Althea's, I'd sealed the photocopies of the mysterious mailings in a big manila envelope I'd taken with me. Now, getting out of the Bronco, I held the envelope prominently in my right hand as a reassurance, a false one, of course, to Jocelyn. I might as well not have bothered. Like the tattooed man at the Gardner kneeling before the John Singer Sargent portrait, Jocelyn was on her knees before Christina's half of the gravestone. Her hands were tightly wrapped around a wicker basket that held an arrangement of pink tulips and white daffodils. Her eyes were closed. Her lips moved in what could only have been prayer. After a moment or two, she placed the basket on the new turf in front of the stone. Her late husband's fresh grave was bare. Any wreaths, sprays, or bouquets left there after the funeral on Saturday must have withered and been cleared away, or had perhaps been moved to other graves by mourners doubly stricken by grief and poverty. In any case, although it was Peter Motherway's barren, unmarked grave that seemed to call for flowers, Jocelyn paid tribute only to Christina. When she rose, I could see tears running down her cheeks.

Without handing her the envelope, I said gently, as if speaking to an injured animal, "Jocelyn, I don't know the details of the situation you're in, but I know you need help. I have a good friend who will know what to do. I want you to come home with me. We'll find a safe place for you."

My offer succeeded only in provoking another freakish smile. "The only safe place," Jocelyn said bitterly, "is right here with Christina." Like a dog snatching an unguarded steak from a kitchen counter, she grabbed the envelope from my hand, dashed to the old Ford pickup, and drove away.

With no reason to linger, I returned to the Bronco, which started on the first try. Heading for the main gate, I reached the old part of the cemetery, where I slowed to a safe crawl to avoid endangering the birders, fitness walkers, and other visitors who were taking advantage of the early-summer evening to enjoy the garden cemetery as its founders had intended. When I neared the main gate, I could see Jocelyn's old black truck, which had halted with its brake lights on and its left-turn signal blinking. One of the buses or trackless trolleys that run along Mount Auburn Street must have discharged a throng of passengers; pedestrians were passing along the sidewalk in front of the truck. When the sidewalk cleared, Jocelyn edged ahead, but had to wait for a break in traffic. Tonight, Mount Auburn Street was jammed with commuters heading home to Watertown, Belmont, and Newton, and after-work shoppers going to and from the big Star Market a block away from the cemetery gate, on the opposite side of the road. A group of tourists clutching maps of the cemetery crossed in front of my car.

As I started to move forward, an ordinary-looking beige car emerged from one of the cemetery streets that join in at the main gate. It pulled in back of Jocelyn's truck. With the pavement ahead of me clear, I added my Bronco to the little two-car line. I signaled for a right turn, thus activating the windshield wipers. Now that I was directly behind the beige car, I could see that it was a Mercedes. Its left-turn signal was blinking. Its wipers were not embarrassing its driver by sweeping nonexistent rain off a dry windshield. I confess to the impulse to shove my foot on the gas and slam my dented, malfunctioning Bronco into the nearest vehicle that had cost more than my yearly income, a vehicle conveniently located about a yard ahead of my front bumper. And the rich S.O.B. had a car phone, too! He was using it right now. The Mercedes probably had a fabulous sound system instead of a tape player that ate tapes. Posh upholstery. Air conditioning that did ninety degrees to sixty-five in ten seconds. If so, the driver evidently had it while it turned off or was wasting gas and money by running it while a window was open. The driver had ended his call and was now stretching. His left hand and forearm appeared through the window. On the arm was a large tattoo. The driver had dark, curly hair. Easing ahead, I strained to look into the rearview mirror of the Mercedes. I managed to catch sight of the driver without locking eyes. His head was turned to the left. In fact, he seemed to be admiring the tattoo, or maybe just the muscles of his arm. I was too far away to see the tattoo in detail, but even at the Gardner, when I'd taken a close look, I hadn't been able to tell what it was supposed to represent. But I recognized the man, the art student, as I persisted in thinking of him. I'd seen him at Mount Auburn before. Once, he'd been alone. The second time, he'd been at Peter Motherway's funeral. Now, his car was directly behind Jocelyn's truck. Like Jocelyn, he was signaling for a left turn. I rapidly switched my turn signal from right to left. Jocelyn finally pulled into Mount Auburn Street, with the Mercedes on her tail and my Bronco close behind.

Maybe Jocelyn's terror was justified. As Rita, the psychologist, always says, just because you're paranoid, it doesn't mean you're not being followed.

Chapter Twenty-five

ON THE LAST DAY of his life, Peter Motherway drove to the cargo area of Logan Airport, where he shipped three puppies. Peter never made it home. The terminally ill Christina Motherway also perished during what was, in another sense, a journey home. A third member of the Motherway family, Jocelyn, was now heading home. Or so I assumed.

After failing to persuade Jocelyn to accept whatever sanctuary Rita and I could find for her, I'd resolved to enlist Kevin Dennehy's help. Jocelyn was, it seemed to me, too acutely terrified and too chronically cowed to act in her own interest. If she wouldn't voluntarily seek refuge from the violence she obviously feared, then she belonged, I decided, in protective custody. I had no idea how protective custody worked or what it meant for the person in its grips, but it couldn't be worse than what Jocelyn faced alone. If she were taken to a police station for questioning, or even arrested and locked in a jail cell, she'd be in the care of people whose job it was to make sure she didn't share her late husband's fate. Just how rational or irrational *was* Jocelyn's panic? Indeed, how rational or irrational was the woman herself? Her husband had in fact been brutally murdered; his body had been propped against the Gardner vault at Mount Auburn.

There was, however, no comparable evidence that Christina Motherway's death had been unnatural; the notion might be Jocelyn's delusion, a symptom of her need for psychiatric help. In mailing a series of mysterious packets to a near stranger, Jocelyn had acted senselessly. A person of sound mind seeks help by enlisting the aid of someone qualified to provide it; Jocelyn, instead of cogently relating her suspicions to a police officer, a private detective, or a psychotherapist, had sent cryptic messages to a dog trainer! The choice was crazy. What was I supposed to do about the whole mess? Housebreak it? Peter's widow had not *imagined* his murder. Still, the true meaning of everything she'd sent me might not be murder, after all, but her own madness. Yes, the Motherway family evidently had secrets that its members wanted kept as just that, family secrets. So did every other family! Wasn't it characteristic of the mad to fabricate sinister connections between unrelated events? To quake at inner demons projected outward?

In Harvard Square was a wild-acting man who alerted passersby to evil schemes concocted by professors, including his stepfather and his own mother. The man's demeanor undermined his credibility. If he'd been hell-bent on convincing people that the sun rose in the east, he'd have turned all eyes westward at dawn. When he was in an agitated mood, he planted himself in the middle of the street to bellow warnings about electrical currents and laboratory rats. At other times, he lingered in doorways to stage-whisper bits of his secret knowledge. The man was blatantly deranged.

As I followed the Mercedes that tailed the old Ford truck, I had to wonder whether I was now being taken in by a subtle madness that I'd failed to see for what it was. Jocelyn Motherway's appearance was unremarkable; she was a tall, dowdy woman with poor posture. Or did she? To me, a near stranger, she'd mailed what were, in effect, tangible bits of secret knowledge. It was I who had fought to discover sinister connections. Althea, of all people, who had enlisted Althea in my efforts. Althea, of all people, the fanatical Holmesian whose greatest delight came from following, or in this case from concocting, a sinister plot! Just beyond the Star Market, Belmont Street forks to the right. Jocelyn bore left, staying on Mount Auburn Street, with the Mercedes and my Bronco trailing after her truck. For a second, I saw the three vehicles as a mockery of a funeral cortege. As an empty hearse trailed by mourners, the old black pickup was a bad joke. There were no flowers, no tears. And far from driving toward a cemetery, we were crawling away from one. Caught in rush-hour traffic, we moved from Cambridge to Watertown with funeral slowness. Jocelyn got stuck at a red light. When it turned green, our procession moved through an intersection, but was soon brought almost to a standstill near Kay's Market, an Armenian greengrocery that also sells tenderly fresh Syrian bread, exotic spices, pistachio nuts, taramosalata, Greek olives, and other specialty foods so literally attractive that hordes of customers are forced to double-park.

When one of the double-parked cars pulled out between my Bronco and the Mercedes, I thought about taking its spot. For all I knew, the unfortunate Jocelyn suffered from delusions of persecution so severe that the Motherway family hired someone to keep an eye on her whenever she left home. Maybe the family's determination to keep Christina out of an institution had been innocent and kindly. If so, family feeling might extend to an equally strong determination to keep Jocelyn out of a mental hospital. Her terror was unquestionably genuine. Its source? I'd seen her as the potential victim of violence. Was she in reality its source? Tormented by guilt, criminals sometimes surrendered to satisfy an underlying need for punishment. True? On television and in movies, anyway. Jocelyn was strong enough to have garroted her husband and strong enough to have carried or dragged his body a great distance. She had no alibi. Maybe Kevin Dennehy's view of marriage as murder was justified after all. If so, there was no reason for me to follow the Mercedes that tailed her truck. Its tattooed driver might be an odd sort of bodyguard, an eccentric, of course, a man with a bizarre crush on Isabella Stewart Gardner, but a guard nonetheless, a hireling whose task was to prevent Jocelyn from committing new acts of violence. B. Robert Motherway had shown no affection for Peter. But would he shield the woman who had murdered his son? As

I'd heard myself, Christopher had quarreled bitterly with his father. And as Jocelyn's son, Christopher might protect her. All along, what I'd seen as Jocelyn's oppression, her relegation to the status of household help, might represent the family's weird effort to contain her violence. On the other hand, genuflecting before the John Singer Sargent portrait of Mrs. Gardner wasn't exactly what Rita always calls "appropriate behavior." Jocelyn's inner demons might not be the only threat she faced; now and then, paranoia coincided with reality. If the man in the Mercedes planned to waylay her, my presence as a witness should deter him.

In the heavily congested approach to Watertown Square, a feat of Boston-driver maneuvering landed me in the right-hand lane, still with only one car between mine and the Mercedes. By now, the driver of the Mercedes had a teal minivan between his car and his quarry's truck. Jocelyn's right turn onto Main Street supported my assumption that she was heading home. Main Street in Watertown would lead her to Main Street in Waltham. A half mile or so past the center of Waltham, she could take Route 117 or veer left staying on Route 20. Either road would take her home.

By obeying what is evidently a Massachusetts traffic law, I interpreted the yellow light as an injunction to pick up speed, and thus managed to jam the Bronco among the other cars clogging Watertown Square. After that, the traffic eased a bit. The teal minivan remained between Jocelyn's truck and the Mercedes, which made no effort to pass. I deliberately let a second car slip between mine and the Mercedes. After what seemed like hours, we crossed a railroad bridge and descended to the part of Main Street in Waltham that's thick with pizzerias, storefront offices, and discount this-and-thats. A working-class town and proud of it, Waltham is also home to lots of high-tech companies, but the impressive new office and industrial buildings cluster along Route 128, America's Technology Highway. Ages ago, Waltham was Watch City, USA, but you'd never call it a Little Switzerland; these days, in downtown Waltham, there's not much to watch.

I was listening to "All Things Considered" on National

EVIL BREEDING / 159

Public Radio. The traffic thickened in the center of town. Soon after we passed City Hall, on the left, then the public library, on the right, an NPR segment ended. The announcement that followed raised my hackles. All I remember about the segment is that it had nothing to do with dogs. What remains clear in my mind is that funding for it had nonetheless been provided by the Geraldine R. Dodge Foundation. Grrr! Catching Rowdy's eye in my rearview mirror, I exclaimed, "A gross miscarriage of dog-loving justice! A crime against caninity! By rights, buddy boy, her whole damn eighty-five million should've gone to the dogs!"

During the second my eyes had been off the road, a gigantic refrigerated truck had appeared just in front of the Mercedes. A block or two ahead, on the left, was a big supermarket; the truck would probably turn there to make its delivery. When it did, Jocelyn's pickup would reappear. In accordance with Massachusetts custom, the teal minivan signaled for a left turn before veering right into the parking lot of a convenience store. Moving ahead, I could see that the tattooed driver of the Mercedes was again using his car phone. He hung up. Then, with no signal, he made an abrupt right turn. While I'd been fuming about NPR and the Geraldine R. Dodge Foundation, he'd presumably kept his eye on Jocelyn. The gigantic truck hadn't blocked the view of her pickup after all, I decided. Rather, the driver of the Mercedes must have seen her turn into the parking lot of this fast-food restaurant.

It was one I'd visited before, mainly because—surprise!—it was near or on the way to various hotbeds of dog activity. Leah and I sometimes took the dogs to obedience matches and breed-handling classes at the nearby Waltham Boys and Girls Club, or followed the scenic Route 117 to dog-training classes and seminars in towns west of 128. Stopping at the fast-food place had become a habit for the usual reason: dogs. It used to be that if you had a dog in the car when you went to the drive-up window, you'd get a free dog biscuit along with your food. Even after the dog treats were discontinued, I kept on stopping there. Ah, the lasting power of intermittent positive reinforcement! Not that the results were all that positive. On the contrary, Rowdy and Kimi learned to expect cookies whenever we went to a drive-through anything, and would rattle their crates and yelp gleefully at ATMs. Little did my trusting dogs suspect that on most days my bank balance wasn't enough to buy two dog treats.

The Mercedes parked in a spot right near the restaurant's main door. The driver got out and entered. I was puzzled. To reach the drive-through window, you had to go around to the back of the building, where you shouted your order through a microphone. Then you continued the circuit of the building and stopped at the window, where you paid, got your food, and failed to get free dog biscuits. When I hadn't seen the black Ford pickup, I'd thought that Jocelyn must be in back of the building yelling her order into the microphone. So why was the guy going *inside* the restaurant?

As it turned out, he entered the restaurant to order and devour enough burgers, fries, ice cream, and cold drinks to fill a large tray. But I've jumped ahead. In search of Jocelyn's truck, I circled the parking lot, looked up and down Main Street and the side streets bordering the fast-food place, and saw no sign of the pickup. Damn! It must have been ahead of that semi after all. Yet the driver of the Mercedes hadn't followed. Instead, he'd pulled into this fast-food joint. Why? The phone call? Had he received instructions to drop his surveillance? Passed on the task to someone else? Was it possible that he hadn't been tailing Jocelyn at all?

It was, I decided, useless for me to try to catch up with her. She had at least a five-minute head start, and I had no idea whether she'd taken Route 117 or Route 20. At Mount Auburn, she'd rejected my offer of sanctuary. Despite that dismissal and despite my increasing doubts about Jocelyn's innocence, I'd done my best to see that she reached home without falling victim to the kind of fatal assault that had killed her husband. When I got home, I'd turn the whole problem over to Kevin Dennehy.

The time was now an almost incredible six-thirty. The traffic on Main Street had eased. With luck, I'd be back in

Cambridge in half an hour. No time at all. Except with a full bladder. I parked in a spot near the side door of the fast-food place, went in, and used the ladies' room. Emerging from it, I saw the Mercedes man, who was seated alone at a table for two with his back toward me. Not that it mattered. Why would he remember someone who'd sat at a table next to his at the Gardner Café, someone he might have seen briefly at Mount Auburn, someone he'd never met? Besides, he wasn't looking around. Rather, he was concentrating on the tray in front of him. At the moment, he was raising a double burger to his mouth. If anyone had ever told him to keep his elbows in when he ate, he hadn't listened. The sight of bad table manners and the man's messy tray shouldn't have stimulated my appetite, especially after all the shortcake I'd eaten at Ceci and Althea's, but I instantly craved food, the greasier the better. Impulsively, I joined the shortest of four lines, waited, and ordered a fish sandwich for myself and, I confess, a cheeseburger for Rowdy.

Back in the car, I fed him his unearned treat, which he downed in one gulp. I ate with a bit more decorum, but I'm not sure I didn't linger; the cuisine and surroundings weren't conducive to elegant tarrying. Besides, it was past Kimi's dinnertime. I wanted to get home. Either I took longer than I remember, or the Mercedes man bolted his food at a speed to rival Rowdy's: Driving out of the lot, I saw that the Mercedes was gone. So what? I wasn't following it anymore. At least not knowingly.

Retracing my route, I made it back to Cambridge in less than half the time it had taken me to reach Waltham during the rush hour. I want to emphasize that I was not trying to follow the Mercedes. For all I knew, it had gone in a completely different direction. It wasn't the Mercedes I saw, anyway, but its driver, and the only reason I spotted him was that he jaywalked across Mount Auburn Street directly in front of my car. He didn't notice me. What attracted my attention was, in fact, his weird look of alert and purposeful oblivi- ousness. His gait was more a trot than a walk, and his head was tilted upward at an awkward angle. As he crossed in front of my car, I couldn't actually see his nostrils, but I'd have bet anything that they were twitching. Everything about his gait, his posture, his facial expression was intimately familiar to me. I know all too well the unmistakable air of a dog who's up to something.

Chapter Twenty-six

IF HE'D BEEN CROSSING from the cemetery side of Mount Auburn Street to the Star Market side, I'd probably have decided that the worst he was up to was shoplifting. In my dogs, that up-to-no-trouble air often heralds a spree of food-stealing. But he was making his strangely abstracted yet resolute way across the street to the sidewalk that runs by the cemetery fence. Mount Auburn Cemetery is, I might mention, the largest fully fenced yard in Cambridge. It's much larger than Harvard Yard, which is walled rather than fenced, and the walls are, in any case, rendered almost completely useless by the wide-open gates. Imagine! An institution of so-called higher learning where dogs can't pursue advanced obedience skills because it's unsafe to work them off-leash! And with Harvard's endowment! Disgraceful! There's no excuse.

Mount Auburn does have an excuse: disrespect for the dead. Eager though I am for a clean, attractive, spacious, and fully fenced area right near my house where I can train and exercise the dogs off-leash, I have to admit that it would be a little unseemly to allow even such splendid and civilized animals as Kimi and Rowdy to lift their legs on B. F. Skinner or Mary Baker Eddy. Skinner's presence, though, sustains my hope. Skinner? Harvard psychology professor. Renowned behaviorist. Pigeons, not dogs, but learning is learning, or so Skinner maintained. Best publicist that operant conditioning ever had. Anyway, there lies Skinner, cold and mute, when, damn it, if I could just warm him for a minute or two of animated chitchat, he'd come up with a clever solution to the vexing problem of how to train dogs not to pee on tombstones. The other part I've solved myself. The owners carry plastic cleanup bags. The plan as a whole is perfectly sound. There's ample precedent. From the beginning, Mount Auburn has been more than a place to bury the dead. Since 1831, it's been an arboretum, a nature preserve, a sculpture garden, and a bird sanctuary as well as a cemetery. Precedent! Precedent for its reincarnation as the world's largest and most beautiful training facility and off-leash dog park. The transformation wouldn't cost a thing. You'd just have to persuade visitors to close the gates.

Gates. The fence. That's where we were. As I was starting to say, in contrast to Harvard Yard, which has high, solid, uniformly expensive-looking brick walls on all sides, Mount Auburn Cemetery has a stretch of handsome, obviously costly wrought-iron fencing on either side of the main gate, which is a towering gray stone, Egyptian-looking affair that somehow fits the popular conception of the gates of hell, but with a different inscription and radically different intentions, of course. The point of a garden cemetery cum bird sanctuary and dog park and so forth is to urge people to reclaim hope, right? Not to abandon it. Anyway, the wrought-iron section wouldn't have disgraced Giralda, but having sensibly put their money up front, where it shows, the Mount Auburn people have economized around the rest of the cemetery's perimeter, most of which is bounded by chain-link, *good* chain-link, mind you, quality stuff, but not in a class with wrought iron. Not that I'm complaining! The Committee for the Canine Reclamation of Mount Auburn is perfectly satisfied with the existing dog-containment system. The chain-link is heavy and sturdy, and it's high enough all the way around to prevent dogs from leaping over. People, too.

The cemetery had closed for the day. The main gate was shut, as the back gate undoubtedly was, too. If the tattooed Mercedes man intended to enter, he'd need to force a gate, scale the fence, or cut a hole in it. On the night of Peter

Motherway's murder, someone had apparently climbed over. The gates hadn't been tampered with. The chain-link hadn't been cut. Rather, someone had hauled the body over the fence before transporting it to the Gardner vault.

Whatever the man's intentions, he wouldn't carry them out here on Mount Auburn Street. Now, even after the rush hour had ended, cars and trucks passed, their headlights on. The Star Market was busy. Streetlights shone on pedestrians. I'd had practice in sneaking a dog into Mount Auburn when it was open to the public. Now, stopped at a red light, I quickly tried to plan what I'd do if I wanted to enter unobserved after dark. If I walked along the fence in the direction the man was taking, I'd come to Coolidge Avenue, where I'd turn right and continue to make my way along the boundary of Mount Auburn. The inhabitants of the big, handsome houses on the opposite side of Coolidge Avenue would be arriving home late from work, leaving for evening activities, walking dogs, and otherwise coming and going. After a quarter mile or maybe a half mile, the houses would give way to the grounds of the Cambridge Cemetery, which has a magnificent view of the Charles River, but is otherwise an ordinary cemetery, lacking as it does Mount Auburn's magnificent monuments, impressive vegetation, imaginative landscaping, and famous remains. Ah, the eternal town and gown! Still, there's a fairness about death. Residents on both sides slept the same six feet under. Even along that stretch, Coolidge Avenue wouldn't be deserted; it served as a convenient short-cut from Cambridge proper to several large condominium buildings, a tennis and fitness club, and a big shopping mall. But tall trees grew inside and, in some places, outside Mount Auburn's fence. Furthermore, somewhere along Coolidge Avenue was a gate I'd seen in daylight when the dogs and I took this route to the river. I vaguely remembered the gate as small. I'd never paid much attention to it because it was always closed and secured with a length of chain; a permanently locked, evidently unused entrance was no place to sneak in a dog.

When the traffic light turned green, I drove past the turn at Brattle that would have taken me home and past the man, who was now moving swiftly. At Coolidge, I made a right and cruised by the big, illuminated houses. Somewhere to my right, not far beyond the fence, was the fine old Mount Auburn neighborhood that included the Mary Baker Eddy Monument and the Gardner family vault. The tattooed man had prayed before Mrs. Gardner's portrait at Fenway Court. Did he also worship at her grave? If the vault was his destination, he might scramble over the fence soon after turning onto Coolidge. But maybe not. The discovery of Peter Motherway's corpse had generated lots of media attention. Especially near the Gardner vault, people would be on the alert, wouldn't they? Cemetery guards, residents of Coolidge Avenue, passersby. As I'd expected, lights were on in the houses along Coolidge, but no children played on the front lawns, and no one sat on the steps or porches by the front doors. There wasn't a dog in sight. These suburban-style houses had side yards and backyards, many of them fenced. What had I been thinking? This wasn't an area where neighbors visited back and forth to gossip on front stoops or where children played anywhere near the street. The yards probably had teak benches and those expensive wooden structures that combine swings, ladders, slides, and gymnastics equipment with adorable little tree houses. Cambridge being Cambridge, Mommy and Daddy sat outside congratulating themselves on the papers they'd just had accepted by peer-reviewed journals. Cambridge being Cambridge, the kiddies prepared for adult life by imaginatively scaling the ladder from assistant to associate to full professor upward, ever upward, toward the tree house, transformed by the infant vision of the future into the ivory tower of academe. The family dog, a black Lab, kept hopefully dropping a tennis ball. No one threw it for him. Why bother? You don't get tenure by playing with your dog.

The traffic was lighter than I'd predicted. For a skilled interloper, almost anywhere along here would offer access to Mount Auburn. I began to look for a place to pull over, preferably a place where I could sit in my car and reconnoiter. A row of parked cars would have camouflaged mine; here, not a single car was parked on the street. What's more, its age and dents made the old Bronco distinctive; the man could have noticed it on the way to Waltham or at the fast-food place. My car was more recognizable than I was, I thought. Bigger, too. On foot, I could become all but invisible in the dark. I could flatten myself against a tree trunk or lurk in a shadow. I had to get rid of the car.

Just after turning onto Coolidge, along the stretch with the big houses, I'd passed a couple of narrow side streets, one of which dead-ended at the Shady Hill School. Like other elite private grade schools, Shady Hill would have liberated its students at the end of May or the beginning of June; there'd be no parent-teacher meetings or school plays tonight. On the other hand, the school's parking area might be gated shut for the night, or there might be a security guard who'd have my car towed. The access road undoubtedly had permit-only parking; my Cambridge permit was good for my own neighborhood but not for this one. What's more, the area around Shady Hill had the kinds of fancy houses that attract burglars; my disreputable Bronco might be mistaken for a getaway car. Feeling outclassed, I ended up leaving the Bronco much farther from Mount Auburn Street than I'd have liked, in the parking lot of the older of two condo complexes near the intersection of Coolidge and Grove. I pulled in, parked, and killed the engine. In his crate, Rowdy stirred. When he shook himself, the tags on his collar jingled. He's always thrilled to go anywhere.

"Sorry, boy," I said. "I'll be back as soon as possible."

I hated to leave him. I always hate to leave my dogs. Rowdy is, however, a big, flashy showman who knocks himself out to become the center of all eyes. He carries his plumy white tail over his back. Except in a complete blackout, you can see his white face, and it's hard to miss the watch-me wag of that magnificent tail. Unobtrusive he's not. Tonight, I wanted to pass unnoticed.

In the absence of Rowdy and Kimi, I imagined their leashes in my hands and their familiar rear ends surging ahead of me as I set off back down Coolidge Avenue on the side opposite Mount Auburn. A short stretch of sidewalk ended, a guardrail appeared, and I found myself forced into the road. On this side of Coolidge, though, I was free from the irrational fear that the man would vault over the fence from inside the cemetery to plummet on top of me. I always walk fast; ever since I first toddled, my pace has been set by big dogs. Now I almost trotted. It still seemed to take me forever to cover the ground. I felt a strange, senseless annoyance at the absence of lights in Mount Auburn. The place was closed to the public. Why waste electricity? The only living people who belonged there were guards, who certainly carried flashlights and knew their way around, and maybe a few of those topflight birders who were rumored to possess cemetery keys. What bothered me, I realized, was the contrast with the cozy, residential atmosphere of Mount Auburn by daylight. The cemetery had its Chestnut, Oak, Spruce, and Magnolia avenues, its Pond Road. The graves, too, bore familiar names. Julia Ward Howe, Winslow Homer, and their neighbors weren't just *buried* at Mount Auburn; they *lived* there. Immortality was the point, wasn't it? The nighttime darkness of the Cambridge Cemetery, on my right, felt normal. Mount Auburn, however, was a charming little town abnormally blackened by a massive power failure.

Soon after I passed the Cambridge Cemetery, just before the access road to Shady Hill, I heard the approach of a car behind me. So what? A few others had passed in both directions. Those cars, however, had been speeding along. This one was moving slowly. Before its headlights reached me, I impulsively stepped to the right, flattened myself on the ground between a hedge and a fence, and peered. What I was seeing might, I thought, be known as a town car. Or was that seeing a big American car, not a limousine, but the kind of long, dark car from which a uniformed chauffeur could emerge without surprising anyone. As the car crept by, I read the license plate. The tiny bulbs mounted above it struck me as ridiculous: A license plate was not a work of art that deserved to be admired in good light. What really drew my dog-person's eye, though, was the vanity plate. You can't attend a dog show without seeing hundreds of vanity plates: DACHSLUV, MALS R AI, DALPROUD, and all kinds of others printed with breed brags and abbreviated kennel names.

This vanity plate? HSM GSD.

To a dog person, GSD means one thing: German shepherd dog. Having decoded the second part of the license plate, I understood the first. HSM: Haus Motherway. Haus Motherway German Shepherd Dogs. B. Robert Motherway's kennel. Then I finally recognized the car as the limo-like one I'd seen in the Motherways' barn. B. Robert Motherway's vanity plate. B. Robert Motherway's car. Was he in it? Was Christopher? Jocelyn? Two of the surviving Motherways? All three? Only a short distance ahead of me, the car came almost to a stop before turning right onto Shady Hill Road.

Feeling foolish, I imitated war-movie G.I.'s by crawling flat on my belly to the end of the fence and the hedge. The big car halted. For a minute or two, it just waited there, its engine running, its headlights on. A soft glow came from the interior of the car, but I couldn't see in. The windows were tinted, I realized. Also, my position on the ground made a wretched vantage point. Suddenly a dark figure crossed from the opposite side of Coolidge Avenue so quickly that it almost seemed to materialize at the front passenger door of the big car. I'd noticed the purposeful air of the tattooed man. His purpose, or part of it, was now clear: He was keeping an appointment. In response to his presence, the door opened. The interior lights went on. My view was now unimpeded. At the wheel was Jocelyn. In the passenger seat, holding a gun to her head, sat B. Robert Motherway. I understood his purpose, too. He was delivering Jocelyn to her executioner.

Chapter Twenty-seven

HERE IN CAMBRIDGE, if you want to spend a pleasant, companionable afternoon in the outdoors, you and your friends stroll through Mount Auburn Cemetery. You chat, admire the trees, and walk on the remains of dead people. In Maine, where I grew up, you do more or less the same thing. You stroll through the woods chatting and admiring the trees, but instead of passively treading on corpses, you create them. Then you take them home and eat them for dinner. They aren't human, of course. Still, the recreational similarities outweigh the differences: fresh air, camaraderie, nature, death.

I am a decent shot. I own two guns. My twenty-two was at my father's place in Maine. My Smith & Wesson revolver might as well have been. It was safely and uselessly stored in the bedroom closet in my house on Concord Avenue. Besides, I was a dog writer and a dog trainer. The cop was Kevin Dennehy. Jocelyn's fears had been rational; her life was in jeopardy. It was time to call the police. Or it would be, as soon as I could get away. For the moment, I didn't dare to move. I'd taken refuge on surprisingly cold and damp earth between the scratchy hedge and the wooden fence. Now that the man had appeared and the car door was open, I was afraid that any movement I made would set the shrubbery rustling. I'd stuck my head out far enough beyond the end of the fence and hedge to discover that they bordered a driveway. It offered no cover. If I leaped out and bolted, I'd be dead. For now, I could do nothing but listen and watch.

There was little to hear. B. Robert spoke softly to Jocelyn. He must have ordered her to move the car beyond the driveway and then turn off the engine and the headlights. She did. The door reopened and the interior lights again came on. I could see that he was holding a silver flask, the kind of old-fashioned one I associate with flappers, Prohibition, and bathtub gin. The gun was in his left hand, the flask in his right. He put the flask down for a moment. I couldn't see what he was doing, but he must have produced some pills from somewhere, because when he spoke, he said, "Swallow them. All of them." Jocelyn must have complied. It was her habit. Without a gun at her head, she'd probably have obeyed. I couldn't see her, but I heard gasping and sputtering. Maybe the flask really did contain gin.

B. Robert was unsympathetic. "Pig! Look what you've done to my dashboard. Dirty pig!"

I remembered reading somewhere that as an epithet, *pig* was far more insulting in German than in English.

As B. Robert repeated it, the tattooed man moved around the car to the driver's side and opened the front door. "The keys," he told Jocelyn.

Reaching toward the ignition, B. Robert said, "I'll take them. You get her. Gently! Not a mark on her! Suicide, suicide, suicide! The dirty little pig will soon be all nice and clean. Off we go!" With that, he stepped out of the car, waited until Jocelyn had done the same, and then threw a switch on the door, an automatic lock, I assumed. I heard a click. Then both doors closed. Motherway didn't suffer from my sense of vehicular social inferiority. With Jocelyn between them, the men crossed Coolidge Avenue and disappeared into the darkness by the fence. Was the locked gate here? It seemed to me that it wasn't across from the houses, but across from the Cambridge Cemetery, in other words, between me and my car.

I forced myself to count to sixty. Then I did it again four more times before wiggling from under the hedge and emerging on Shady Hill Road. Trying to adopt the unobservant, inner-directed manner of a fitness walker on her regular route, I made no effort to conceal myself, but strode boldly to the corner, turned left, and headed toward my car. The impulse to sprint was almost overwhelming. I restrained it. As I'd done on the way from the car, I avoided the Mount Auburn side of the street. Casting my eyes in that direction, listening hard, I neither saw nor heard a thing; Jocelyn and her captors must already have entered the cemetery. Even after I passed the entrance to the Cambridge Cemetery and found myself squeezed into the road by the guardrail, I persisted in my superstitious resistance to crossing Coolidge Avenue. Instead, keeping an eye out for cars, I broke into a run at the edge of the blacktop. Pounding along, I managed not to worry about Rowdy. Instead, I focused on the location of the nearest pay phone. At the Mount Auburn Star Market? Or in the opposite direction, at the shopping mall on Arsenal Street? The two spots were about the same distance from my car, weren't they? So the direction didn't really matter. Whichever way I went, I'd be talking to the police in no time. And if Christopher Motherway were lurking around somewhere? If he were part of the plan? If he were meeting his fellow conspirators inside Mount Auburn? Or keeping a lookout? Well, the chances were negligible that he'd noticed the Bronco in the parking lot by the condo building. If he had? Why would he break into my car and steal Rowdy, for heaven's sake? Not that Rowdy would have put up a fuss. On the contrary, Rowdy'd have happily gone with Christopher Motherway or anyone else. In the short time it took me to reach the parking lot, my heart shifted to the middle of my chest, where it kicked hard in an alarming effort to escape captivity. I leaned my weight on the Bronco and peered through the windows. Rowdy's crate was there. It looked empty.

Then his tags jingled. I gave myself a second to recover before I opened the door. Flopping into the driver's seat and jamming the key in the ignition, I said, "Rowdy, I am always glad to see you. The mall it is. I think it's a minute or two closer than Mount Auburn Street."

In response, he stirred. Again, I heard his tags. I heard them clearly. Why? Because the damned Bronco made not a sound. The engine didn't even try to start. The battery didn't whine. It didn't whir. Still, I couldn't stop myself from turning the key. I removed it from the ignition, reinserted it, and tried again. Nothing. I held my foot on the gas pedal and again turned the key. Nothing. I waited thirty seconds. Then I turned the key ten times in a row. At a minimum, the battery was dead. Possibly, the whole car was.

Damn, damn, damn! Should I go to the lobby of the condo building and plead with someone to call the police? But I'd need to talk to the police myself. Among other things, I'd need to make it clear that sirens were taboo. If wailing cruisers zoomed into Mount Auburn, Mr. Motherway would abandon the plan to fake a suicide. Instead of holding the silent gun to Jocelyn's head, he'd shoot her, wouldn't he? Could I convince someone in the condo complex to let me use a phone? I was covered with dirt I'd picked up crawling on the ground. My face was stinging where the hedge's branches had scratched me. Did I look persuasively desperate? Or just disreputable?

Damn it! Mount Auburn Cemetery simply *had* to be patrolled at night. It was a sculpture garden! Every museum had security guards. Mount Auburn was an outdoor museum. There had to be security guards who prevented theft and vandalism. As soon as Peter Motherway's body had been found at the Gardner vault, the security precautions had probably been doubled. At no distance from me, just over the Mount Auburn fence, were trained professionals whose principal task was to protect the cemetery from intruders. I'd seen no sign of them because I'd stuck to the wrong side of Coolidge Avenue. Did the guards carry guns? I hoped so. But they certainly had walkie-talkies of some kind. Who'd hire guards without providing a means for them to summon help? And that rumor about the keys given to top birders? The idea was pure Cambridge; it had to be true.

At the back of my mind lurked memories of the Gardner heist. The thieves had succeeded for one reason: Contrary to explicit orders never to admit anyone to Fenway Court, the museum guards had opened the door to robbers who'd masqueraded as members of the Boston police. Then there was the matter of Peter Motherway's body. The night he'd been garroted, the night his corpse had been taken to Mount Auburn and transported to the Gardner vault, there'd been guards on duty, hadn't there? Fewer than there must be now, I told myself. For all I knew, B. Robert Motherway, Jocelyn had already been saved by a courageous key-carrying birder. Still, lackey were already in custody. For all I knew, Jocelyn had hypervigilant. Now there'd be plenty of guards. Now they'd be purely as a matter of form, I assured myself, as little more than a courtesy, I had to make sure, didn't I? And whatever I did, wherever I went, I had to go on foot. But not alone.

"Come on, buddy!" I said inspiringly to Rowdy, who, of course, would've been perfectly comfortable walking alone through the middle of a cemetery crowded with the newly risen ghosts of everyone ever interred there. "We're going for a nice little stroll by the graveyard at night. And we're not going to be afraid, are we? Not us! And you know what we're going to do? We're going to whistle past that graveyard! We're going to whistle a song that says you never walk alone. Because *you* don't, do you, chum? Not when *I'm* around."

Thus did the bold alpha leader of our two-creature pack boost the confidence of her trembling subordinate. So successful was her pep talk that within half a minute, she was trotting along behind him, his leather leash clutched in her sweaty palm. "The bit about whistling," I confessed in a whisper, "was strictly metaphorical. I'm not actually going to whistle *aloud*, okay? Especially after we cross the street and get to the cemetery fence. No cars coming! Rowdy, this way!" Across the street we went and onto the grass that carpeted the area between the pavement and the chain-link. Now that we were practically inside the cemetery, I directed my attention to looking and listening for a sign of a guard on night patrol. Birders would be silent, wouldn't they? Or did they night-visit in chattering flocks?

Rowdy expressed his anxiety about murderers, graveyards, and assorted other petrifying threats both real and imaginary by casually lifting his leg on the fence and then on a utility pole. The streetlight mounted atop the pole cast none of its light into Mount Auburn. Its principal effect was to dim my night vision. Through the chain-link, I saw nothing in the cemetery and, indeed, nothing of the cemetery. It might have been a black hole in outer space. Not five minutes earlier, I'd assured myself that Mount Auburn would be thick with armed guards. If so, they were on stealthy patrol. The call notes of birds or birders? There were none. I strained to hear footfalls. Ah, but would the guards necessarily be on foot? Mount Auburn had more than ten miles of roads and paths. In the daytime, maintenance crews used trucks and golf carts. If Rowdy and I just kept heading along the fence toward that never-used gate, I was sure to see the lights of a patrol car and to hear the comforting sound of its engine. For all I knew, the guards kept watch from outside the cemetery as well as from within! At any moment, Mount Auburn guards or maybe even uniformed members of the Cambridge police force might cruise along Coolidge Avenue. Moving quickly behind Rowdy, I shifted my eyes hopefully back and forth between Mount Auburn, a few inches to my left, and the Cambridge Cemetery across the street. Maybe it, too, had guards! To my annoyance, however, Coolidge Avenue remained almost as deserted as the burial grounds that bordered it. I began to feel an irrational anger at the families and loved ones of the people buried for acres and acres around me. Why did cemetery visits have to be daytime events? Foolish custom! Why not floodlight the monuments and turf, throw open the gates to flower-bearing nocturnal mourners? Wasn't it on lonely nights that the departed were most acutely missed? If fair were fair, these forsaken grounds would be open twenty-four hours a day! Supermarkets were. Why not cemeteries? Which was more likely to strike at three A.M.—grief or hunger?

A few cars passed. Not one looked even remotely like a cruiser. As Rowdy and I drew opposite the gate to the Cambridge Cemetery, the grass verge on our side of Coolidge Avenue widened, and trees appeared between the pavement and the Mount Auburn fence. Almost clinging to the fence, I felt sheltered by the trees and took advantage of the sense of concealment to halt briefly and once again focus on the far side of the chain-link. As before, all was as dark and silent as the proverbial you-know-what. We'd covered the distance from the car in what felt like an unnaturally short time. The unused gate to Mount Auburn must be along here somewhere. I cursed myself for failing to study the terrain by daylight when the dogs and I had taken this route to the river. I'd driven by here many times. Why hadn't I noted the mileage from landmark to landmark? From Shady Hill Road to the border of Cambridge Cemetery? Why hadn't I memorized the precise location of the unused gate? Because it hadn't mattered, that's why. Landmarks hadn't been landmarks. Until now.

The gate was even closer than I expected. My memory had distorted its size. Perhaps because the double doors were always closed, I'd remembered the gate as a single, narrow panel. But I'd been right in recalling a length of heavy chain. As usual, the gate was closed. My hands found the chain, which was deceptively looped around the panels of the double gate as if to lock them together. I found one end of the chain, then the other, and ran my fingers slowly along the links. The gate was indeed shut and chained. But it wasn't actually locked. Despite the mildness of the night, a shiver of cold ran down my arms. This had to be where B. Robert Motherway and the tattooed man had led Jocelyn into Mount Auburn. When? At a guess, twenty minutes ago. Was Jocelyn dead now? At a guess, twenty minutes ago. Was Jocelyn dead now? Murdered? This gate was the men's bolt-hole, wasn't it? Any second now, it could open. When it did, I'd collide with Jocelyn's killers face to face. No guard dog, Rowdy would nonetheless do his best to protect me if he understood that I was under threat. But he wouldn't understand a gun. And he'd be as vulnerable to bullets as I was.

From inside the cemetery, I heard a muffled, distant cry. The voice was a woman's. Was she weeping? Calling out? Pleading for help? All that reached me was a single high-pitched note, all the more heartrending for its brevity. Without hesitation, I reached into my pocket, found a nylon slip collar, and slid it over Rowdy's head. Transferring the leash to the slip collar, I removed Rowdy's buckle collar with its jingling tags. After cramming the leather collar into my pocket, I unlooped the chain and eased open the gate as slowly and cautiously as if I'd been afraid of waking the dead. When I'd created an opening just wide enough for Rowdy and me to slip through, I paused for a second. The cry did not repeat itself. I heard no footsteps. Rowdy was silent. I heard no change in his breathing. His white tail was waving lazily over his back. Otherwise, he was almost motionless. Although I could see him only dimly, I felt his eyes on me. Nothing escapes a dog's keen nose and acute ears. If Rowdy perceived the presence of anyone but me, he showed no sign of it.

I shortened his leash, gave him a light, bracing pat on the shoulder, then slipped through the barely open gate, Rowdy on my heels. With almost unbearable impatience, I inched the gate shut and replaced the chain as best I could. Now that Rowdy and I were actually on the grounds of Mount Auburn, I understood the folly of my plan for round-the-clock visits. By daylight, Mount Auburn was a visitor's delight. But in the dark, what lay beneath the sod were not the deep, thick roots of old trees, but the decomposed and decomposing bodies of dead people. The monuments that rose around me, no matter how fanciful, moving, or even amusing by day, were stripped by darkness of their brave effort to make light of death. Simple, grand, angular, reverent, picturesque, all were now tombstones, nothing more.

Again, there was a soft, muffled cry. It came from somewhere to my right. At what distance? Not close. Not far. A paved road crossed in front of the gate. Another stretched in front of us. Rowdy and I moved straight ahead. In seconds, we reached an intersection, where Rowdy made a quick, eager move away from my left side. I assumed he wanted to take the lead. In a way, he did. It was Rowdy who came upon the uniformed body, Rowdy who sniffed it, Rowdy who raised his great head to me in confident expectation. Rowdy trusted me. He suffered from the humbling illusion that I would know what to do.

Chapter Twenty-eight

I'D FINALLY FOUND a Mount Auburn guard. I fumbled at his wrist for a pulse. Finding none, I forced myself to put my fingers on his throat. Although I knew that Peter Motherway had been garroted, I'd avoided dwelling on the details of how he must have died. Consequently, it took me a second to interpret the thin, sickeningly unnatural indentation in the bristly flesh. When I did, my hand sprang away all of its own accord, as if my fingers had brushed a hot iron. The reaction was instantaneous and involuntary. This, I told myself, was an unconditioned reflex, a primitive reaction from deep in the brain. Stimulus: sudden and unexpected physical contact with a dead body. Response: a startle of revulsion. Once my hand had fled, I felt pity. There was something pitiful about the stubble on the man's neck, about dying while needing a shave. Still, I found myself compulsively rubbing my hand on my sleeve before I reached out to hold Rowdy.

I knew I had to touch the body again. Were the Mount Auburn guards armed? If this one had carried a weapon, it would be foolish not to take it. But all I found was a walkie-talkie of some sort, a little box clipped to his belt. It felt like a small radio with a series of buttons and a square of plastic mesh that must have covered the speaker. I had no idea how to operate the gadget. Tinkering blindly, I could set off the kind of brassy squawk you hear in police cruisers and taxis; in trying to rouse help, I'd broadcast my presence. In case the guard had dropped a weapon when he'd been attacked, I searched the ground around the body. All I found was a little plastic bottle with the distinctive shape of a nasal-spray dispenser. The poor man had apparently been killed while defending himself against a stuffy nose.

If the attacker approached, Rowdy would warn me, wouldn't he? Not deliberately, I thought. On the contrary, Rowdy would prepare himself to extend his usual happy greeting. On the other hand, he wouldn't just sit there and let someone garrote me. He stands twenty-five inches at the withers and weighs close to ninety pounds. The power of his breed is even greater than the size would suggest. I comforted myself with the memory that in his youth, Tazs, my friend Delores's somersaulting malamute, had often pulled forty times his own weight. Forty times! Tazs, the famous Pulling Machine, had a Working Weight Pull Dog Excellent title and a history of weight-pull triumphs that Rowdy lacked. But the two dogs weighed the same! And Rowdy loved me as devotedly as Tazs loved Delores, which is to say with a concentrated adoration equal to a million times his own weight. I felt certain that Rowdy would bring a physical attack to an immediate, violent halt. I didn't want to see Superdog in action, though. In particular, I didn't want to see bullets penetrate his chest instead of bouncing off.

As if to shield Rowdy, I shortened his leash and forced my way ahead of him. The guard's corpse lay near an intersection of roads. At a guess, it wouldn't have been left where Motherway and the tattooed man would cross it on their return route. From where I stood, with my back toward Coolidge Avenue, the body was on the left. Therefore, I should head to the right. And at another guess, the men had taken Jocelyn to the Gardner vault, which I was quite sure was somewhere to my right. Mary Baker Eddy's monument, readily visible in the daytime from Coolidge Avenue, was definitely to my right. It was the size of a building and was made of pale stone; even at night, it'd be impossible to miss. If I reached it, I'd know I'd gone too far. The Gardner vault was deeper into the cemetery than the Eddy Memorial. I'd need to bear right and cut toward the interior of Mount Auburn. I'd also need to leave the paved roads. The Gardner vault, the family crypt, sat on the shores of a little artificial lake in what might have been a natural valley. Some sort of path ran near the lakeshore, but I was positive that I'd looked down on the vault and its neighbors from a trail on the high ground above. Unfortunately, it also seemed to me that even for one of the old sections of Mount Auburn, the area was an exceptionally tortuous maze of streets, paths, ponds, monuments, and crypts. Worse, it wasn't a section I knew well because there was only one dog monument nearby, and Dr. Stanton, Rowdy's former owner, was buried elsewhere.

If the sounds hadn't led me there, I might never have found it. The voice I heard now was different from the one that had cried out. There were words. I couldn't understand them. The sex was male. The tone was belligerent. Rowdy crowded against me. I could feel his muscles tighten. He has a nose for trouble. On his own, hearing it and smelling it, he'd head directly for its source. With misgivings, I loosened his leash to give him free run within its six-foot length. With a questioning glance at me—*This is what you want, isn't it?*—he confidently hit the end of the leash and justified the view of all the dumb people who'd ever said, ''Hey, lady, who's taking who for a walk?'' Rowdy plainly knew where he was going. More than that! I knew as well as I knew my dog that he was, indeed, gleefully pulling toward trouble. The hitch was Rowdy's varied conception of trouble. Rowdy might be making for human conflict. Alternatively, he could be in ardent pursuit of a meal of plump raccoon.

We suddenly came to a place I remembered, a passageway between walls of polished stone. I couldn't read the names on the walls now, couldn't even remember whether they were cut into the rock or engraved on brass plaques, but I knew they were there. If we followed the passageway and turned sharply right, there'd be a little body of water on our left and, on our right, happily situated on the shore like a row of summer cottages, the quaint buildings that were, in fact, family crypts. The Gardner vault was in the row.

But we didn't follow the passageway. I tugged on Rowdy's leash and managed to persuade him to reverse direction. I didn't need to see his face to read his disgusted expression. I could almost hear him silently groan. My stupid ideas are a great trial to him. By patting my thigh and stepping enthusiastically forward, I convinced him to indulge me. Now that I finally had my bearings, I quickly found the little footpath that ran parallel to the shore of the tiny lake on the miniature hillside above the family vaults. The passing of clouds brightened the sky a shade or two, so I didn't need to grope my way, but moved swiftly until the roofs of the squat crypts were below me and, below them, the water. I could hear movement. There was a soft splash. Someone was mumbling. Jocelyn? Yes. She repeated a series of syllables. The pills had thickened her voice. She seemed to be saying the same thing over and over, but I couldn't make out what it was. I heard whispers. One had a tone of impatience. I was too far away to understand the words.

In frustration, I dropped to my hands and knees and began to creep slowly downhill. I shortened Rowdy's leash and gripped it tightly in my hand. I must not raise my hindquarters and lower my shoulders, I reminded myself; in the universal body language of dogs, the "play bow" is an invitation to start leaping and tearing around. To my relief, Rowdy seemed content to join me in a game of silent stealth. The short distance we covered put me close enough to hear the phrase that Jocelyn was now uttering again and again in a drugged, yet weirdly insistent, voice.

"Brother and sister, brother and sister, brother and sister," she mumbled. Her tone changed to one of surprise. "Brother and sister! Brother and sister! Christina, my Christina!"

"Gerhard, for Christ's sake," B. Robert grumbled, "hurry up! Your orders are clear! Get her head underwater and hold it there! Is that too complicated? First, get her head underwater. Then hold it there! And no marks!"

I could now see B. Robert Motherway's tall figure pace back and forth on what seemed to be a gravel path in front of the Gardner vault. Between the path and the water was a large, low, rectangular object I couldn't identify, a tomb, perhaps, or dignified housing for equipment that pumped water to the artificial lake. Or aired out the crypts? Anyway, Jocelyn was stretched out on it. Facing the lake, Gerhard sat on it in the pose of *The Thinker*. Suddenly, he exclaimed at almost normal volume, "It's concrete! I could smash her head against it!"

"Brother and sister," Jocelyn muttered compulsively, "brother and sister."

"Shut up!" Motherway quietly ordered her. "Oh, for Christ's sake! Why is it impossible to get people to obey orders! It is a terrible thing," he added, obviously to himself, "to lose the strength of manhood. It is a terrible thing to grow old." Again issuing orders, he strutted toward the two figures, pointed a menacing hand, and said, "We have planned all this in detail and at length! Hold her head underwater! Do it now, you moron! Overcome with guilt and remorse, she washes off the stain of murder! Hurry! This should have been over in minutes! You had her in the water! Take her there again! Take her there now!"

"Here lie the remains," Gerhard announced in the tone of a museum guide, "of a public benefactress, a beautiful woman who suffered the slings and arrowroots of outraged—" His voice broke off. My mouth must have been hanging open. *Arrowroots?* Wasn't arrowroot a thickener used in cooking? A type of bland cookie?

In any case, the outraged one was Motherway. "Enough crazy talk! Enough!"

"Mama!" Gerhard cried. "Mama! Your little Jackie is here! Your little Jackie has come back! He has come with presents! You like pretty things, don't you, Mama? All the pretty swastikas on your little house? Your pretty little boy? Your beautiful pictures? Mama, your little Jackie has come back to make sacrifices for you. Mama? Mama?"

Jackie? Isabella Stewart Gardner was Mrs. Jack Gardner. For short, she was Mrs. Jack. Jackie: her only child, the son who died in infancy. Gardner! Gerhard! This Gerhard had not the slightest trace of a German accent; in fact, from his vowels, I'd have guessed that he grew up in one of the suburbs south of Boston or on the South Shore. I felt suddenly certain that he'd taken the name himself, picked it because it reminded him of Gardner.

As I watched, Jocelyn unexpectedly sat up. "Brother and sister," she repeated.

Motherway abruptly lost patience. I saw him reach into his pocket and produce what must have been the handgun he'd had in the car. He stepped stiffly to Gerhard. "Pick her up, take her to the water, submerge her! Do it now!" The one he pointed the gun at, though, was Jocelyn. If Gerhard didn't drown her, Motherway would shoot her. Did it matter which way she died?

If it hadn't been for Rowdy, I'd have lacked inspiration to act. As I struggled to think of almost anything to do, a great many sirens wailed faintly somewhere far away. But not too far for Rowdy's sharp ears. Clicker training, I remind you, increases the frequency, intensity, and duration of target behavior. Does it ever! Raising his mighty head, Rowdy howled back. *Ahhhhh-wooooo! Ahhhhh-wooooo!* Unmuffled by walls, his operatic voice rang through the night air.

I leaped to my feet. A few steps put me on the turf-covered roof of the Gardner family vault. In what I hoped would pass with Gerhard as the elegant turn-of-the-century cadences of Isabella Stewart Gardner, I took advantage of Rowdy's bloodcurdling accompaniment to declaim, "I am Mrs. Jack Gardner! I sleep here in peace! Why do you desecrate my memory?"

My desperate, loony act apparently took in Gerhard. He fell to his knees facing the vault. Motherway's head jerked around to where Jocelyn sat, then jerked back. Could he see me? Could he see Rowdy? Even if he could, he'd have to be a first-rate marksman to hit either of us using a handgun at this distance at night.

Boldly, I added in my Isabella voice, "Do not kill the woman!" Mrs. Gardner, I reminded myself, had owned dogs. I allowed a hint of my dog-trainer assertiveness to slip in. "Save her! Save her life! Do it for *me*!"

Preoccupied with my role and with the weapon in Motherway's hand, I failed to keep an eye in other directions. Motherway still faced the vault. He was just starting uphill toward me when a weirdly identical figure came running at full speed along the path by the lake.

"What the hell is going on here?" Christopher Motherway's voice was a young man's version of his grandfather's.

"Mother left me a note. She must've been desperate."

"Christopher, go home!" Motherway commanded.

Far from being roused by her son's arrival, Jocelyn slid back down. "Brother and sister," she mumbled. "Brother and sister. Christina, I am so sorry! I didn't know! I didn't know! I didn't think he'd do it! I didn't know!"

In ludicrous understatement, Christopher exclaimed, "This situation is unacceptable!"

"Get off your high horse!" his grandfather snapped. "You had no qualms about Peter, did you? And if you had obeyed orders then instead of hiring this crazy Gerhard, this would be unnecessary. But you had to get greedy, didn't you? You couldn't go and pay full price for a professional, could you, Christopher? You had to keep half the fee for yourself. You always were a greedy little boy."

It would have been easy to hear the traded accusations as an ardent family spat about where Christopher had taken a suit to be dry-cleaned. In reality, the grandfather and grandson were quarreling about arrangements for the murder of the grandfather's son, the grandson's father. The full sickness of the family hit me at last.

"Peter could have been bought off," responded Christopher, sounding like his grandfather's identical twin. "And he was a mean bastard. But Mother's done nothing. Not a thing." As if to disclaim any respect he might have for Jocelyn, he added, "She doesn't have it in her."

B. Robert Motherway was haughty. "To the contrary, she is a sneak who has been scheming to reveal everything." He paused. "And I mean *everything*."

"Impossible," Christopher replied. "She doesn't know a thing."

Gerhard suddenly tuned in to the present. "Oh yes she does! I keep telling you and telling you! She *knows*! I don't know how, but she does! She knows about the dogs! She said, Wasn't it a miracle! All those canvases, and they didn't get chewed by dogs! Shepherds! All those shepherds, she said, and they didn't chew the paintings! She said it, she said it, she said it!"

I was the one who'd talked about the shepherds and the paintings. I'd meant Geraldine R. Dodge's dogs and Geraldine R. Dodge's paintings, of course. Although Steve and I had been at Mrs. Gardner's museum, I hadn't been talking about her at all.

I was eager to hear more, but the elder Mr. Motherway finally lost patience. To my surprise, he didn't shoot Gerhard, but slammed him on the head with the butt of the gun. Gerhard fell to the ground and lay motionless.

As if she were the one who'd received a hard blow to the temple, Jocelyn groaned. "Christina, my poor Christina! He brought her back from Germany, you know. She was happy there. He brought her back to case the mansion for him, to tell him what was where! Brother and sister! Brother and sister!"

"Pay no attention to her," the elder Motherway said. "She came from nowhere. Her parentage is unknown. She is a nobody." He moved to Jocelyn and held the gun to her head. The drug that was causing the compulsive babbling seemed also to have made her oblivious to the peril of her situation; she hadn't tried to escape.

"What is she talking about?" her son demanded. Then he asked Jocelyn directly. "What the hell are you going on about?"

"I am cursed with women who *babble*!" Motherway exploded.

"Let her answer!" ordered Christopher, shoving his grandfather away from Jocelyn. "What's this about a brother and sister?"

Jocelyn's voice was wild with melodrama. "He fell in love with her! Oh, he fell madly in love with her! She was so beautiful! Christina! He brought her back to work for the rich old lady, and then he fell in love with her! And he married her."

"The old lady?" Christopher asked, bewildered. "What old lady?"

"No, no!" Jocelyn was getting groggy again. Her voice dropped. "His sister. His very own sister."

The grandfather raised the arm that held the gun. "Christopher, get out of the way!"

Almost simultaneously, Christopher must have understood the personal implication of what Jocelyn had revealed. With a roar, he sprang on his grandfather. "You son of a bitch! You dirty son of a bitch! Parentage! Hah! Parentage! Pig! Filthy pig!" Although grandfather and grandson seemed the same man at different ages, Christopher had no difficulty in wresting the gun from his grandfather. And no apparent difficulty in shooting him, either.

Chapter Twenty-nine

THE CRUISERS AND THE AMBULANCES arrived with sirens silent and headlights off. Still, a short distance behind me, engines hummed, and tires droned. I could have sworn that the temperature suddenly rose a degree or two, warmed by the body heat of a large, yet furtive, presence. Someone, I felt certain, had discovered the slain guard's body; only murder could speedily have summoned a force this large.

I saw no reason to remain at the scene. If my testimony were needed later, I would provide it. All I felt now was the primitive urge to get away and to take Rowdy with me. Rita informs me that I need feel no guilt about the impulse to flee. My horror, she claims, and my overwhelming compulsion to distance myself were normal, indeed, universal human responses to incest. "Hence," Rita says smugly, "the taboo." Human, maybe. But *universal?* Not half so universal as it ought to be, if you want my opinion. B. Robert and Christina. Rather, B. Robert and Eva Kappe. Brother and sister.

Also, I was scared of crossfire. Christopher's bullet must have shattered his grandfather's skull and penetrated the brain, and Gerhard was comatose, at least for now, but Christopher was able and armed. Having come to his mother's rescue, he'd be unlikely to risk a gun battle that could leave Jocelyn an innocent casualty. Still, I couldn't be sure.

The police would certainly approach on Mount Auburn's roads and paths. The paved streets and the trails all around the lake would be under surveillance, if not actually occupied, and there was bound to be a substantial force at the intersection where I'd found the dead guard's body. Consequently, my spur-of-the-moment plan for evading detection called for staying off Mount Auburn's major and minor thoroughfares; wherever possible, Rowdy and I would wend our way from monument to monument, stone to stone, tree to tree. Our destination would be the same gate through which we'd entered. It would be watched now, perhaps barred. But we'd deal with that problem when we came to it. If necessary, we'd go to some distant part of Mount Auburn and hide out until morning.

My advantage over the arriving forces was my recently acquired familiarity with the terrain. In the daytime, visitors who studied street signs and consulted maps still found themselves disoriented. Now, at night, the police were probably unsure of exactly what was where. But in this small part of the cemetery, I knew where I was and where I was going. Rowdy and I would crawl, slither, or dash, as needed, parallel to the trail that ran above the tiny lake. We'd stay uphill, above the path. That course should land us right near the gate to Coolidge Avenue.

All went well until a minor miscalculation of mine led us a bit too far above the trail. Taking one tentative step behind a massive monument, I came close to bumping into a police cruiser. I backstepped so rapidly that I bumped into Rowdy, but luckily managed not to step on a paw. To give myself a minute to regain my composure, I huddled behind the monument with my arms wrapped around Rowdy and my face buried in the warm comfort of his thick coat. As my heart slowed, I realized that the sight of the cruiser, far from alarming me, should have allayed my fears by offering visual confirmation of the conclusion I'd already reached. Yes, the police were indeed here, and in force, too. The cruiser I'd almost smacked into had been the middle car in a row of three. I'd heard more than that. There must be similar clusters of police vehicles throughout the area. Before long, I told myself, a Cambridge-cop voice with a heavy Boston accent would boom down through a loudspeaker into the little valley that contained the tiny lake and the Gardner vault. For all I knew, it might be Kevin Dennehy's voice that issued the warning and the order you always hear in movies: *It's the police. We've got you surrounded! Put down your weapons!*

The vision of Kevin Dennehy and his uniformed and plainclothes associates deployed all around the valley buoyed my confidence. With renewed determination, I rose to my feet, and Rowdy and I set off toward the Coolidge Avenue gate. Despite detours around low iron fences surrounding family plots and a few near tumbles on footstones, we soon found ourselves maddeningly close to our goal. At this point, the path forked. Virtually no distance ahead, both forks ended at blacktop. Somewhere to our right was the intersection where we had come upon the body of the guard. There'd be cops there, as well as at least one ambulance, and who knew what else. Straight ahead was the high boundary fence and, inches beyond it, Coolidge Avenue. If we went straight, then cut right, we'd be at the gate.

Just as I filled my lungs with oxygen, preparing to make the bold move out of the shelter of the trees and monuments and onto the exposed asphalt, I heard footsteps and then muted talk. It proved to be two large uniformed men heading onto the path, which is to say, directly toward us. Damn! Paths and roads converged so thickly here that there was almost no space between them. Immediately to my left, however, was a long rectangular monument with a flat top, the kind of memorial that's unhappily shaped like a coffin. It took no effort to lure Rowdy onto it. With a quick hand signal, I had him posed in a perfect down-stay. A second later, I was on a down-stay myself, flattened on the grass behind the monument, squeezing myself against its cold stone. Unable to speak aloud, I issued silent commands. *Stay! Good boy! Hold it right there! Freeeeeeze!*

As I heard the two men pass quickly by, I decided with relief that we'd entirely eluded their attention. Then a young man's voice said softly, "Hey, sergeant? Hey, wait up!

There's a dog back there." The footfalls stopped. "There's a great big dog on one of the—"

The sergeant guffawed softly. "This place is full of nutty statues. Statues of dogs all over! What you saw was—"

The footfalls resumed. The young officer was trailing after his sergeant. As they departed, I heard the young voice say plaintively, "But, Sergeant? Sergeant? Sergeant! It was wagging its tail! The dog was—"

"It was a stone dog, kid. It didn't wag its tail." The sergeant's voice faded as the men disappeared. "Kid, you must've been smoking something you shouldn't. You been doing that? Huh? What you been smoking? Wagging its tail! Wagging its tail! Jesus, what I gotta put up with!"

Once they were out of sight, I instantly got to my feet, brushed myself off, ran my fingers through my hair, and adopted the supremely self-confident air of utter obliviousness that is the hallmark of Cambridge eccentricity. I pretended to be an updated version of the parrot-walking Miss Whitehead, the near kin of a Cambridge personage so eminent that one could expect almost anything from me . . . and not be disappointed. The Cambridge attitude: *Within the city limits, I am entitled to go where I please when I please with whom I please. My life is the life of the mind! Nothing could be further from my thoughts than the opinions of people I may encounter on my journey.*

With Rowdy beside me in the improbable role of Miss Whitehead's parrot, I marched straight along the asphalt and up to the gate through which we'd entered, where I was only slightly irked to discover that the scene I'd scripted for myself was already being enacted. Indeed, it was immediately clear that I was being radically upstaged by a Cambridge type who'd gotten there first. Unlike me, he was dressed for the part. His peculiar-looking binoculars were harnessed to his chest, he wore a funny-looking hat and a loose vest with dozens of bulging pockets, and he carried a device designed, as he was explaining to a cop at the gate, to enable birders to hear their quarry. Certainly he had a key! His defensive tone suggested that the cop had offensively mistaken a *rara avis* for a guttersnipe. Unlike me, the bona fide night birder was not accompanied by a dog. He was not, however, alone. Hanging back, embarrassed, I thought, by his companion's arrogance, was, of all people, Artie Spicer, the leader of Rita's birding group, the guy we'd had dinner with the night my house was broken into. As the costumed birder strutted before the cop, Artie and I made eye contact and exchanged wry little smiles. Artie carried what I guessed was some fancy kind of night-vision spotting scope, a contraption for seeing birds in the dark.

Fearful that my lack of fluency in the language of birding would give me away, I picked my words carefully. "Hi, Artie," I said as normally as possible. "Anything interesting tonight?" I was hoping he'd mention some avian species so that I could say I'd heard it, too. Before encountering the real birder, I'd intended, if challenged, to brag about detecting the call of a black-crowned night heron, only because it was the only bird name I'd been able to think of that had anything to do with night. I'd felt apprehensive. Maybe the creature never flew north of Florida. Maybe it was voiceless, a cousin of the mute swan. Maybe the guard or the cop at the gate would be a birder with a life list approaching a trillion and would instantly spot me for the liar I was.

After taking down our three names and addresses, the cop waved the condescending birder through the gate. At Artie's side, Rowdy and I followed. Nodding at Rowdy, the cop said, "Good idea. Birds or no birds, this is no place to go wandering around at night."

With a knowing nod and a conspiratorial smile, I replied, "Well, Cambridge is Cambridge!"

The cop knew just what I meant. With a bob of his head in the direction of the costumed birder, he said, "Yup! A lot of odd ducks here, all right. A whole lot of odd ducks."

In Cambridge, attitude is everything.

Chapter Thirty

JOCELYN MOTHERWAY ENDED UP in Mount Auburn. The *other* one: Mount Auburn Hospital. The two parallel universes—pardon me, venerable Cambridge institutions—are only a few blocks apart on Mount Auburn Street. Whether the proximity is depressing or convenient depends on your point of view. Jocelyn Motherway's opinion on the matter was a bit difficult to decipher. She seemed less than overjoyed to be alive.

She was only a little paler than usual, and her hospital gown wasn't any dowdier than what she ordinarily wore. I found it satisfying, however, to see her propped up in a bed she hadn't made, sipping orange juice poured and served by someone else. The basket of flowers I'd brought rested on a windowsill. The arrangement contained a great many daisies and tons of those thick, coarse, cheap ferns, but it was better than nothing, I guess. I couldn't afford delphiniums.

"It was kind of you," Jocelyn told me lethargically. "People here are very kind. Someone washed my hair. And they haven't thrown me out on the street. There's nothing really wrong with me, you know. Most hospitals would've sent me home last night."

"You were in no shape to go home last night," I said. "You were incoherent. You were heavily drugged."

"This is what Christina needed. This kind of care."

Jocelyn patted the neatly made bed. Tears spilled down her cheeks. "This is what she deserved."

"I'm sure you took good care of her. I'm sure you did your best."

"My best wasn't good enough. Not that she was in physical pain. She wasn't. And toward the end, a lot of the time, she didn't know where she was. Or she did, in her own mind. She was in Germany, she was a little girl, she was in New Jersey. . . . You never knew where she was, how old she was. Sometimes she spoke English, sometimes she spoke German, so you'd get a clue that way."

"You speak German?"

"A little. Enough. Christina taught me some. Before she got sick. I understood her pretty well, better than I understood other people, because I learned from her. She used to get so homesick for Germany, and no one else in the house spoke it except *him*, and he made everyone speak English. I mean, supposedly she was born in this country. And you wouldn't have guessed, because she came here when she was young enough, so in English she didn't have a German accent."

"The birth certificate," I said.

"Christina Heinck. I think he picked it because it sounded German. Christina looked German." Jocelyn paused. "She looked like him. Christopher looks exactly like both of them."

I didn't want to be the first to utter that phrase that Jocelyn had repeated so compulsively the night before: *brother and sister, brother and sister.* I hadn't said B. Robert Motherway's name aloud, either. I'd been waiting for Jocelyn. So far, she'd referred to Mr. Motherway only as *he* and *him*. A little exchange I'd had with *him* kept coming back to me. I'd remarked that his stepfather had had a major impact on what he'd done with his life. "With my *wife?*" he'd demanded.

"Her real name was Eva," Jocelyn said. "She liked housework. She liked making things clean. She was beautiful. When she was old, she was still beautiful. If you don't know him, if you don't know what he's like, he's a handsome old man. Christina had that same look." Jocelyn lightly tapped a hand on her face. "Those cheekbones. The very fair coloring.

When he brought her to this country and sent her to that mansion in New Jersey, he made her dye her hair. That was the thing she minded most! He made her dye her hair red! With henna. She used to go on and on about that henna. It was the one thing she never really forgave him for. Funny, isn't it?''

''Christina was supposed to case the house for him,'' I said. ''Giralda, it was called. It really was a mansion. The woman who owned it was a Rockefeller. She was a major art collector.''

''Christina was happy there.'' Jocelyn managed a little smile. ''The woman was nice to her, Mrs. Dodge. That was her name. She was crazy about dogs. They were all over the place. Christina didn't mind. She liked dogs. Christina had her own room. She liked that. Except for the henna, she was very happy there. That's why she kept that letter, because she wrote it when she was happy. She had this 'treasure chest,' she called it. That's where that stuff came from. She liked to go through it, talk about it. It's still there at the house. Under her bed. She used to get me to get it out, and we'd go through it together.''

''Did the, uh, robbery take place?''

''Not that I ever heard of. Not that Christina knew. She would've said something. She used to talk about how the old fascist bastard—my words, not hers—got mad at her because she didn't find out anything. I mean, she didn't find out anything *he* wanted to know. Christina was supposed to find out about a dog show there, and she didn't because she couldn't, could she? She didn't have anything to do with the dog show. She was busy cleaning the carpets and washing the floors. And she was supposed to tell him about the paintings in the house, but all she knew was that there were a lot of them. She was no art expert. She dropped out of high school and went to Germany to be a maid. What was she supposed to know about art? So all she knew was about there being dogs all over the place, and I guess that security was pretty tight. Well, if the woman was a Rockefeller, it would be, wouldn't it? I didn't know that about her. I don't know if Christina knew that. It wouldn't have meant much to her. Christina was the kindest person I ever knew, but she wasn't . . . . He was al-ways trying to get her to read, but he didn't have much luck. Not that she was stupid or anything. She just wasn't very complicated. She was very loving. And very friendly. Unlike him. I mean, that's the main thing he was afraid of. No matter where she went, even at the end, like to a nursing home or a hospital, she would've talked to people, not necessarily in English, but you can never tell who's going to speak German, can you? *He* didn't give a sweet goddamn if she ended up in an institution. He just didn't want her talking where anyone but us could listen in."

"You weren't, uh, bothered by what you heard?"

"Well, a lot of it wasn't news to me. I mean, I was mar-ried to Peter, wasn't I? I mean about the art, not the other business. Peter didn't know about that. Like I said, he didn't speak German, and back when she was her-self, Christina wouldn't've told him, and then after her mind was wandering, she made Peter nervous, so he didn't spend a lot of time with her."

"The blackmail?" I asked.

"Yeah, that."

"That was about . . . ?"

"That was my fault. I shouldn't have told Peter. I was the one who knew about it. Soloxine. You knew what that was, right?"

"Yes. A fair number of the shepherds are on it? Uh, *his* dogs? They're hypothyroid?"

"Just about all of them. It's no big deal. You just shove these pills down their throats, and they're fine."

"That's sort of true." I couldn't restrain myself. "But they still shouldn't be bred."

"Oh," said Jocelyn. "Why?"

"Because it runs in families. If you breed hypothyroid dogs, what you get are hypothyroid dogs."

Jocelyn actually looked surprised. "Well, be that as it may, it was how I knew what he'd done, because the pills . . . You know what they look like? They're kind of a bluish green. And Christina . . . When I came in, after it was too late, well, I could see she'd thrown up. This green-blue stuff.

The same color. And none of the medicine she took, the medicine she was supposed to take, was that color. It wasn't anything like that color. Most of what she took was liquid, anyway, and I was the one that gave it to her, so I knew right away. *He'd* been there, in her room. He'd been there alone with her."

"You decided not to say anything?"

"No! No, I loved Christina. I told Peter right away."

"And Peter . . . ?"

At last, Jocelyn began to sob.

I spoke softly. "Peter didn't go to the police. He went to his father instead. He didn't care about avenging his mother. He used what you told him to try to blackmail his father." I couldn't bear to go on. Christopher was, after all, Jocelyn's son. Last night, when grandfather and grandson had quarreled, Jocelyn had been too doped to understand the dispute. For the moment, she didn't need to hear that B. Robert's response to Peter's attempted blackmail had been to order Christopher to hire an assassin to kill Peter. The grandfather married and then murdered his sister. Their son tried to use his knowledge of the murder to blackmail his father. The grandfather then enlisted the grandson in a scheme to murder the grandson's father.

"The stingy old Nazi bastard," said Jocelyn, sipping her juice. "Money would've fixed Peter, you know. If we hadn't been so damned hard up, none of this would've happened, but *he* was a stingy son of a bitch. He could've bought Peter off, but he was just too stingy. You know, for that matter, he could've bought me off, too. I shouldn't've sent you that stuff. It was a mistake."

"Why did you?"

"I was upset about Christina."

"Why me? Because of the dog? Wagner?"

"Yeah. That took some guts. It's a nasty dog." She sipped more juice. "You struck me as a nervy woman."

"Is that why you stayed with them? With Peter? And then with, uh, *him*? Because you weren't"—I hesitated—"nervy? I assumed you were afraid someone would kill you, too."

The freakish smile reappeared. I'd almost forgotten it.

Why, I can't imagine. It haunts me now. "I was, sort of. But, really, nerves had nothing to do with it," Jocelyn said. "I'm in the old man's will. So is Christopher." She laughed. "You didn't guess? Yeah, it's all ours. It's all ours now. And Christopher will be all right. I mean, who's going to send a boy to jail for saving his mother's life?"

Chapter Thirty-one

I **WAS WRONG** about Gerhard," I told Althea, who was seated in her wheelchair on the wide terrace that overlooks the long, sloping backyard of the house she shares with her sister. Despite the heat of the day, Althea was wrapped in a fuzzy pink wool shawl. I wore thin cotton jeans, a black tank top, and my Geraldine R. Dodge hat. Rowdy and Kimi had been given the liberty of the large fenced yard, but after a few minutes of tearing around, they'd returned to the terrace, to pant in the shade under an iron table.

"Have you ever noticed," I continued, "that if someone keeps harping on something, then you tend to dismiss it? Well, I do. And that's what happened. Kevin Dennehy has this twisted view of families. He's always going on about matricide, patricide, mate murder, the Menendez brothers, Susan Smith, notorious crime families, *The Godfather, Paris One Through Ten Thousand*, cousins murdering cousins, until he's covered all the ground and all you can think of are the exceptions. And there are some! Strangers kill strangers! There are plenty of criminal organizations that aren't composed exclusively of blood relatives."

Althea smiled gently. "Not to mention the occasional family or two in which no one murders anyone else."

"Exactly, Althea! And in which everyone works for an honest living instead of banding together to go around robbing museums and fencing stolen art and murdering people. So how was I supposed to guess that Gerhard was a cousin? Gerhard Woolf? Have you ever heard a more made-up-sounding name? He doesn't have a German accent, he doesn't look German, and he doesn't look anything like Mr. Motherway or Peter or Christopher. And nobody called him 'Cousin Gerhard,' or anything. Not that he's all that close a relative. He's something like B. Robert Motherway's mother's sister's great-grandson. I think I've got that right. And Christina's mother's, too, of course. Eva Kappe's mother's sister's great-grandson? Maybe I'm off somewhere. Anyway, it's the part of the family that Eva—in other words, Christina—went to in Germany when she dropped out of high school in New Jersey. Later on, B. Robert told the family in Germany that she died here. And he told people here that his sister died in Germany. The German part of the family just thought he'd married a woman named Christina, which he had, of course, only it was the same woman. Eva.''

"Appalling,'' said Althea, "but not unprecedented. There was a couple in Spain, wasn't there? Brother and sister. Ceci and I heard about them on National Public Radio, if I recall. They had two children. They were allowed to marry. The parents, that is, not the children, although one does have to wonder. . . . But it's interesting to observe, isn't it, that in this case, the madness one tends to associate with inbreeding shows itself most blatantly in a family member, this Gerhard, who, so far as one knows, is *not* the child of close relatives.''

"Peter Motherway didn't even look all *that* much like his father,'' I pointed out, "even though his parents apparently looked quite a lot alike. There was a family resemblance, but nothing out of the ordinary. That kind of thing happens with dogs all the time, of course. You can linebreed two beautiful dogs of a similar type and get a whole litter of funny-looking puppies. Good dogs aren't necessarily good producers. They can throw all kinds of stuff you wouldn't expect.''

"Three heads,'' Althea said mischievously.

I smiled. "Not exactly three heads. Missing teeth, bad bites, incorrect coats, all kinds of faults you don't see in the parents. And the kind of strong resemblance between B. Robert and Christopher does sometimes crop up in dogs, including between grandsire and grandson.''

"And evil, too?'' inquired Althea. "Does evil, too, run in canine families?''

"Certainly not! Althea, you're teasing me. No, evil has nothing to do with dogs. There are dogs with bad temperaments, and there are a few vicious dogs, but evil is an exclusively human characteristic. I don't think it has a thing to do with genetics. The person who really got B. Robert Motherway started was his stepfather, who was a small-time crook. Christina told Jocelyn about it. The guy—''

Althea blanched.

"Pardon me. The man, the Mr. Motterway who adopted B. Robert, ran what was really a junk shop rather than an antique shop, but he had higher ambitions. When he returned from Germany with his German bride and her two kids—children, pardon me—he also smuggled some stuff with him. And I think that's when he discovered that the boy, B. Robert, could be useful to him.''

"Fagin!'' Althea exclaimed. She concentrates on Sir Arthur Conan Doyle, but reads Dickens on the side. "*Oliver Twist*,'' she informed me.

"Yes,'' I said. "And the stepfather also seems to have pumped his stepson full of grandiose ideas about the glory of Germany and about rising to the aristocracy and so forth. And then when B. Robert got to Princeton—Princeton University—he happened to find himself in the same class as Hartley Dodge, Jr., who was in the same *Princeton* class, 1930, but in a whole other league from the townie son of a junk dealer. Christina told Jocelyn that B. Robert was totally obsessed with Hartley Dodge. He used to keep clippings about Hartley Dodge from the school newspaper, and sometimes he actually followed him around. When he saw Hartley Dodge, he saw a manifestation of the person he desperately wanted to be. Only he couldn't, of course. For a start, he didn't have any money. But the image was there: the glamorous, risk-taking heir to Remington Arms and to part of the Rockefeller fortune, the mansions, the show dogs, the incredible art collection! It was who he tried to become.''

"You know quite a bit about your Mr. Motherway now," Althea commented. Her eyes narrowed.

"He isn't *my* Mr. Motherway. And he isn't the only villain in the piece. Far from it. The stepfather seems to be the origin of a lot of what went wrong. For one thing, Christina sort of hinted to Jocelyn that the stepfather was the reason she was sent back to Germany. She was a pretty girl, a beautiful girl, young, and not his biological daughter. In fact, he'd never adopted her the way he had her brother. And the idea is that he was paying her inappropriate attentions, so her mother got her out of the country and away from him. There's no way to know for sure. Anyway, the stepfather died rather sadly. He hanged himself in 1929. He hadn't had a lot to invest, but he'd put it in the market, and after the Crash, he killed himself."

"As did others," Althea commented.

"Yes. But strangely enough, his wife, B. Robert's mother, died right after that, too. B. Robert was in his senior year at Princeton. He was living at home, naturally. He had a scholarship, but nothing beyond that. Until his mother supposedly hanged herself."

"Supposedly?"

"She'd managed to keep up the payments on a small insurance policy."

"Ah-hah!"

"But it was assumed that she was overcome with grief and shame about her husband's suicide, and followed suit. Anyway, by then, Eva was in Germany, and before long, our Mr. Motherway, B. Robert, had a degree in art history from Princeton. When he graduated, he took over his stepfather's business, mostly the shady part of it, and his stepfather's dogs, but he apparently decided he needed a better cover than a junk shop. That's when he moved here, to Massachusetts. He got a job teaching art history at exactly the kind of prep school he wished he'd gone to, and he had the perfect excuse to keep going back and forth to Europe: escorting student tours. And he liked what he saw in Germany in the thirties: the art, the music, the tidiness, the nationalism. What impressed him most of all was Eva. He hadn't seen her since

1926. She was beautiful. She liked housework. She was a simple person. She was the ideal Aryan woman. And she looked like him! After that, things get foggy for a while. What's clear is that he discovered an elite employment agency in New York that Mrs. Dodge used, and Eva Kappe came to this country, and she was a big hit there. She really did have good recommendations, and her training in European household service was practically designed to appeal to wealthy American employers. And then there was an opening with Mrs. Dodge. One of her dogs had bitten a maid, so she'd fired the maid. And Eva got the job. She kept them in what she called her 'treasure chest.' I've read them. So far as casting the place went, she really was useless, except that she did give a picture of tight security. Anyway, he finally pulled her out of there."

"The war began," Althea said.

"Yes, but he didn't go. He had a heart murmur. And flat feet. But he sure did go to Germany after the war. It was paradise for shady dealings in art, and he spoke fluent German. That's when he really made a bundle. By then he'd married Eva, who was now Christina. He brought her to Massachusetts. Peter was born in 1946. From what Peter told Jocelyn, I gather that there was trouble from the beginning. Really, I think that B. Robert had the world's worst case of sibling rivalry about the baby. He didn't want to share Christina's affection. Nothing Peter did was ever right. He got into trouble in school, kept flunking out of prep schools, and eventually got drafted and sent to Vietnam. When he got back, he moved into a cottage, a hovel, way at the back of his parents' property, and just sort of stayed there, doing kennel work, yard work, odd jobs, drifting along. And assisting his father in other ways, too. Then he met Jocelyn, who didn't know she was adopted until just before she got married. Her parents decided to tell her. And she stupidly told B. Robert, who threw a fit about having his family tainted with blood from God knows where. Can you believe it? Of all people?"

"Oh yes," said Althea. "I certainly can believe it."

"But strangely enough, when Christopher was born, his

grandfather moved in and took over. It reminds me of what Marcellus Hartley did. He was M. Hartley Dodge's grandfather. He basically *was* Remington Arms and a lot else. His daughter died in childbirth, and he raised the baby, Marcellus Hartley Dodge, who, of course, married Geraldine Rockefeller. So in sort of the same way, Christopher became his grandfather's son. And B. Robert did everything he could to poison the relationship between Peter and Christopher. Christopher lived in the big house. Peter and Jocelyn were still stuck in a hovel."

"With expectations of inheritance."

"Yes. Justified expectations, too. They really were included in B. Robert's will. Both of them. Separately. He wasn't stupid. He knew how to use people. He knew how to keep Peter and Jocelyn where he wanted them. Obviously, the strategy was effective."

"And Gerhard?"

"A German import, so to speak," I said. "Mr. Motherway brought Gerhard here from Germany when Gerhard was ten. I have a hunch that the immediate use he had for Gerhard was to help him smuggle something from Germany. Just as his stepfather had used him, of course. Once they got here, he must have made plans for Gerhard. He really kept Gerhard in a kind of servitude. Christopher got the education B. Robert had wanted for himself. Gerhard's job was to do what B. Robert said when he said it. Jocelyn says he was a docile boy, not very bright, pitifully eager for approval, very shy and very isolated, socially awkward. He had artistic ambitions, but no talent. He couldn't even draw. He didn't finish high school. He became B. Robert's lackey and, to some extent, Christopher's. He took care of the cars, drove for Mr. Motherway, did what he was told. As far as I can tell, it was all the same to him. Polishing the car, murdering Peter, following Jocelyn and reporting back to Mr. Motherway. He was at Mount Auburn when I gave her the envelope. He called Mr. Motherway to tell him. Once Mr. Motherway was sure she was on her way home, he waited for her there. He sent Gerhard back to Mount Auburn. They talked on Gerhard's car phone. Mr. Motherway wanted Peter's murder explained. Jocelyn's suicide was supposed to do that. The police were supposed to decide that she drowned herself where she'd left her husband's body."

"At the Gardner vault. Whence that eccentric interest in Isabella Stewart Gardner?"

"What Gerhard tells the police, Althea, is that it began after the heist. He's confessed to that. He says he was one of the actual robbers, the men disguised as Boston police officers. He says that Fenway Court was the most beautiful place he'd ever been. His words are, I'm told, that he was crazy about it the second he walked in. Of course, he's also confessed to ten or twenty other art thefts and to assorted other crimes. For example, the kidnapping of the Lindbergh baby."

"He wasn't born yet."

"He says he was. He also helped Lee Harvey Oswald to assassinate John Kennedy, and that was before he was born, too. What's not imaginary is his obsession with Isabella Stewart Gardner. He lived in a room in the basement of the Motherways' house. Kevin Dennehy, my friend who's with the Cambridge police, told me about it. He heard the place was a shrine to Mrs. Gardner. The walls were plastered with reproductions of works at Fenway Court, and there were tons of clippings about the robbery. What also seems to be true is that Gerhard cracked up about the time of the Gardner heist. Until then, he was peculiar and isolated. About that time, he started having what I guess were psychotic episodes. Jocelyn won't say much more than that. She doesn't want to talk about it. It occurs to me that she thinks a lot about the reward."

"Five million dollars? There's a good deal of room for thought there."

"Yes," I said ruefully. "Unfortunately, there's a lot of room for thought and no proof at all. What does seem clear is that leaving Peter's body at the Gardner vault was strictly Gerhard's idea. On Mr. Motherway's orders, Christopher was supposed to hire someone to kill Peter. Instead, Christopher got Gerhard to do it. He was supposed to make it look as if Peter had been attacked at the airport or on the way home by some random assailant. But Gerhard wanted to offer a sacrifice to his heroine. So he did."

"Holly, tell me, do you honestly believe that he was, in fact, involved in the Gardner robbery?"

"There is no proof, Althea. There is no proof."

And there isn't. What I know is that since being taken into custody, Gerhard has rambled wildly about many crimes and many people, me among them. Indeed, when he realized that the police didn't believe he'd robbed the Gardner, he cited me, of all people, as a corroborative witness. He explained that while sitting at a table next to mine at the Gardner Café, he'd heard me reveal knowledge of the robbery that I could not have read in the papers. Not surprisingly, I'd been talking about the Gardners, Gerhard claimed. I'd mentioned, for example, that Jack Gardner had died of apoplexy, as he had. I remember talking about apoplexy. Steve and I had been discussing Mrs. Dodge, of course. I'd said something about her husband's death. We'd joked about his having died of apoplexy when his wife got yet another dog. What convinced Gerhard of my inside knowledge, of course, was my remark that it was a miracle that all those priceless artworks hadn't been chewed or otherwise damaged by dogs. Furthermore, Gerhard insisted, I even knew the breed that had had brief access to the Rembrandts, the Vermeer, and the other works lifted from Fenway court. If I hadn't been privy to the hidden truth about the heist, how could I have known that the potential chewers were German shepherd dogs? Gerhard also makes much of my having stared at the tattoo on his arm. I did stare at it; he's right about that. As you know, I had no idea what it was supposed to represent. According to Gerhard, it portrays a special item he selected during the Gardner heist: the finial from a Napoleonic flag.

B. Robert, of course, had dismissed Gerhard's suspicion of me as delusional paranoia centered yet again on Isabella Stewart Gardner. Gerhard followed me from Mr. Motherway's all on his own. It was, I am convinced, Gerhard who broke into my house and trashed my study. There did, after all, turn out to be one object missing, something I hadn't noticed while straightening out the mess. The object was a book. It was the guidebook Steve had bought for me at the Gardner, the guide to Fenway Court. Gerhard had clearly found nothing else in my house to connect me to knowledge of the famous heist.

A few last words. The book is done. Elizabeth and I have submitted it to our publisher. It has been accepted. It's nonetheless a disappointment to me. It says nothing about Nazi spies. Were there any at the old Morris and Essex shows? There may have been many. I do not know. I know of only one. The proof was in Christina Motherway's treasure chest. It consisted of a document in German, a letter to her husband that she had secretly kept because she was proud of him for serving the Fatherland. So there was a Nazi spy at Morris and Essex. His name was B. Robert Motherway.

My financial situation is improving. I had the Bronco fixed. It starts most of the time. I'm showing Rowdy and Kimi again. I scrape together the fees. But my hopes are great. I have applied for a grant, you see. I don't know whether I'll get it, but I'm optimistic. The funding agency is bound to love me. I have applied, you see, to the Geraldine R. Dodge Foundation. I am applying for a grant to write dog books. It is the perfect topic. I am the perfect candidate.

About the Author

SUSAN CONANT, a three-time recipient of the Maxwell Award for Fiction Writing given by the Dog Writers' Association of America, lives in Newton, Massachusetts, with her husband, two cats, and two Alaskan Malamutes—Frostfield Firestar's Kobuk, CGC; and Frostfield Perfect Crime, CGC, called Rowdy. She is the author of twelve Dog Lover's Mysteries. Look for her (lucky) thirteen, *Creature Discomforts*, in hardcover from Doubleday at your favorite bookseller in April 2000.

RITA MAE BROWN & SNEAKY PIE BROWN

"Charming . . . Ms. Brown writes with wise, disarming wit."
— *The New York Times Book Review*

Sneaky Pie Brown has a sharp feline eye for human foibles. She and her human co-author, Rita Mae Brown, offer wise and witty mysteries featuring small-town postmistress Mary Minor Haristeen (known to all as Harry) and her crime-solving tiger cat, Mrs. Murphy.

WISH YOU WERE HERE
___28753-2 $6.99/$9.99 Canada

REST IN PIECES
___56239-8 $6.99/$9.99

MURDER AT MONTICELLO
___57235-0 $6.99/$9.99

PAY DIRT
___57236-9 $6.99/$9.99

MURDER, SHE MEOWED
___57237-7 $6.99/$9.99

MURDER ON THE PROWL
___09970-1 $6.99/$9.99

Ask for these books at your local bookstore or use this page to order.

Please send me the books I have checked above. I am enclosing $_____ (add $2.50 to cover postage and handling). Send check or money order, no cash or C.O.D.'s, please.

Name _____

Address _____

City/State/Zip _____

Send order to: Bantam Books, Dept. MC 43, 2451 S. Wolf Rd., Des Plaines, IL 60018
Allow four to six weeks for delivery.

Prices and availability subject to change without notice.   MC 43 3/99